AN
INADMISSIBLE
SOURCE

RAY HOBBS

Wingspan Press

Published in the United States and the United Kingdom
by WingSpan Press, Livermore, CA

The WingSpan name, logo and colophon are the trademarks
of WingSpan Publishing.

ISBN 978-1-63683-072-8 (pbk.)
ISBN 978-1-63683-940-0 (ebook)

Printed in the United States of America

www.wingspanpress.com

Also by Ray Hobbs and Published by Wingspan Press

An Act of Kindness	2014
Following On	2016
A Year From Now	2017
A Rural Diversion	2019
A Chance Sighting	2020
Roses and Red Herrings	2020
Happy Even After	2020
The Right Direction	2020
An Ideal World	2020
Mischief and Masquerade	2021
Big Ideas	2021
First Appearances	2021
New Directions	2021
A Deserving Case	2021
Unknown Warrior	2021
Daffs in December	2022
A Worthy Scoundrel	2022
Fatal Shock	2022
Last Wicket Pair	2022
Knights Errant	2022
A Baker's Round	2023
Confusion to Zeus	2023
Ways of Gentleness	2023
An Eye to the Future	2023
Stage Direction	2023
Dogs in Daft Outfits	2024
Taking the Stick	2024
People are Like Bottles	2024
A Family Effort	2024
A Future Denied	2024
Segue	2024

Published Elsewhere

Second Wind (Spiderwize)	2011
Lovingly Restored (New Generation P ublishing)	2018

As ever, I am indebted to my brother Chris, who provided the initial germ of an idea, who advised me on the curating of historic buildings and their contents, as well as acting as a sounding board for my ideas and helping to fuel my enthusiasm throughout.

1

THE POWER OF IMAGINATION

The green surgical garb was less than flattering, but with her mask now down, he could see that the new dentist was rather attractive as well as tall and slim. Her hair, what little of it he could see beneath her head-covering, was fair, a little fairer than his, in fact.

Nick offered his hand. 'Miss Bramhope? I'm Nicholas Burnett.'

'How do you do, Mr Burnett? Come in and take a seat. I believe you used to see Mr Grimshaw, who's now retired.'

'And not before time,' said Nick good-naturedly, taking his place on the chair. 'With a name like "Grimshaw", he shouldn't have been allowed to practise dentistry.'

She laughed lightly. 'There are worse names. Believe it or not, I had a professor called Payne.'

'Deed poll was invented for such people.'

She laughed again. 'That's a bit harsh, isn't it? What do you do, Mr Burnett? You're not in the Fire Service, I imagine?'

'No, I'm not. I'm a teacher at Frederick Delius High School.'

'Oh yes,' she said, looking at his record. 'What do you teach?'

'History.'

She gave a polite smile of approval, and said, 'I always enjoyed history at school.'

'I'm pleased to hear it.' It wasn't the kind of response he was used to hearing, which made it all the more welcome. More often than not, people were inclined to question the usefulness of the subject.

Returning to his record, she said, 'Now, you're not on any regular medication. Have you had any dental problems since your last appointment?'

'No.'

'Have you any allergies?'

'None that I'm aware of.'

'Good, I'm just going to take you back to examine you.' She lowered the back of the chair, placing him in a horizontal position with a bright light above him, and donned a new pair of surgical gloves and a facemask. 'Open wide.'

It was reassuring to know that one item of terminology remained comprehensible, because the string of dental technicalities she then dictated to the nurse meant nothing to him. It also occurred to him that it was one of the few instances when it was possible to gaze into the friendly, blue eyes of an attractive woman without feeling awkward or being accused of anything. It was possibly the only perk dental treatment allowed.

Satisfied with her examination, she said, 'There's nothing to worry about, Mr Burnett. I'll just give your teeth a clean while you're here.'

Ultrasonic cleaning had never been Nick's favourite experience, so he gripped the chair arms and looked forward to the moment when Miss Bramhope would switch off the offending instrument. It was inconceivable that his teeth could have accumulated so much scale in six months, but it seemed an age before the high-pitched whistling eventually stopped.

'There, Mr Burnett, all done.' She re-elevated the chair so that he could resume his sitting position and said, 'Have a rinse.'

He obliged, feeling as awkward as he always did when he spat into the tiny basin.

'You know,' she said, 'if you stopped smoking, you could consider having your teeth whitened.' She sat at her desk, drawing the fabric of her surgical boiler suit, or whatever it was called, more tightly over what now appeared to be a rather appealing figure.

'I could,' he agreed. 'My girlfriend gives me a lot of grief about it, and I have to admit I'm a slave to the habit.' Only recently, at the British Library in London, he'd had to take two breaks for nicotine relief, each involving the lengthy and compulsory readmission process.

He was the first to admit that it was an awful nuisance, and a self-imposed one at that.

'I see you're twenty-seven,' she said, looking again at his record.

'Almost twenty-eight,' he reminded her, guessing her age at roughly the same.

'You still have most of your life ahead of you. Why do you jeopardise it by smoking?'

'Why indeed?' He wasn't actually thinking about the health risk, so much as her earlier suggestion about whitening. When an attractive and desirable woman remarked negatively on the appearance of your teeth, some kind of action was indicated.

'You're with Lister Road Surgery, aren't you?'

'I believe so.' He hadn't consulted a doctor for quite some time, but he remembered the name of the surgery.

'If you pop in there, you'll probably find leaflets about ways to help you defy the habit.'

'I'll do that.' He got up to leave.

'Be sure to brush and floss twice a day, and make an appointment for six months' time.'

'I will. Thank you, Miss Bramhope.'

She removed the glove from her right hand to shake his. 'Are you interested in any particular period in history?' she asked.

'Yes, I'm researching the effects of Cromwell's Protectorate on the local community.'

'Ah.' She nodded, possibly to let him know that she'd heard of Cromwell. Most people had. 'How's it going?'

'Not at all well. Sources of information are scarce, to say the least. I'm afraid the Puritans were too good at covering their tracks.'

'Oh well, good luck with it.'

'Thank you, Miss Bramhope.' Catching the silent nurse's eye, he said, 'Thank you both.' He hated to see anyone left out, and he'd no wish to be responsible for it. 'Goodbye, ladies.'

'Goodbye, Mr Burnett.'

'Goodbye.'

He left one surgery and headed for the other, which was only a little out of his way. It was fortunate, considering the seemingly endless drizzle.

When he reached the desk, one of the doctors' receptionists offered to help him.

'I'm just looking for some reading matter,' he told her. 'Thank you, anyway.' Looking at the leaflets on offer, he arrived at the conclusion that men were the poor relation. He found one on breast-feeding, another on oral contraception and one on menorrhagia, which sounded vaguely feminine and certainly gruesome. '*Time to Quit*' was hiding beneath '*Breast Enhancement and Reduction*'. He showed it to the receptionist, who wished him luck.

* * *

He arrived home to find Amanda spoiling, if not for a fight, at least for a few rounds of acrimonious disagreement. The situation was tiresomely familiar.

She asked, 'What's the new dentist like?'

'Outwardly reassuring, but deadly with a pair of pliers.'

'I meant, did you and he hit it off?'

'She, actually.' He delivered the information in a matter-of-fact way, so that only Amanda could possibly read anything into it.

'A female dentist, eh? Next thing you know, you'll be seeing a female doctor. Then you'll know what it's like.'

Nick winced, knowing what was to follow. 'So you keep telling me.' It was one of Amanda's favourite moans. She was a selective feminist, the kind who complained about inequality, but who nevertheless expected the special treatment that they felt was due to their sex.

Undeterred, she aired her resentment. 'Women have had to talk to male doctors about their troubles since the year dot. We've had to be examined and prodded and probed as well, and now you're miffed because you've suddenly got a woman dentist.'

'I'm not at all miffed, Acid Drop. I don't know what's given you that idea.'

'You mean you're not admitting it out loud, and I wish you wouldn't call me that silly name.'

'Okay.' It was time for some straight talk. 'I'll stop calling you "Acid Drop" if you'll stop pretending to know what I'm thinking, because you couldn't be further wrong.'

'There's no pretence about it, Nick. I know you better than you think.'

'I'm not in the mood for an argument, Aci... Amanda. Are we eating in or out this evening? It's your shout.'

Amanda raised one sardonic eyebrow. She was quite an attractive woman, dark-haired and with a slender face, features that had appealed to him in the first instance, before he'd had time to experience one of her sour looks. 'You can see how much marking I've got.' She pointed unnecessarily to the pile of exercise books beside her chair.

He couldn't resist saying, 'Don't tell me you've been doing some proper teaching.'

'Oh, ha-ha-ha.' Amanda taught PE and Geography at the local middle school, and she resented references to the fact that PE required no marking. Setting that aside, however, she asked, 'What about tomorrow night?'

'I've got a meeting with Norman Lumb tomorrow.'

'And of course nothing has to come between you and Professor Lumb, has it?'

'It's important,' he agreed.

'It's more than important. It's become an obsession with you. I sometimes think you'd pay more attention to me if I wore a lace bonnet and voluminous skirts, or else dressed up as Oliver Cromwell himself.'

It was evident to Nick that romantic relations were off the menu. In a way, it was a relief, because he was tired of pretending.

* * *

Parking was by permit at Airedale Polytechnic, but Nick usually found a place on the cobbled street leading down to the canal, and he still had only a ten-minute walk to the History Department.

The friendly administrator was about to leave when Nick arrived, but she spoke to Norman briefly on the internal phone, and invited Nick to go up to his office.

The door was open when Nick reached the top of the stairs, so he called out a greeting, and Norman invited him in. The two men shook hands and sat down, Norman doing so with a sigh. 'I don't know about you,' he said, 'but I'm sick to death of hearing endless post mortems about this damned election.'

'Tomorrow's history, Norman.' Nick reminded him with a mischievous smile. Then with the air of someone whose memory has just received a prompt, he asked innocently, 'Has it been and gone? You know, I'd forgotten all about it until you mentioned it just now, so whoever won will have managed it with neither help nor obstruction from me.'

'Are you serious, Nicholas?' Norman eyed him suspiciously.

'Absolutely. Who did win, anyway?'

'The Conservatives, as everyone expected. I'm amazed you didn't know. Does no one talk politics in your staffroom? If that's the case, I'd seriously consider swapping jobs with you.'

'I'm sure they do, but I've been giving the place a wide berth lately. I'm completely caught up with this business at Newbury Hall, and staffroom chatter is a distraction I can do without.'

With a look of some concern, Norman said, 'Research has a way of taking over your life, Nicholas, and believe me, that's not healthy. You must find a balance.'

'It's difficult, Norman.'

'Why?'

'To begin with, my relationship with my girlfriend is heading for the hills, which means that the atmosphere at home is less than pleasant.' As he spoke, he realised it was the first time he'd admitted it to anyone. 'Also, the last two years have been generally difficult, ever since I lost my parents.'

'I'm sorry, Nicholas. I'd no idea. Was it an accident?'

'Yes, a collision on the M-Sixty-Two. They both died, actually within two days of each other.'

'How awful. I can't even imagine how that must have affected you.'

'Yes.' Nick had no wish to dwell on it. 'The point I'm making is that the research is more than ever important to me because, other than the daily grind, it's the only thing in my life that's constant. It's actually more constant than I'd like it to be.'

'How's that?'

'Basically, I know exactly where I stand with it, because I'm completely stymied.'

'Tell me about it.' Norman leaned forward, perhaps thankful that he was able to offer some support.

Nick set about describing the frustrating circle his project had become. 'Folklore has it,' he began, 'that in August, sixteen fifty-five, Sir William Newbury and his family were murdered by Roundhead troops, who caught them sheltering a fugitive from what, in those days, they called justice, and the incident is somewhat central to my enquiry. Naturally, the whole thing would be hushed up, as the only crimes for which Cromwell sanctioned the death penalty were murder and treason.'

'There must have been a great many in authority,' said Norman, 'who took the law into their own hands, if only because they could. Power does that to some people, and they'd always be able to destroy or falsify the evidence.'

'I'm sure of it, Norman, but one thing they couldn't falsify was the death date on the headstones in Saint Radigund's churchyard. It shows that the whole family ended their lives on the tenth of August, and that's something that would have been more than unlikely if the cause of death had been a natural one.'

Norman was thoughtful. Eventually, he said, 'If you remember, when you first showed me your proposal, I warned you about the paucity of primary sources of information from the period. The most helpful thing I can tell you, now, is that it's sometimes better to admit defeat than to pit your wits endlessly against the impossible, and it's particularly true when, clearly, it's clouding your judgement.'

'How do you know it's doing that, Norman?'

'You've as good as admitted it.'

* * *

Nick was enjoying the best kind of dream. In the way only the unconscious mind could arrange such a glorious liaison, Miss Samantha Bramhope had surprised him by inviting him over to her place.

It didn't surprise him at all that she lived in a Tudor house with tall chimneys and leaded, mullion windows. Crossed rapiers were suspended above a gigantic fireplace that hosted a generous fire, even though it was June, and a flamboyantly-feathered hat hung beside the oaken staircase. With a sense of growing excitement, he climbed the stairs with her. Curiously, she said nothing, but was clearly happy to invite him into her bedchamber.

He watched her remove her green, surgical suit beside the four-poster bed, unveiling each exquisite feature in turn until, shedding her face mask and gloves, she pulled aside the covers and joined him. He couldn't actually remember undressing or getting into bed, but that didn't matter as he slipped one arm beneath her to draw her towards him. It was a beautiful experience, and it was about to become even better—

Much to his disappointment, that was the point at which he woke up and realised that the warm body beside him was Amanda's.

'No,' she murmured sleepily, but still in a tone that discouraged persistence, 'go to sleep.'

* * *

It was Saturday morning, and Amanda was umpiring a cricket match. Girls' cricket at Holdsworth Junior High School was a new development, and one that Nick applauded and might normally have supported in person, but on this occasion, he used the freedom the occasion allowed to visit Newbury Hall.

As he drove, his thoughts returned to the dream he'd had, and not simply because of its content, appealing though that was, but because of the contrast it presented with life as he currently knew it.

The fact was, he no longer liked Amanda. Her negative disposition had eroded any cohesion that had existed between them, and it was equally likely that his inflexible stance hadn't improved their relationship either, although that was no more than a reaction to her abrasive manner.

Love had never been a part of their arrangement. He'd met her at a party and, on learning that she was looking quite urgently for somewhere to live, offered her temporary accommodation in his house, which she accepted readily. It was quite remarkable, he thought, how easily frequently-available sex could paper over the cracks of a dysfunctional liaison, although not for long, as events had demonstrated.

He turned into the grounds of Newbury Hall and continued to the visitors' carpark, and then into the parking bay that was convenient and so often empty that he'd come to think of it as his own.

Newbury Hall was a magnificent house, built during the Tudor period in the shape of a letter 'H', with the main hall providing the central part that connected the two parallel wings.

He entered by the huge doorway used by visitors, and greeted the first assistant he met. 'Good morning, Malcolm.'

'Good morning, Nick. Come to soak in the atmosphere again?'

'It seems there's little else I can do.'

Malcolm smiled sympathetically. 'The Newbury family's important to you, isn't it?'

'Yes, too important, it seems.'

Shaking his head in sympathy, Malcolm said, 'I can only wish you luck, Nick. I'm going to put the kettle on, so come and join us when you've done what you have to do.'

'Thanks, I will.' Nick continued on his way to the north staircase, smiling to himself as he set foot on the first oak tread. It might almost have been the staircase he'd climbed in his silly dream; in fact, there was no doubt that his familiarity with Newbury Hall had influenced it. It was rather interesting, how previously unconnected experiences so often came together in that way, and whilst Nick was no psychologist, he reckoned the phenomenon would probably be a damned sight easier to research than his current line of inquiry. Anything had to be.

The stairs led to the part that some called the 'minstrels' gallery', although in truth it was nothing of the kind, but simply an extension of the landing that led to several rooms, bedchambers and dressing rooms. One appeared to be a tiny study, although it might originally have been a dressing room.

It was one of the bedchambers, however, that always lured him in, at least, as far as he was allowed. The short four-poster bed, the dressing table and wash-stand were all protected from public contact by a stout, hemp rope, leaving only a limited, free area from which visitors could view the artefacts, although it was admittedly a larger area than those in the other rooms. Despite that restriction, however, Nick felt drawn frequently to that same room, where he could scent linen and old timber, and visualise the family members and servants who had lived and worked there four centuries earlier. The most wonderful thing about historic buildings and their original contents was the direct connection they provided between their own time and the present day. They were tangible and recognisable objects of the past that had survived long after their owners. The modern-day enthusiasm for time capsules was no more than a naïve attempt to reinvent the kind of sensation already created by places such as Newbury Hall, although he would have welcomed something of that kind, or indeed, any kind that would help him in his research.

He stood in the viewing area, conscious as ever that he might never find the evidence he was seeking, but content for the moment merely to absorb the atmosphere and history of the room.

The adjacent room was of a similar size and was connected to it by an adjoining door, suggesting that they were the sleeping quarters of the master and mistress of the house. Presumably, when the urge came upon him, the master would come visiting, whilst at less demanding times, each would occupy his or her own bed. The contents of the room that held Nick's interest suggested that it was that of the mistress. 'Lady Catherine Newbury.' He uttered the name aloud, correcting himself immediately. As the wife of a baronet, she would be known simply as 'Lady Newbury'. He spoke the name again, because to hear it in that bedchamber made her all the more real and alive, and to speak it made him feel as if he were addressing her directly.

Imagination, he decided, was a vulnerable and sensitive property capable of being triggered by the merest thought or stimulus, because he was now conscious of a change in the atmosphere, a fall in temperature, in fact. It was nonsense, of course; the temperature on that unusually cool day in June was equalised, give or take a degree, throughout the building. One room couldn't be noticeably colder than the rest, although goosebumps had already formed on his bare arms. He rubbed them, dismissing the sensation as a product of his fancy. Maybe Norman Lumb was right, and he really was letting his frustration affect his reasoning.

It was then that he was aware of something else, separate from the cold, although that was still very much in evidence. The new sensation was of a different kind, an awareness that, whilst his eyes told him he was completely alone, it was as if there were someone else with him in the room.

2

CLEARING THE MIND

He returned home to find Amanda surrounded by two sport bags, three full carriers and two suitcases. He'd heard the word 'baggage' used to describe emotional impedimenta, and she certainly had no shortage of that, but he could only marvel at the extent of her physical belongings, which seemed to have multiplied during her stay. If that had him wondering, though, the reason for the assembly of luggage was quite evident, and the words with which she greeted him confirmed it.

'I'm moving out.' She delivered that information in her customary monotone.

'I got that impression.'

She faltered momentarily, possibly because his response was less than she'd anticipated. She said, 'I'm going to stay with my dad for the time being.'

'Give him my symp— my regards.'

'Is that all you've got to say?' Her eyes challenged him in the way that no doubt made her feared and respected on a hockey pitch, but which he found simply tiresome.

'What do you want me to say? It's your decision.'

She treated him to a smouldering look that she possibly shared equally between ex-boyfriends and children who failed to bring their PE kit to school. Then, seemingly thrown off-balance by his casual acceptance of the situation, she asked, 'Don't you want to know why?'

'I've got a rough idea, but I've no doubt you'll enlighten me if you want to.' He took the electric kettle to the sink and filled it. Life would continue with or without Amanda and, if he were honest, he found her impending departure a welcome surprise. There was a bonus, too, in that the removal of her cases and bags meant that the box room could resume its original purpose as his darkroom. He hadn't been able to use it since Amanda's arrival.

'You're a cold-blooded bastard, Nick.' She glared at him, no doubt expecting a reaction, but perhaps not the one she got. 'What are you laughing at?' she demanded pettishly.

'A kettle calling a pot "grimy-arse".'

'Oh, ha-ha-ha. I'll tell you why I'm going.'

'Go on, end the suspense.'

'I'm leaving because you care more about your precious research than you do about me. You certainly spend more time with it, and it somehow manages to get you excited, which is a damned sight more than I can manage nowadays.'

He couldn't disagree with any of that. All he could say was, 'I suppose I have been rather preoccupied.'

'Preoccu…pied?' In her anger, she stumbled over the word and then recovered. 'You're bloody-well *obsessed* with it! It's taken over your whole life!'

He made no response. Her accusation was too close to the truth; he'd been thinking about that ever since his experience at Newbury Hall that morning. That was something else he wasn't about to share with Amanda. Attempting to discuss even an imagined supernatural experience with her would be the ultimate pointless exercise. Instead, he decided that one of them should be civilised. He asked, 'Can I give you a hand taking your luggage out to your car?'

'I'm probably fitter than you are, but go on if you want to.'

He picked up the two suitcases because they looked as if they might be the heaviest items, and carried them to her car. Judging by the ease with which she picked up the rest of her stuff, he reckoned she was probably right about their relative fitness. He really had to start exercising again.

He waited for her to unlock her car and lift the tailgate, and then placed her cases gratefully inside. What she'd packed in them was one of those feminine mysteries. He just hoped the Chevette's suspension was equal to the challenge.

Having loaded the two sports bags and the carriers into the back of the car, Amanda got into the driving seat and opened her window to initiate the demisting process.

He felt one of them should say something at such a time. Concealing his feeling of mischievous celebration, he leant forward to say, 'Goodbye and good luck, Acid Drop.'

Typically, she made no response other than to start the engine and pull out into the road, earning an angry horn blast from a van driver, who just managed to avoid her.

Nick returned to the house and, pleased with the way things had turned out, brewed some coffee and sat down to consider his earlier experience at Newbury Hall.

He knew of places that were said to be aware of their history. Auschwitz Concentration Camp, Glencoe Pass and Sanctuary Wood sprang to mind as locations that wildlife shunned, or were, in the case of Glencoe, shrouded in a gloom of such menace that denial of the massacre that had taken place there was impossible. Such phenomena were largely accepted, so could it be that, in its own way, Newbury Hall retained a sense of the atrocity committed there? He pondered that possibility before he remembered being aware of the difference in temperature between the mistress's bedchamber and the landing outside it. Only feet away, the air felt much warmer. The difference was too great, too abrupt to be dismissed easily. Could it be, then, that Amanda and Norman were right? Was he so blinkered and driven in his search for evidence that he'd become obsessed to the extent that his imagination was following its own path, and his judgement had become unsound? His eye fell on the leaflet he'd picked up at the doctors' surgery, and he made a positive decision. A healthy mind would thrive better for being associated with a healthy body. He would stop smoking, reduce his alcohol intake, and take exercise, which meant reverting to an earlier regime that involved getting up early each morning for a swim before work. Then, he might clear his mind and stop imagining bloody silly things.

* * *

The leaflet *Time to Quit* told him that most of the nicotine inhaled by smoking left the body within hours, and that any withdrawal symptoms after that were largely psychological. Consequently, he'd smoked his last cigarette at eleven-thirty on Saturday night, using the hours of sleep to rid his system of the stuff, and forty-one hours later, he still felt fresh and liberated. He hadn't told anyone; no one ever took such claims seriously, but he didn't feel the need to share the news, anyway. It was sufficient that he knew he'd stopped.

He'd cut down the alcohol to half a bottle of wine, as well, and he thought that compensated in some way for failing to keep his third resolution. He'd switched off the alarm that morning and reset it so that he slept until his usual time. Consequently, the early-morning swim never happened, but tomorrow, he told himself, was another day.

* * *

Determined to keep to his fitness regime, Nick resisted the urge to reset the alarm on Tuesday morning. Instead, he got ready and arrived at the pool in time to secure one of the individual, private showers before his swim.

It was about six forty-five, and there was only a small number of people in the pool. Even so, they were taking their exercise seriously, and Nick followed their example, putting in two quick lengths and then two slower ones. He reckoned if he alternated quick and slow, he would achieve the result he wanted without overstretching himself. After his second spell of two lengths of front crawl, however, he lingered at the shallow end to catch his breath.

As he stood there, he heard two women in conversation. One was saying, 'Nag, nag, nag, and it's always about money. There'll be no holiday this year. In fact, I wouldn't put it past him to cancel Christmas an' all.' Nick looked up to see the two talking on the poolside. Laughing, the other one said, 'Who does he think he is? Oliver Cromwell?'

Immediately, Nick felt a frisson, not the cold rush of blood caused by the kind of adrenalin charge he'd experienced watching *Hammer House of Horror*, but a strange, cold, tingling sensation that lasted maybe ten seconds. When it was over, he climbed out of the pool and went to change and to ponder.

He'd overheard a woman complaining about her husband's behaviour, a perfectly commonplace conversation in itself, and her companion's reference to Cromwell was almost as unremarkable, so why had his nervous system reacted to it in that way? Like his research problem, the question seemed to have no obvious answer.

* * *

On arrival at school, he paid his usual lightning visit to the staffroom to check the substitution and exam invigilation lists. 'A' levels, the last of the now-superseded 'O' levels and the exam component of Sixteen-Plus still dominated the school day, but happily, he wasn't required until that afternoon. He was surprised, though, to find Geoff Harrison, Head of Art, hanging pictures on the staffroom walls.

''Morning, Geoff,' he said. 'I've often thought this school would benefit from a whiff of culture.' The only kind in evidence was provided by the school's music department, which was appropriate, given that the school was named after a celebrated local composer.

'I think you and I are in a minority, there, Nick,' said Geoff.

'Well, I can't see the point.' The voice of philistinism, and therefore the untutored majority, was that of Ann Moresby, one of the deputies and a member of the Needlework Department.

'If I could make you see the point of it, Ann,' said Geoff, 'I'd bask in the satisfaction for evermore.'

His remark seemed lost on her, because, instead of rising to it, she asked, 'What is that, anyway?'

'*Luncheon of the Boating Party* by Pierre Auguste Renoir.'

'I've never heard of him,' she said dismissively.

'Renoir was a celebrated French Impressionist,' Nick told her, winking at Geoff as he spoke.

'Oh, yes?'

'Highly celebrated,' he assured her.

'Was he any good?' She squinted at the picture, possibly trying to judge its merit for herself.

'Any good?' said Nick. 'Not only was he brilliant, he was also astonishingly versatile. He did Charles de Gaulle and Toulouse Lautrec, and his impression of Maurice Chevalier singing "Any Old Iron" never failed to bring the house down.'

'I never get any sense out of you two,' she said, making her exit while Geoff dismounted the stepladder for safety.

'How's the research going, Nick?' he asked when he was recovered.

'Don't ask, Geoff. I'm beginning to think I've chosen the worst possible area to study.'

'Oliver Cromwell, isn't it?'

'Not him specifically, but the effects of his regime.'

'He was a humourless shit. That's all I know about him.'

'I don't know that he was all that miserable. The Puritans condemned what they called "excessive laughter", but Cromwell wasn't above an occasional chuckle.'

Geoff seemed to have missed the immediate message, because he said, 'Those Puritans were so down on people having a good time, it makes you wonder how little Puritans happened. Was Cromwell such a villain, Nick?' It sounded like a genuine enquiry.

'I'm not convinced that he was. I don't think he was anything like the brutal dictator he's been made out to be. He rid the country of a corrupt and absolute monarchy, and he did a lot for the universities and schools of the day, as well as achieving some success abroad. He did create the Irish problem that's still with us today, it has to be said. Otherwise, though, he favoured religious tolerance, even though he was a Calvinist with some very strong views about worship.'

'Did he really?'

'Yes, even the Roman Catholics fared better under him. I suspect that the excesses during his time were largely the work of minor officials abusing their power.'

The information evidently took Geoff by surprise. 'So he wasn't the monster we've been led to imagine.'

'Absolutely not. I think we owe him a great deal.'

Geoff nodded slowly, digesting what he'd been told. Then he said, as irreverently as ever, 'It's a pity he didn't take a leaf out of Renoir's book and do impressions on the side. He might have put smiles on a few faces as well as those other things you mentioned.'

As Nick left the staffroom, he was more inclined to regret the fact that the soldiers of the Protectorate hadn't left behind more in the way of documentation. There was always the possibility that the on-going restoration at Newbury Hall might uncover something, but he was clutching at straws or, at least, at oak beams and panels.

3

ANXIETY AND REASSURANCE

Two girls waited until the rest of their class were almost out of the room, before speaking to Nick. It wasn't unusual; in fact, he'd come to regard it as a normal occurrence. There were always those who preferred to air their curiosity in comparative privacy rather than raise their voices so that the class could hear them. Mockery was seldom hard to find, and shyness was a merciless inhibitor.

'Yes, Louise? How can I help you?'

The small, dark-haired girl began diffidently. 'Sir, was Florence Nightingale as good as what they say she was?' The girl by her side appeared to be there as moral support, because she said nothing. That was also common, as girls seemed to go everywhere in pairs. He couldn't blame them.

'You know, Louise, I believe she was.' He was aware that such a straight answer alone would have satisfied the child's curiosity, but he still felt obliged to explain his opinion. 'She was a very clever person. As well as being the founder of modern nursing, she was a statistician. Do you know what that means?'

'No, sir.'

'It means that she used numbers to prove things and make comparisons. She was quite a pioneer in that, and it's all the more remarkable because it was so unusual for a woman in those days to be at all interested in maths, let alone be any good at it. She also campaigned for hunger relief in India and for women's rights. She's best known, though for saving countless lives and relieving untold suffering. You know she was called "The Lady With the Lamp", don't you?'

'No, sir.'

'It was the name the newspapers gave her. They say she used to walk through the wards at night with a lamp, making sure her patients were settled for the night and that no one needed attention, and her patients would kiss her shadow as it fell on them. They loved her for what she did for them, and that wasn't all. She made them feel that someone cared about them, and that was more important than you might imagine. When you consider the harsh way the Army treated them in those days, she must have become the most important person in their lives.'

Both girls stared at him, silent but evidently fascinated by what he had to say.

'Something else that made her great,' he told them, 'was the way she got everything she needed for her hospital from some very high-up Army officers – generals and so on. It was a very unequal society in the mid-nineteenth century, and a woman making demands in those days was unheard-of, and yet she convinced them of the rightness of her cause. Yes, I think she was a very special person indeed.'

The other girl raised her hand quite unnecessarily and said, 'I want to be a nurse when I leave school, sir.'

'Do you really, Vicky? Well, if you go about it with the kind of determination Florence Nightingale showed, and follow her example, I think you'll do well. Now, off you go, both of you, or you'll be late for your next lesson.'

'That's all right, sir,' said Vicky, 'it's only Maths.'

'Well, you mustn't keep your teacher waiting.' He liked children to get their priorities in order, and putting History before Maths was a laudable start, but good manners were also important.

He had a marking period next, and two piles of books stood waiting for his attention, but rather than start immediately, he considered the conversation he'd just had. Those children were genuinely fascinated by the achievements of Florence Nightingale, but they doubtless had other interests. In that respect, they were an example to him in his preoccupation with the Newbury family.

He hesitated there, side-tracked for the moment. He called it a preoccupation; he recalled using that word more than once, but Amanda had called it an obsession. Now, given that she was less than rich in vocabulary, and that she shared the popular practice of devaluing emotive words by using them in careless exaggeration, he asked himself once more, could she be right? Had he become obsessed without realising the fact? Did obsessives ever realise it was happening to them, and if it came to that, at what point did a preoccupation become an obsession? Maybe, rather than happening at a given moment, it was more of a continuum, a gradual slide through the funnel of preoccupation into the receptacle of obsession. He had to avoid that. If it meant switching his thoughts from Cromwell to Henry the Seventh, to Sir Francis Drake, to Guy Fawkes, to the Duke of Wellington to Sir Winston Churchill, he had to resist the luring cone of that funnel. He took the first exercise book from the pile and made himself concentrate on his marking.

* * *

Driving home, he reflected on the unfortunate coincidence that, on the day he'd resolved to defy the threat of obsession, his last lesson had been on the Norman Conquest, the invasion that had brought with it the doctrine of the Divine Right of Kings, the licence to rule as an absolute monarch, that had led to the English Civil Wars.

In view of what he'd told Geoff Harrison, which was what he truly believed, it seemed ironic that he should be so involved – he avoided the 'p' or 'o' words now, even in his private thoughts – in an inhuman outrage perpetrated in Cromwell's name. Such atrocities, though, had to be made known.... Realising he'd slipped back, however fleetingly, into his old ways, he made himself think about something else. One topic of immediate interest was that of his need for a research degree if he were ever to enter higher education, and what area of study he could possibly adopt, should he abandon his current obsess— project. The difficulty in making such a change lay, not so much in finding a suitable lacuna for his research as, in gaining the approval of the validating body. The Council for National Academic Awards was notoriously difficult to satisfy, and a candidate changing research areas without what they considered an acceptable reason was unlikely to be viewed sympathetically. It was actually more likely that his request would be rejected.

He could, of course, continue with his current interest whilst turning a blind eye to the Newbury Hall atrocity, but the unsolved mystery would always be at the back of his mind, a constant and embarrassing reminder that he'd given up on it.

One minor mystery he had to lay to rest was the fall in temperature in the mistress's bedchamber, and he knew how to do that. As a last-minute decision, instead of parking outside his house, he continued up Thornton Road towards Newbury Hall. It seemed to him that he would be much happier if he could dismiss that anomaly as a minor malfunction in the ventilation system. Otherwise, it must have been a trick of the imagination or a brief and unexplained reaction, like a dizzy spell or a wave of nausea, not that he'd ever been given to funny turns.

* * *

He arrived at Newbury Hall to find another assistant by the door. He knew her well from past visits. 'Good afternoon, Angela.'

'Hello, Nick. It's nice to see you again. Things have been very quiet today. Is there anything I can help you with?'

'There is, Angela,' he said. 'I believe you have a system of recording temperature. Is that right?'

'Temperature and humidity, yes. It's to safeguard artefacts and fabric against the atmosphere.' She gave him an odd look. 'Does that interest you?'

'If you can check the temperatures retrospectively, it does.'

'We can do it within reason. We haven't had the equipment all that long.'

'I'm interested in last Saturday morning. I was in what I believe was the mistress's bedchamber.'

'Lucky you.' Angela was a married woman in her late forties, so she could get away with that kind of flippant remark.

'Not so lucky, really. At one stage, the temperature fell suddenly and quite dramatically.' He added, 'At least, it felt as though it did. I'm beginning to wonder.'

'Come this way.' She took him through to the office, searching briefly before finding the record for Saturday. 'What time did this thing occur? Just roughly – you don't have to remember the time to the nearest minute.'

He thought. 'Between nine and ten, I suppose.'

Evidently relieved to be doing something that took her away from the normal routine, she scanned the roll happily. 'It makes it easier,' she said, 'that it was at the beginning of the day.' Peering at the data, she asked, 'Are you sure about the time?'

'Positive. My then girlfriend was umpiring a match at school, so I took the opportunity to come here. She was less than supportive about my research,' he said. There was no need for her to know it was a classic understatement.

'Oh, dear,' she said, looking up from the roll. 'I'm sorry to hear that, but a nice, good-looking chap like you shouldn't be alone for long. Was it very sudden or threatened?'

'Threatened, overdue and very welcome.'

'Ah.' She held up the record for him so see, no doubt feeling that further enquiry might be intrusive. 'The temperature at nine, nine-thirty and ten was steady at fifteen degrees. In fact, it only crept up one degree by noon.' With some feeling, she said, 'It never gets warm in here.'

The evidence was there, literally, in black and white. 'Angela,' he asked, 'will you do me a favour?'

'Oh, I don't know,' she teased.

'I know it sounds as if I'm round the bend, but will you come with me and stand in the mistress's bedroom, where I was standing when I felt the temperature fall?'

'Why not?' she said. 'As offers go, it doesn't sweep me off my feet, but it's the best I've had for a while.'

They took the stairs to the gallery and entered the mistress's bedchamber. Looking around, Nick said clearly, 'Lady Newbury.'

'Why did you say that, Nick?' asked Angela.

'It was just after I said it last Saturday that the temperature fell.'

She gave him an odd look. 'It feels quite normal to me.'

'Me too.' He was almost disappointed.

'Tell me,' said Angela, 'do you make a habit of walking into a room and addressing someone who's been dead for three centuries?'

'No, I was thinking about her, and I spoke her name, sort of thinking aloud.'

She touched his arm and said, 'An hour or so in a darkened room might well be in order, but all I can offer you for now is a cup of tea. I think you need one.'

'I'll take you up on that, Angela.'

As they turned to leave, Angela said, ''Bye, Lady Newbury.'

They went downstairs to the office and Angela filled the kettle. 'Do you think,' she asked in her deadpan way, 'you may have encountered the ghost of Newbury Hall?'

'I hope not. To be honest, I didn't know there was one.'

'I don't know that there is. Mind you, they say these old houses are all haunted. I just thought we should consider all the possibilities. Milk and sugar? We may have some biscuits, too, if that gannet of a trainee has left us any.'

*　*　*

Nick drove home reasonably satisfied that his earlier experience at Newbury Hall was a one-off 'turn' that might be worth a mention on his forthcoming visit to the surgery. He'd no intention of spending more time there than he had to, but he'd been invited the following week to a well-man clinic with Dr Wheeler. Meanwhile, he had an evening of marking ahead of him.

4

PHANTOM OR FANCY?

Nick got up when his number appeared on the screen, and walked cheerfully down the passage to the consulting room. 'Hello, Mr Burnett,' said Dr Wheeler when he walked in. 'Come in and take a seat.'

'Thank you.'

'How have you been recently?' He consulted his record to refresh his memory in readiness for Nick's reply.

'Quite well, thank you. Within the last few days, I've stopped smoking, I've reduced my alcohol intake, and I'm exercising regularly for the first time in more than a year.'

The doctor raised his eyebrows in agreeable surprise. 'All very laudable,' he said, 'but what prompted you to make those changes all at once?'

Nick had to think about his answer. He could hardly cite a desirable dentist, much less an experience that might have been supernatural but which was more likely to be born of indigestion or some other temporary imbalance. 'I decided to make some lifestyle changes,' he said, 'to break out of what I can only describe as an unhealthy preoccupation.' He deliberately avoided the word 'obsession' in the ostrich-like hope that in doing so he might actually avoid that trap.

'Oh? Would you like to tell me about this preoccupation?'

'I'm doing some research for a higher degree, and I've reached a dead end. I simply can't find any documentary evidence of an atrocity that took place not far from here in sixteen fifty-five.'

'During the Protectorate,' mused the doctor.

'Yes.' Nick tried not to sound too surprised.

'Cromwell made himself Lord Protector in 1653, didn't he?'

'That's right.'

'I did it at "A" level.'

Now Nick thought he was allowed to be surprised. 'I thought doctors did Chemistry and Biology,' he said.

'And History, in my case.' Dr Wheeler smiled at his response. 'It makes me almost human, doesn't it?'

'I'd never accuse you of anything less,' Nick assured him.

'You're doing the right thing in taking regular exercise, Mr Burnett. I also recommend developing outside interests. I mean interests other than your research.'

'I take your point, Dr Wheeler.'

'So, apart from that, you're not aware of any current problems.'

'Not really.'

'You don't sound terribly sure.'

He thought it was worth mentioning. 'It's not a problem as such. Just out of interest, what kind of thing might cause a sudden reduction in body temperature?'

'Has it happened to you?'

'Yes.'

'It could be one of a number of things.' He consulted his record again and said, 'You're not on regular medication, I see, but we'd better have some blood tests, just to rule out thyroid deficiency and diabetes. Did this happen recently?'

'Yes, a couple of weeks ago, at Newbury Hall.' Without mentioning his interest in Lady Newbury, he described the incident. 'I had goosebumps,' he told him, 'and the hairs on my arms... bristled, I suppose.'

He nodded. 'Were you short of breath?'

'No.'

'Did you feel at all faint?'

'No.'

'Did you have much to drink the previous night?'

'No, that was when I first cut it back to two glasses of wine per night.'

Dr Wheeler nodded. 'What had your weekly intake been prior to that?'

It was one of the questions Nick had always anticipated with some apprehension. Nevertheless, he had to be honest. 'My girlfriend and I would have a gin-and-tonic when we came home at the end of the day, sometimes two if it had been a tough day. Then we'd have a bottle of wine, or maybe more, with dinner. Otherwise, if we went to the pub, I'd have three or four pints of bitter.'

'Hm.' Dr Wheeler looked again at his record. 'Withdrawal from alcohol might have caused it, but I'd be surprised. Your consumption was excessive, but not in the heavyweight class. Even so,' he concluded pointedly, 'you were right to cut down. I believe you told me you'd stopped smoking. When was that?'

'Not until that night, after the incident.'

'Had it happened before, or was it just the one instance?'

'That was the only time.'

He put Nick's record card down and said, 'It was most likely a momentary aberration. Maybe you climbed the stairs a little quickly, or maybe you were affected by the general ambience. I've only been there once, but I must confess I found the place dark and forbidding. At all events, it doesn't sound terribly serious, but do tell us if it happens again.'

'I will.'

'All right. Let's listen to your heart, and then I'll check your blood pressure.'

* * *

It was a busy time for Nick. Exams were tailing off, but he was required as starter at both Sports Day and the Swimming Gala. Why the PE Department saw him as the ideal member of staff to wield the starting pistol, he had no idea, but it seemed the job was his for life, or at least for as long as he worked at Frederick Delius High School.

As a change from firing the starting pistol, or so it seemed, he bought a number of cream cakes and took them into the staffroom. A feature of orphanhood was that, with the exception of a few close friends, no one knew it was his birthday. Naturally, he didn't go about telling people, but the cream cakes told their own story, and his colleagues were generous with their birthday greetings.

A less welcome aspect of the end of term was the usual plethora of staff and departmental meetings, of which the latter presented a particular problem for Nick. His head of department, Ronald Eccles was looking forward to retirement at Christmas and was consequently doing as little as possible beyond actual teaching, which meant that relying on him for any kind of direction was a lost hope. Departmental meetings included Kirsty Watford, a junior member of the English Department timetabled to teach some History, and therefore also in need of direction from above. After a typically unproductive meeting with Ronald, she asked Nick, 'How am I supposed to teach Year Nine History without a syllabus?' In anticipation of the expected legislation, the school had already adopted the new numbering of the years, and the thirteen-year-old intake were now known as Year Nine.

'Come to my room, Kirsty, and I'll give you the scheme of work I wrote for myself. It's the one I've been working from.'

'Really? Oh, Nick, that's really good of you.' As they walked to his teaching room, she said, 'I hope the new Head of History's going to be more helpful.' Then, as the question occurred to her, she asked, 'Did you apply for it?' The post had been advertised for some time.

'No, I'm not interested.'

She looked at him in surprise. 'Aren't you?'

'No.' He didn't elaborate. Kirsty was a nice enough person, but she tended to contribute generously to staffroom chatter, and he preferred not to have his career discussed around the hot water urn, or anywhere else.

On entering his room, he went to the filing cabinet and found the scheme of work in question. 'There you are,' he said, handing it to her, 'all you need to know about teaching the Norman Invasion *et ainsi de suite*, as the Normans quite possibly called the aftermath. If you photocopy it and then let me have it back, I'll be grateful.'

'Thank you, Nick. This is very good of you.'

'Not in the least. I was in the same boat as you when I wrote this, so I can hardly stand by and watch you struggle.'

'I'll let you have this back as soon as I've copied it.' Clearly with the long term still in mind, she said, 'I believe they're interviewing for Head of History next week. One chap's already been for a look around.'

'Has he really? He must be keen.' Visiting a school and collecting an application form at the same time was a widely-practised gambit among candidates as a means of creating an early impression. Headteachers were aware of it, and some were less obliging than others, but it still went on.

'Someone told me you were doing a research degree, Nick.'

'Yes, that's true.'

'What's your particular field?'

'The aftermath of the English Civil Wars.'

'Oh,' she said, narrowing her eyes in distaste, 'that awful Oliver Cromwell.'

He smiled at her reaction, because by then he was used to it. 'The same,' he said.'

'How's it going?'

'So-so.' Again, he didn't feel inclined to say too much to a staffroom gossip. Also, he was still trying to find the necessary balance that Norman and Doc Wheeler had mentioned, so he was reluctant to discuss it with anyone. Instead, he just said, 'I'll get there in the end.' He hoped he would. Meanwhile, at the risk of upsetting the balance, supposing he were anywhere near it, it might be interesting to see what progress had been made at Newbury Hall. The last he'd heard, a child's glove, of all things, had been found buried in the plaster of a kitchen wall. He'd seen the glove and wondered how it came to be encased in plaster, but that had been only an idle thought. Recent experience had told him that it didn't pay to become too inquisitive.

* * *

He waited for a coach filled with excited children to leave the carpark, before heading for his usual place. The school party was an indication that it had been a special day at the Hall, so he was glad he'd arrived as late as he had.

There was no one about when he stepped inside, so he tried the office, where he found several members of staff in Jacobean costume. They were all drinking tea, no doubt after an exhausting afternoon.

'It wasn't until I arrived that I realised you'd been having an activities day,' he said. 'Am I still welcome?'

'As long as you behave yourself,' said Angela, 'not like some of the lot we've had today.'

'Hard work, were they?'

The worn-out expressions of those around him told their own story. Angela asked him, 'Do you fancy a brew?'

'Thanks, but I won't intrude on you any longer.' He could imagine all too easily how they must feel.

'It's a shame you weren't here today,' said Malcolm. 'It was a Jacobean day, as you can see, and you're the closest we know to an expert on the period.'

'My period's rather later, and I certainly don't think of myself as an expert. Anyway, I'll leave you all to recover.' He re-crossed the Main Hall and started up the shallow steps.

Reflecting on his conversation with Dr Wheeler, he failed to see how any reasonably-fit person could find himself out of breath after climbing that staircase.

With all the arguments, theories and reassurances behind him, he still hesitated before entering the bedroom, although when he did, he found it as it had always been, completely unchanged by time.

He stood for a while, imagining Lady Newbury seated at the dressing table. It wasn't difficult; after months of intense study, he felt he almost knew her. He also knew that one thing had not changed, and that was the fact that, for all his efforts to maintain a sense of perspective, he had only to stand in the room again to become gripped by the story of the family's tragedy.

With a deep sense of pity, he said softly, 'Oh, Lady Newbury, what loathsome people those Roundheads must have been to commit such a terrible crime.' As if in agreement, a gust of wind hurled a welter of rain at the window.

His feelings were so intense that he was unaware for some time of the change in temperature and, when he did become conscious of it, the difference was unmistakable. Again, the hairs on his arms and, it seemed, elsewhere, were erect. He had to check the temperature outside the room before it changed again. Urgently, he walked out on to the landing, feeling the difference immediately, because it was like stepping into a warm blanket. He stood for a moment, convincing himself of the change that had taken place, and then he re-entered the bedchamber. Immediately, he was aware that the air was as warm as it had been on the landing. Self-consciously, although there was no one

28

to see him, he crossed the threshold repeatedly, checking and double-checking that there really was no difference in temperature.

His confused thoughts were interrupted by a voice from below calling, 'Closing time, Nick!'

He had to leave it there. Turning to leave the chamber, he stopped and, for some reason of which not even he was aware, said, 'Farewell, Lady Newbury.' He left, still on the dividing line between acceptance and disbelief.

When he reached the ground floor, Angela asked him, 'Did you have a nice chat with Lady Newbury?'

'What?' For one embarrassing moment, he thought he'd been overheard, or maybe he'd been the butt of an elaborate prank.

'I'm sorry, Nick. I shouldn't tease. I know that story's important to your studies.'

'Yes, I'm sorry I took so long.'

Angela shrugged easily. 'You were only up there a few minutes. Anyway, off you go before you really do outstay your welcome.'

5

HEADSTONES AND HEADACHES

Questions crowded Nick's thoughts as he left Newbury Hall. His brief conversation with Angela had eliminated the possibility of a mischievous trick on the part of the museum staff, and that left him wondering if he were going round the twist, or whether he really had experienced a brief but significant fluctuation in temperature between the adjacent spaces.

When he arrived home, he went through his various notes and accompanying documents until he found the wax crayon rubbing he'd taken from the headstone in St Radigund's churchyard. He'd despaired when he first found the grave and saw that the inscribed names and epitaph had been worn almost smooth by three centuries of erosion. Then he remembered encountering the same problem when he'd taken a school party to the plague village of Eyam in Derbyshire. The discovery had cost him two reams of paper and several packets of wax crayons, with which most of the children had been able to take rubbings of the faded details and epitaphs they found. It turned out to be an educational trip for him, as well, because, armed with that experience, he was able to return to St Radigund's with the necessary equipment.

Now, with the rubbing on his desk, he made out the inscription:

Here lye the mortal Remaines of
Sir William Edward Newbvry, Bart.
Borne 1622.
Departed this Lyfe 10th. Avgvst, 1655.

There was no mention of Lady Newbury, who would most certainly have been buried with her husband, had she died with him. On the other hand, had she survived him, it might have been considered judicious to keep her name from the public gaze in case the perpetrators returned to ensure her silence regarding the event.

Turning to the following sheets, he read:

Here lye also the mortal Remaines of
William Newbvry
Borne 1651.
Departed this Lyfe 10th. Avgvst, 1655.
Mary Newbvry
Borne 1652.
Departed this Lyfe 10th. Avgvst, 1655.
Edward Newbvry
Borne 1653.
Departed this Lyfe 10th. Avgvst, 1655.
James Newbvry
Borne 1654.
Departed this Lyfe 10th. Avgvst, 1655.

"Svffer little Children to come vnto me."
(The Gospel according to
St. Matthew, ch. 19, v. 14.)

He was horrified to learn that James, the baby, was a year old at the most, and even the eldest, William, was only about four. He wondered what kind of inhuman bastards could have murdered four little children.

After a while, he replaced the rubbings in the file, took out fresh paper and a crayon, and drove to St Radigund's. He had one more headstone to find; at least, he was fairly sure he had.

He pulled in beside the churchyard, being careful not to park under the lime tree beside and overshadowing the lychgate. A previous visit had cost him a bottle of car shampoo and half-an-hour's hard work in ridding the car of the sticky residue.

His plan was to use the family grave as a starting point, and he was making his way there when a voice said, 'Hello, there.' He looked around him to see who was greeting him. After his experience that afternoon, the last thing he needed was to be addressed by a disembodied voice, but he was relieved to see the vicar approaching. He was carrying an umbrella, and his lean and active figure as he walked up the graveside path was reassuringly lifelike.

'Hello,' said the vicar again, 'you're the chap who's researching Newbury Hall, aren't you?' He was young and he seemed very pleasant.

'That's part of it, Reverend. I'm Nicholas Burnett.' He offered his hand.

'Michael Ellison,' said the vicar, shaking his hand. 'It's good to see you again.' Eyeing the paper and crayon, he asked, 'What are you looking for?'

'The grave of Lady Catherine Newbury. I imagined it would be quite close to the family grave.'

'Quite close,' confirmed the Reverend Ellison. 'Short of purchasing a plot in advance, the mortality rate in those days made it impossible to guarantee one, but I can take you to it.'

'That's very kind of you, Reverend. Thank you.'

' "Michael", please, and it's no trouble.' He led the way past the Newbury family grave to another above which the headstone was similarly eroded. 'Feel free to take a rubbing,' he said. 'It's the only way you'll ever be able to read it.' The thin drizzle became heavier, and he opened his umbrella. 'There,' he said, 'we can both shelter under my brolly.'

'Thank you, Michael.'

'It's no trouble.' As he watched Nick rub the headstone with the duster from his car to remove what moisture he could, he said, 'The poor woman is said to have witnessed the slaughter of her family by Roundhead troops, but that's no more than folklore, and we know what folklore is, don't we?'

'Do we?' Nick was trying to concentrate on the task as well as the conversation.

'Folklore is gossip that has endured long enough to earn a kinder name. Unfortunately, the Register of Burials for the time is missing, so we have no record of the deaths except these headstones, which say what they were allowed to say. The Parliamentarians had a lot to answer for.'

'The Puritans had,' said Nick, 'but we mustn't blame Cromwell for everything.'

'No, he's been greatly maligned. Now I think of it, there's the story of a Quaker wearing a crown of thorns and riding into London on a donkey. He intended it as a celebration, an act of worship, in fact, but the Puritans, acting on what they presumably regarded as their own initiative, accused him of blasphemy and tortured him almost to death.'

Nick nodded, relieved that for once he was spared having to play the role of Cromwell's advocate.

'I believe, when it came to Cromwell's notice, he was horrified that anyone could be treated in such a way.' Smiling, almost to himself, he said, 'I'm preaching to the enlightened, I know, but I have to say that Cromwell wasn't the monster we read about in *Children of the New Forest.*' Returning to the question of the headstone, he asked, 'Can you make anything of it so far? I'm talking about the inscription.'

'It's much clearer now,' said Nick. It read:

Herein lye, expecting the seconde Comminge
of our Saviovr Christ Jesvs,
the mortal Remaines of
Catherine, Ladye Newbvry,
Widowe of Sir W^m. Newbvry, Bart.
Borne 1634,
Departed this Lyfe 23rd. July, 1657.
Nowe revnited wythe her Familie.
"Verilye I saye vnto thee,
thov shalte be wythe me today in Paradise."
(The Gospel according to
St. Luke, Ch. 23., verses 42, 43.)

He handed it to Michael, who read it soberly, commenting, 'Only "reunited", not "blissfully reunited", but I suppose the Puritans frowned on bliss.'

'Yes, they were as uncompromising about epitaphs as they were about most things.' Nick spoke almost absent-mindedly; he was actually thinking about the dates of Lady Newbury's birth and death. They showed her to have lived approximately twenty-three years. The date of her death, however, was of particular interest, occurring almost two years after the slaughter of her family. 'Michael,' he said, 'this may seem an odd sort of question to ask a clergyman, but do you believe in ghosts?'

'It's not an odd question at all, and the answer is yes, I do. I believe in the Holy Ghost. We know that Christ on the cross "gave up the ghost". The Greek word *"eidolon"*, used in the scriptures, means, literally, "ghost", and his spirit appeared before Mary Magdalene at the tomb, and then before his disciples, so it's not at all unusual for a clergyman to believe in ghosts.' He smiled as he delivered his conclusion.

'I can see that, Michael, but I'm thinking more along the lines of what they used to call "unquiet spirits".'

'Oh, have you encountered one?'

'I may have.'

Michael seemed unsurprised. 'I don't doubt it for a minute, Nicholas. Christ's spirit was restless after the crucifixion, until he'd completed his ministry. His final task was to demonstrate the substance of his promise of life after death. Once he'd done that, he ascended into Heaven, so yes, I can imagine other souls being in limbo for various reasons. As I often tell my parishioners, his isn't a bad example to follow.'

Nick laid his hands on the headstone and closed his eyes for a few seconds of silent sympathy before taking his leave of the vicar. Oddly, he'd been conscious again of a fall in temperature, but he was careful not to react. 'Thank you for your time, Michael.'

'You're most welcome, Nicholas. I don't wish to pry, but did your experience take place in Newbury Hall?'

'Yes, it did.'

Michael seemed unsurprised. 'Such places tend to resonate with their history, almost as if there really is a presence from the past.'

'I agree, and I want very much to find evidence of the atrocity committed there.'

'In that case, I wish you well. God bless you, Nicholas.'

* * *

As the final week of term hurried towards its conclusion, Nick became aware of two things. The first was communicated to him in a familiarly distant way by his head of department.

'We're probably getting a PGCE student in the department next term,' said Ronald.

'Oh, yes?' It was normal procedure for post-graduate teaching students to have a short teaching practice towards the end of the autumn term, and a longer one in the spring term.

As if reading his thoughts, Ronald said, 'This time, Leeds are doing it differently. Instead of coming in for an introductory day or two before starting the practice, he's going to spend two separate weeks with us, one in late September or early October, and then another nearer his practice. That way, they reckon to be able to use the practice more fruitfully. Instead of observing for a few days, he'll start teaching straight away.'

'I see. Thanks for telling me that, Ronald.' It was possibly the fullest information Nick could remember receiving from his superior, and he was wondering what could be behind it when Ronald spoke again.

'Because you're a young chap and up-to-date with the latest developments, Nick, I want you to be this student's mentor.'

'Ah.' That explained it. Ronald didn't want to be bothered with the job, so he was passing it down the line. It was only to be expected, and it was to be hoped the poor old sod wouldn't find retirement too demanding. Those roses didn't tend themselves. 'Okay, Ronald,' he said, 'I'll guide his footsteps.'

'Thanks, Nick. I knew I could rely on you.' He wandered off, presumably to find more things not to do.

Nick's second discovery came in the form of a surprise meeting with the recently-appointed head of department, due to start in January. Nathan Thorganby was a neat, dark-haired man, whose glasses seemed to have been designed for a larger face, and which therefore gave him the unfortunate appearance of a condescending owl. Ann Moresby, the 'Doomsday Deputy', as she was known, introduced him in the staffroom, thus reminding Nick, if a reminder were necessary, that it was a good idea to avoid the place whenever possible.

'Nick, this is Nathan Thorganby, your head of department as from January. I'll leave you to get on.'

'A bold assumption,' said Nick.

'What is?' enquired the new man importantly.

'That we'll "get on".'

Mr Thorganby blinked, as owls were wont. Then, like someone dictating policy, he said, 'I don't see why we shouldn't.'

Even with those lenses, thought Nick. Then, feeling he should sound positive, he said, 'Let's be optimistic.'

'Yes, let's.' It seemed that Ann Moresby had briefed him, because he said brightly, 'I gather you're pursuing a research degree, Nicholas.'

'Yes, as hotly as I can,' confirmed Nick. 'I haven't caught the bugger yet, but there's still time.'

With a look that Nick hoped he'd misread as one of condescension, Mr Thorganby asked, 'What's the subject of your research?'

'The effects of Cromwell's Protectorate on the local population.'

'A particular interest of yours?'

A silly question from a thirteen or fourteen-year-old was one thing, but a head of department, even newly-appointed, had no excuse. Nick shook his head dismissively. 'Not really.'

'Well, I suppose it's better not to get too personally involved with one's research.'

In the circumstances, it was possibly truer than he realised, a fact that Nick was careful to keep to himself.

'What's your role? Sceptic or Advocate?' The Owl had an unfortunate way of asking a question whilst giving the impression that he was humouring an inferior. It was also clear from his question that he didn't know the first thing about post-graduate research.

Nick feigned thought, as if he'd never really considered the question, and said, 'I suppose I'm more of an observer. I'm waiting to see how it turns out.'

'Oh, well, as long as it doesn't get in the way of your teaching, I suppose it's harmless enough.'

'Oh, I don't bother with that sort of thing.'

'With what sort of thing?' He really was slow.

'Teaching. That sort of thing. I just sit behind my desk and read about Cromwell's home policy. Sooner or later, the kids grow tired of chucking paper snowballs at each other and start reading. That way, the job takes care of itself.'

Some hitherto hidden clue evidently told Mr Thorganby that Nick wasn't being entirely serious, because he said, 'I was told you had a sense of humour.' He made it sound like chronic flatulence.

'It helps in this job.' In Nick's view it was essential. So far that day, it had helped him cope with an indolent head of department and his condescending heir apparent. In fact, the only area of concern in Nick's life that defied a sense of humour or any other resource was the riddle at Newbury Hall. It was a shame, because he would have to visit the place again, and he found the prospect daunting.

6

A Change of Haunt

School holidays were a good time for work to be done on Newbury Hall, and the work currently in progress was highly necessary. The building was Elizabethan, and four hundred years was a long time for its fabric to withstand the demands made on it. The kitchen floor was under repair and, in the perverse way that repairs on elderly buildings had, one job frequently uncovered or created another. A section of one wall, weakened by the removal of a floorboard, had already fallen apart, its horsehair plaster having supported itself for four centuries and finally given up the impossible task as well as the child's glove that Nick had seen.

When he arrived, the work was still on-going, but no more interesting discoveries had been made. He hardly knew the people on duty, so he exchanged just a few words with them before going up to the bedchamber.

It came as a surprise to him that his feelings were strangely ambivalent; part of him still feared for his mental stability, yet he still felt strangely and compellingly drawn by the mystery.

It was a curious feeling, then, returning to the scene of his recent experience, delusion, or whatever it had been, and he had to admit to himself that he would be relieved if it turned out to be an isolated, if unexplained, scrap of nonsense. Even so, he walked respectfully into the room and stood with an eye on the doorway so that he would know if one of the staff were to come upstairs. He'd no wish to be disturbed, but if he must be, he preferred to have some warning of it. It would be helpful, too, to have warning of any unexplained fall in room temperature, but that was asking a great deal. If it were to occur again, he would simply have to take it as it came.

As the thought passed through his mind, he noticed a trail of dust on the windowsill and he wondered why the window had been opened. He assumed it had, because he wasn't immediately conscious of a draught. Purely for his own satisfaction, he passed his hands around the window frame, but he felt little movement. Returning his attention to the dust, he thought it seemed odd that it had been left unswept, as the staff were normally meticulous in such matters.

His eyes wandered to the dressing table, and he tried to imagine Lady Newbury brushing her hair and attending to the mysterious functions that seventeenth-century women observed. As he did so, he was surprised to find dust on the dressing table. Looking more closely, he saw that it was similar to that on the windowsill. It was very odd, although he imagined there would be a normal explanation for it, just as he still hoped to find one for the fluctuation in room temperature.

Footsteps on the stairs turned out to be those of one of the staff, a young woman Nick had seen maybe a couple of times in the past, but with whom he'd never exchanged more than a few words. She saw him through the doorway and came to join him. 'Are you particularly interested in this room?' she asked.

'Yes, it's quite important in my research.'

'Oh, what's that, then?'

'The effects of the Protectorate on the local community. I'm doing an M.Phil. at Airedale Poly.'

'What's that?'

'Airedale Polytechnic?'

'No, that M-whatsit you mentioned.'

'A master of philosophy degree.'

'Well, good luck with— Oh, no.'

'What's the matter?'

'Just look at that dust. Have you had the window open?' She sounded like an admonishing parent.

'I wouldn't dream of touching anything in this house.'

'Well, somebody has.'

He told her helpfully, 'You'll find some more on the dressing table, and I've no idea who was responsible for that, either.'

Staring in disbelief, she said, 'I don't know how that got there. I'll fetch a duster.'

'I'll come down with you. It's time I was away.'

When they reached the ground floor, another assistant asked, 'Are you off, sir?'

'Yes.'

'Have you signed the visitors' book?'

'No, I signed it some time ago. I'm a regular visitor,' he explained.

'I see. I hope you enjoyed your visit, today. Do you know about the closure?'

'Closure? No, no one's said anything to me.'

'It's not surprising. It was only decided last week. With all the restoration that's going on, the Hall's going to be closed to visitors for the next four-to-six weeks.'

'From when?'

'From today.'

'That's a blow.' Still, it wasn't as if his research was going anywhere, so maybe it wasn't such an impediment. He drove home no wiser than he'd been when he arrived.

* * *

Considering his chosen area of interest, it was perhaps appropriate that Nick should drink at the King's Head and, having been absent for some time, he was less than surprised when he received a degree of ribbing from those present.

'We thought you'd signed the pledge,' said Mike Shuttleworth, seeing him at the bar.

'No, I had a difficult girlfriend.'

'You say, "had",' said David Turner. Does that mean we're going to see more of you?'

'Yes, she's off to pastures new.'

'Good girl,' said Mike. 'I always knew she'd do the decent thing in the end.'

'What's up?' asked Shaun Gray.

'Amanda's walked out on Nick,' said Mike. 'You can see the poor bugger's heartbroken, can't you?'

'I'll be all right when I've had a pint,' Nick assured them.

'You'll be all right, anyway,' said David. 'Judging by the number of kids on the streets, your long holiday's just started. That should put a smile on your face.'

As if by popular request, the darts came out, and girlfriends and long holidays were forgotten as the four squared up to each other in competition.

Mike threw a double twenty, a one and an eighteen; Shaun threw a nine, a twelve and a five, and David threw two ones and an eighteen. They all waited, then, to see what the absentee would do.

Nick took the darts and examined them, shaking his head doubtfully.

'You know what they say about a poor workman and his tools, don't you?' said David.

'No, I never listen to idle gossip.' Nick's first dart scored treble twenty, his next did the same, and Mike said, 'If he gets another sixty, I'm goin' to top meself.' He was spared that unpleasant task when Nick scored a mere double twenty with his third throw.

'How do you do it, Nick?' asked David.

'I practise in the long holidays.' He added unsurely, 'I thought that was what they were for.'

'A likely story when you haven't been in for weeks on end,' said Mike.

'Well, I knew you wouldn't believe me if I told you the truth, that I'm really a descendant of—'

'Not Robin Hood,' said Shaun with bored irony.

'I was going to say Eros.'

There was a silent chorus of puzzled frowns, and then Mike asked, 'Isn't he that bloke who stands on a podium in Leicester Square?'

'Piccadilly Circus,' Nick told him. As a rule, he tried not to correct his friends, but he was a teacher, after all, and they had as much right as anyone to know the facts.

'I knew it were one of them places.'

'That's right. He used to go around loosing off arrows at people, and whoever he hit was sure to get his leg over, that very night. Of course, that's if he was feeling up to it after being shot.'

'I expect most blokes would make an effort,' said Shaun. 'I know I would.'

David rubbed his chin thoughtfully and said, 'He sounds like a

41

useful lad to have around. Mind you, he'd be an embarrassment in a darts match, I mean if you were playing against him.'

'Who'd be interested in darts, with him around setting up nailed-on opportunities for his mates?' asked Shaun.

It was the kind of conversation Nick had been missing, and his return to the fold was so enjoyable that he broke another resolution by drinking rather more than he'd intended. Still, he was in a happier frame of mind than of late when he walked home.

He let himself into the house and, after a cup of coffee to round off the evening, he went up to bed. Unusually for late July, it was rather cool as well as wet, and he closed the bedroom curtains to defy the foul weather, tucking them safely behind the ornamental Roundhead helmet that stood on the windowsill. Then having undressed, he switched off the light and crawled gratefully beneath the duvet. Now warm and comfortable, he drifted easily towards sleep with what could only be an imaginary picture in his mind of Lady Newbury.

It was sheer conjecture, as he'd never seen a painted portrait of her. The only hard fact in his possession was that she'd died at twenty-three, so the rest was up to him. In those days, ladies wore their hair pinned up. Why they didn't just have it cut short was beyond him, but that was the custom. He liked to think of her with her long, medium-brown hair down and in loose waves. She would most likely have a centre parting and, he thought, a slender, gentle face with blue eyes and delicately-formed lips. He saw her nose as... fine. Yes, he liked to think of her with a finely-shaped nose, and her complexion would be fair and unblemished. She would have long eyelashes, he felt, and her eyebrows would be uncultivated but neat. As for her figure, she'd had four children within a brief timespan, but he knew women who'd done much the same and managed to maintain their figure, so he decided to make hers slim and appealing, too. After all, it was his fantasy, and he was allowed whatever he wanted. Returning to his inventory, he considered her hands. They said so much about a woman, he mustn't leave them out of his picture. He imagined they would be small and delicate, with manicured nails. To his shame, he wasn't at all sure whether women had their nails manicured in those days, or whether they simply trimmed them, but again, he had complete licence.

So much for her hands, then. What about the rest? It was doubtful that her breasts had ever seen the light of day, except when she was alone and in her bath, but he felt they should be of modest proportions and reasonably— He was suddenly aware that the temperature in the room had fallen, and he heard a buffeting at the window, followed by lashing rain. Then, just as suddenly, there was a crash, as if something fairly heavy had fallen to the floor. Hurriedly, he reached for the bedside lamp and switched it on. For a moment, he could see nothing unusual, although the crash had sounded real enough. He looked around the room again, and it was then that he saw the Roundhead helmet and its stand on the floor. It was inconceivable that a draught from the window could have rocked it sufficiently to tip it over, so he could only wonder. If the strange occurrences at Newbury Hall had now transferred themselves to 24, Sycamore Avenue, he wondered also about their timing. It was easily past midnight, and that kind of thing might well become a habit if it were allowed. He had to make a stand. He'd spoken to her earlier, so why not again?

'Lady Newbury,' he asked, 'are you there?' It was a silly question, he knew, but he had to make contact somehow. 'If you are Lady Newbury,' he said, 'I'm very much in sympathy with you regarding the events of the tenth of August, sixteen fifty-five, but I should be grateful if you would be kind enough to come back in the morning. It's late, I'm tired, and I need to sleep.' He waited, and nothing happened. However, it occurred to him that the request, 'come back in the morning' might not be immediately meaningful to someone who'd last bandied words in the seventeenth century idiom. He tried again. 'Lady Newbury, pray be kind enough to return on the morrow.' The temperature began to rise again, and being the optimist he was, he regarded that as a sign that she was signing off for the night. Leaving the Roundhead helmet on the floor for the time being, he switched off the lamp and pulled up the duvet.

As he drifted towards sleep, he wondered if Lady Newbury might have been startled at having her physical form imagined in detail. Such an experience might easily shock a lady of her time. Naturally, he wasn't sure that ghosts were able to read the thoughts of those they haunted, but he resolved to keep them under tighter control in future.

7

A Note From the Past

With his eyes now open, and focus re-established, Nick wondered at first if the events of the previous night had really taken place. The whole sequence had a dreamlike quality that inevitably raised that question, at least initially. Now that he was fully awake, however, and the helmet lay as he remembered it, on the floor beneath the window, he was certain he hadn't imagined any of it.

He got out of bed and went to the bathroom, confident that if Lady Newbury were to catch him at the loo or under the shower, the shock would surely ensure that the visit was her last.

Later, as he stood beneath the shower, enjoying the soothing cascade of warm water, he rather hoped she would call on him again. Now that he was reasonably sure he wasn't going round the bend, he felt he should respond to her…. What could he call them? Appearances? Approaches? He decided it didn't actually matter what he called them. He and she knew what was happening, and that was all that mattered. Content with that decision, he reached for the shampoo and worked some into his hair while he thought about the kind of conversation they might have. Then, turning to rinse out the shampoo, he became conscious of a cool draught from behind him. It was only for a few seconds, and when he was able to open his eyes again, he realised that the draught must have come from the opened top window. Recent experience was making him over-sensitive.

He dried himself and dressed without experiencing any appreciable variation in temperature, and conjectured as to Lady Newbury's sleeping habits. Did she sleep late? Did she sleep at all? Like his research project, the situation raised many questions without providing a single answer.

Normal life beckoned, however, so he took his swimming trunks from their drawer and a towel from the airing cupboard, and set off for the swimming pool.

* * *

With the school holiday in full vigour, the place was naturally busy, and it wasn't long before Nick encountered children he knew. It was as easy to recognise the boys as it was for them to identify him; the girls, however, were a different matter. Swimming caps made them all equally anonymous, and he had to explain the problem each time he asked them who they were. It seemed to him that, after seven weeks at school without a break, they might have avoided any teachers they happened across, and got on with enjoying their holiday, but they chatted happily to him as if he were a normal part of their leisure activity. Eventually, though, he had to say, 'It's good to see you all enjoying yourselves, but I really must get on and do my six lengths.'

One of the girls asked, 'Can you really do six lengths, sir?'

Her question prompted one of the boys to say, 'Six lengths is nowt. I can do ten.' That provoked a lively disagreement between the boys, for whom competition was a way of life. It also provided Nick with an opportunity to bid them farewell and get on with the business of swimming.

Keeping to his usual routine of two fast lengths, two slow and two more fast ones, he finished his sixth length and stood at the shallow end, regaining his breath. A woman close by smiled at him as he caught his breath, and said, 'You mustn't overdo it.'

She had a very appealing figure and she seemed somehow familiar, but the swimming cap defeated him once again. 'You should have seen me a few weeks ago, when I started swimming again,' he told her.

'Good for you. Keep it up.' Looking up at the large wall clock, she said, 'I must go. I'm due at the surgery at ten.'

That was when he penetrated the disguise. 'The dentist,' he said, searching his memory for her name. 'I'm sorry, Miss Bramhope. Those swimming caps do it every time.'

'I know.' She pulled off the cap and shook her hair free. 'It's nice to see you again. Goodbye.'

'Goodbye.' It was more than nice to see her, especially without the impediment of her green dentist outfit, although, to be fair, it had made its contribution to a classic among erotic dreams. That was where it had to end, though. He could only imagine that dentists, like doctors, were required to keep their patients at arm's length. In her case, it was an awful waste, and it was with that distressing knowledge that he climbed out of the pool and went to change.

As he drove home, he thought again about the events of the previous night, and he wondered if the temporary closure of Newbury Hall and the goings-on at his home were coincidental. He concluded that he would never know, so there was no point in conjecturing about it.

* * *

Later, that afternoon, he came in from shopping to find the message lamp on the answering machine flashing. He'd no idea who might be trying to contact him in holiday time, but he pushed the button to play the message.

'Hello, Nick,' said a woman's voice. 'It's Angela at Newbury Hall. I've just heard something quite amusing. I'm sure you'll appreciate it, so give me a ring when you can.' She left Newbury Hall's number, but he already had that. He also had things for the fridge and the freezer, so he put them safely away and made a cup of tea before phoning Angela.

The first couple of times he tried, there was no reply. He couldn't imagine how the staff occupied their time when the place was closed to visitors, so he was a little surprised. He left it for a while before trying again, and when he did, it was answered almost immediately.

'Newbury Hall. How can I help you?' It was one of the helpers or a trainee. It sounded like a young lad's voice.

'Hello, it's Nick Burnett returning a call from Angela. Is she available?'

''Ang on. I'll see if I can find her.'

It seemed that the 'How can I help you?' was an isolated example of courtesy, but it was a start. Nick waited patiently. His tea was currently too hot to drink, and he had nothing else to do in the meantime.

After a minute or so, Angela answered. 'Hello, Nick. I'm sorry to take so long, but there's great excitement here. The workmen have discovered a document of some kind behind the panelling in the room we call the "Study". You know the one I mean, don't you?'

'I do, but "of some kind" doesn't tell me a lot, Angela. Can't you make out what it is?'

'It's difficult. As you can imagine, it's covered in damp mould and it's far too delicate to be handled, but it seems to be a sort of register, a list of names. That's all I can tell you, except that the letterhead, for want of a better term, bears the name of Sir William Newbury, Justice of the Peace.'

So he was a magistrate. That was interesting. 'Look, if I come over, do you think you could let me see it? I know the place is closed to the public, but this is important.'

'Sorry, Nick.' She sounded genuinely apologetic. 'It mustn't be handled. Someone's coming from the University this afternoon to take it away for repair and conservation.'

'Can't I have even a quick look before he or she arrives?'

'No, Nick. I've told you everything I've been able to make out, but it's in loose scroll form – the twine, or whatever it was that bound it must have rotted away – and it would be impossible to straighten it without causing serious damage. You'll have to be patient.'

'All right, so it's a list of names made, presumably, by Sir William Newbury in his capacity as a magistrate. Is that all you know?'

'That's all, Nick. The university have said that no one is to touch it, and I'm just passing that on, so don't shoot the messenger.'

Now he felt guilty. 'I'm sorry, Angela. I didn't mean to be impatient, but the Newbury family is important to me, as you know.'

'I know, but I'm sure the university will let us know as soon as they're able to read it.' Sounding more relaxed, she said, 'Be that as it may, it's not the reason I phoned you. The discovery happened since then.'

'Go on.' He put his disappointment aside and waited to hear what she had to say.

'Do you remember coming in to ask about the temperature in here? I believe I turned up the records for you.'

'Yes.' Now he was interested.

'Well, someone told me something quite interesting shortly before we closed. I couldn't phone you earlier, because I've been on leave, and I didn't have your number.'

47

'Okay, what was it?'

'Apparently, there have been two occasions in the past twenty years or so, when visitors have reported unusual goings-on in that very bedchamber, including dramatic fluctuations in temperature. Isn't that interesting?'

'Very. Do you know who the visitors were, or anything about them?'

'I'm afraid not, Nick, but I thought you'd be interested to hear about it.'

'I am, Angela. Thanks for telling me.'

'It was no trouble. Anyway, I must go. I think the technician from the university is here now. 'Bye, Nick. Give my regards to Lady Newbury if you see her.'

'There's not much hope of that. 'Bye, Angela, and thanks again.' He replaced the receiver, excited by the discovery, but disappointed that he wasn't allowed to see it. It actually made a deal of sense when he thought about it. A document that had lain in a damp place for more than three hundred years would be.... Delicate didn't describe it. It was best left to the technicians at the university. As for the other matter, he'd be surprised if Lady Newbury ever visited him again.

8

Rest and Recuperation

phone call to Airedale Polytechnic told Nick that Norman
Lumb was away on leave for the next two weeks. In his
absence, he spoke to Trevor Raymond, one of the senior
lecturers.

'It's about a document that's been discovered at Newbury Hall,' Nick
explained. 'From what I can gather, it could be central to my research, and
I just don't want to lose track of it while it's being treated and restored.'

'Hold on a minute,' said Mr Raymond. 'What sort of period are we
talking about?'

'I'm sorry.' In his anxiety, Nick had gone straight to the problem
without explaining the nature of his research. 'I'm doing some work
on the way Cromwell's Protectorate affected the local population. The
document was written by Sir William Newbury some time before sixteen
fifty-five.'

'Right. Seventeenth century, then. It'll most likely need a lot of
stabilising and restoration. Where have they taken it?'

'Bradford University.'

'I see. Who owns Newbury Hall?'

'Bradford City Council.'

'Well, as the document is the council's property, and Bradford have
the facilities for preserving it, it should be handed to them, so you've
nothing to worry about. Once it's been handed over, you'll get a microfilm
copy of it easily enough.'

Nick was sure his relief was tangible, even on the phone. 'Thank you,
Mr Raymond. That's a weight off my mind.'

'You're welcome, and it's "Trevor", by the way. Are you a newcomer
to research?'

'Fairly new.'

He laughed gently. 'It's good that you're so passionate about it. One word of warning, though. Don't expect anything to happen in a hurry. A document of that age will have to be stabilised and then treated for all the ravages it's suffered over the three hundred years it's been lost and forgotten.'

'At least I know I haven't lost it. Thank you, Trevor.'

'You're welcome. Good luck with your research.'

'Thanks. Goodbye.'

As he put the phone down, he felt reassured if impatient, and wondered what he might do next. As far as his research was concerned, the answer was obvious, so he turned instead to what was possible. He needed a break from everything, and that meant a holiday of some kind. In normal summer weather, a spell of walking would certainly have appealed; the Pennine Way, or at least part of it, might have been attractive, had it not been for the seemingly incessant rain. He brooded about that for a while until it occurred to him that it was the walking, rather than the location, that the weather precluded. As far as roads allowed, he would follow the route by car, making leisurely progress, not via youth hostels, but from one bed and breakfast facility to another, because he wanted to spoil himself. Now enthused, he made his preparations.

* * *

Rather than drive to Derbyshire and join the route in the normal way, he decided to start at Malham, for no better reason than that it was one of his favourite spots.

Feeling distinctly more cheerful, he drove through Shipley, Bingley and Keighley, and picked up the A65 from Skipton, leaving the main road at Gargrave and eventually arriving in Malham.

As he'd suspected, the foul weather had discouraged all but the hardiest and the most determined of travellers, and a room was available at the first B and B he tried. Having booked that, he went on to the nearest pub for lunch and a pint, or possibly three. The weather was worsening rapidly, and a cosy afternoon by the fire beckoned.

He was enjoying that luxury when a man, presumably a rained-off walker joined him.

'Not walking, then?'

Nick confirmed that he wasn't currently walking.

'Don't blame you. Don't know what we've done to deserve this.' It appeared that he preferred not to speak in full sentences. He went on to say, 'Won't be long before I pack it in, at this rate. Hm?'

'Very wise.' It was also good news to Nick. He hoped the decision would follow soon.

'I'm in animal feed. Just taking a bit of time off.'

'Are you really?' His bushy moustache and ill-kempt eyebrows hinted at a bucolic way of life.

'What do you do?'

'I'm a teacher, but I'm on holiday now.' He thought a hint might give the right message.

'You lot are always on holiday, aren't you? Hm?' The attempted witticism came with a slap on the knee and hearty laughter.

'Of course we are. We're not daft.' People never expected that, and it was fun, seeing them struggle with it.

Seemingly untroubled by Nick's riposte, the man continued to pursue his agenda. 'Mind you,' he said, 'don't talk to me about education.'

'I'll try not to.'

'Trouble with education today is there's too many silly ideas. Hm?'

Nick presumed that the 'Hm?' was intended to invite agreement, so he ignored it.

'Mean to say, it was straightforward enough in my day. Teacher stood there and told you what was what, and you learned. Hm? Not good enough nowadays. They even have training courses for teachers. I ask you.'

Nick resisted the urge to point out that such courses had existed for a very long time.

'Courses for 'em to learn how to teach, and even then, kids still can't read and write. Not only that, teachers can't keep order. That's why there are so many juvenile delinquents about. Hm?'

'Is that right?'

The man looked at Nick as if he were stupid. Then he said, 'Stands to reason. I wouldn't put up with half of what teachers let 'em get away with.' After an interrogatory glare, he emitted the obligatory 'Hm?'

Nick waited for more, but it seemed he was expected to contribute something to the conversation. 'Good for you,' he said.

'What subject do you teach, then. Hm?'

'History.'

'History?' His response was one of disbelief rather than a request for confirmation.

Even so, Nick felt impelled to repeat the information. 'History.'

'That just bears out what I've been saying. Instead of teaching them useful subjects, such as maths and science, you teach them dates. What is the point in learning history? Hm?'

He'd asked, so Nick told him. 'It keeps me in a job and enables me to come here for rest and recuperation. That's if I'm allowed a little peace. Unfortunately you seem to have other ideas. You said, "Don't talk to me about education", and I've tried not to, whereas you've spoken about nothing else, in spite of your woeful ignorance of the subject, a shortcoming you've demonstrated most amply.'

'I see,' said the man, standing up. 'It's like that, is it? And I was going to offer to buy you a drink. Well, it's a pity they didn't teach you any manners on that so-called training course. Hm?' He went to the bar, no doubt seeking other ears to bend. As he did so, a member of the bar staff placed a fresh log on the fire, and Nick snuggled more comfortably in his chair and watched the flames leap around it. It was infinitely cosier than passive prejudice.

Presently, a young woman came to the fireside with a smooth and appealing dog. She took a seat on the settle and smiled across at Nick. 'It's so peaceful in here, isn't it?' she said. She was quite attractive, he thought, in an English rose kind of way.

'You should have been here a few minutes ago,' he told her, 'but you're right, it's very peaceful now.'

A young man joined her with two drinks. The dog glanced at him over its shoulder before returning its attention to the fire. Nick caught a little of the conversation going on behind him. A familiar voice was saying, 'That's another thing. Dogs in public bars. Hm? Shouldn't be allowed.'

The young man across the fireside gave him a frosty look, but the barman answered the challenge. 'It's management policy to welcome dogs and most people in here. Whether or not you choose to share the bar with a well-mannered dog is your choice, but the dog is most welcome.'

Nick didn't catch the grunted rejoinder, but he was pleased to see the disagreeable man make for the door.

'Good riddance,' said the young woman.

'I agree,' said Nick. On hearing him speak, the dog turned its head and studied him briefly before getting to its feet and coming over to him.

'Bertie,' said the young woman, 'don't.'

'He's all right,' said Nick, now sure of the dog's gender. He stroked his smooth fur and asked, 'What is he?'

'He's a German pointer.'

Nick stroked him again, feeling that he should say something. '*Du bist ein sehr hübscher Hund,*' he said.

The woman and the man both smiled. 'He doesn't understand German,' said the man.

'My mistake.' Speaking again to the friendly animal, he said, 'You're a very handsome dog.'

Bertie moved closer and allowed Nick to stroke him behind his ears.

' "Bertie" is a friendly name,' said Nick, 'unusual, but no worse for that.'

'It's after Bertie Wooster,' the man explained. 'He has style, as you can see, but very little brain.'

'Personality is everything, Bertie,' said Nick.

'I'm glad you think so,' said the woman, who was clearly blessed with personality as well as looks.

'I couldn't help overhearing your conversation with the boorish chap who just went out,' said the man.

'That wasn't so much a conversation,' Nick told him, 'as a barrage of bigotry.'

The man smiled. 'He couldn't see the point of history. Maybe he thinks everyone should be as boring as he is.'

'I got that impression.'

The woman was looking at them both unsurely, so her husband explained, 'This chap teaches history. Our friend disapproved.'

'Wretched man.' Then, possibly because she thought she should show some interest in the matter, she asked, 'Is there a period of history that interests you particularly?'

It was inevitable that she should ask him that. She didn't know he'd come away to escape from it. 'I'm interested in the English Civil Wars and their aftermath,' he said.

'The Commonwealth and Protectorate,' said the man. 'I'm a lecturer in history,' he explained, 'at Reading. My area of interest is somewhat later than yours.'

'I sometimes wish I'd chosen something earlier or later for my research. Anything but the Protectorate.'

'Lack of original sources?'

'Spot on.'

'Well, whatever headway you make is bound to attract notice. Good luck, anyway.' He lifted his glass and drank to it.

* * *

After a cosy evening, thankfully without abrasive company, and a comfortable night, Nick set out for his next stop, which was Horton in Ribblesdale, with its neighbouring giant Pen-y-Ghent. The village was traditionally the mustering point for those about to walk or, for those who took life to extreme limits, to run the Three Peaks of Pen-y-Ghent, Whernside and Ingleborough. It seemed to Nick that no one with any grasp on reality would consider such an expedition in the current weather, so he was surprised to learn on arrival at the Pen-y-Ghent Café that two parties had already left, hell-bent on qualifying for the Three Peaks of Yorkshire Club. To do so, they were required to complete the venture in twelve hours or less, and Nick wished them luck, even though they were insane. He preferred to drive the short distance to the magnificent, quarter-mile-long Ribblehead Viaduct, with its twenty-four colossal arches.

As well as providing a glorious vista, it was of particular interest to historians. Nick remembered learning that a great many navvies had lost their lives in its construction, and that the railway had been required to finance an extension to the graveyard to make room for the casualties. It occurred to him that his interests seemed to lead from one churchyard to another. He also reflected that the line was currently threatened with closure. It would be a poor way to treat a memorial to those who'd built it.

A few trenches were all that remained of Batty Green, the village of wooden shacks that had housed them. He'd tried sometimes to imagine the kind of scene, reminiscent of a Wild West prospectors' town, that must have existed there. The village was all they had for accommodation and entertainment, which would inevitably include alehouses and dens of vice.

As he sat at the roadside, viewing the monument to Victorian enterprise and callousness, he noticed a figure in the distance. He or she seemed to be moving with difficulty – it was impossible to see anything clearly through the rain – so he started the engine and drove towards the struggling walker. As he drew closer, he saw that there were two of them, and that one was supporting the other. He pulled in beside them and lowered his window. 'Can I help?' he asked. It was probably a silly question, but they weren't in any position to point that out to him.

The casualty, who turned out to be a woman, moaned with pain, but her companion spoke for her. 'She's twisted her ankle,' he said in a tone that suggested carelessness at the very least, on her part.

'Right, I can offer you both a lift, if you like.'

'Thank you,' said the injured young woman with obvious relief in her voice.

'Right,' grunted her companion.

Nick unlocked the near side door. The young man opened the door and folded the seat, beckoning silently to the young woman to climb into the back.

'Don't you think the lady should ride in the front, where there's more room for her ankle?' suggested Nick.

'Yeah, well, I'm taller than what she is,' said the young man, still holding the front passenger seat back for her. The young woman struggled obligingly and painfully into the rear of the car.

Nick waited for her companion to get in and close the door, which he did with an unnecessary slam. 'Now, my name's Nick.' He looked to his male passenger and, in the absence of any kind of response, asked, 'What's yours?'

'What's my what?'

'Your name.'

'Lee.'

A tiny voice from the rear said, 'I'm Sharon.'

'Glad to meet you, Sharon. Where would you like to go?'

Immediately, Lee said, 'We live in Clitheroe.'

'Sharon,' asked Nick, 'would you like to have your ankle examined in hospital?'

'There's no need,' said Lee.

'This is Sharon's shout,' insisted Nick. 'What do you say, Sharon? Hospital or home?'

'I've told you,' said Lee, 'there's no need for her to go to hospital.'

Nick waited for Sharon to reply. 'It's your ankle, Sharon,' he said, 'so it's your decision.'

'I don't need to go to hospital,' she said dutifully.

'Just take us home,' said Lee.

'Please,' said Sharon, the polite member of the partnership, despite her discomfort.

After a short while, Lee evidently felt obliged to speak. 'Nice car,' he said.

'Thanks. Yes, I like it.'

'You must be doin' all right for yourself. What d' yer do for a livin'?'

'I'm a teacher.'

'Oh, that explains it.'

'What does it explain?' asked Nick, suspecting he was about to come under fire again for his choice of employment.

'How you can afford a car like this.'

'I've got another one like this at home,' said Nick. 'I take them out in turn. This is my Sunday, Tuesday, Thursday and Saturday car, this week, anyway. Next week, it will change over to Monday, Wednesday, and Friday duties. It's all down to there being seven days in a week, you see.'

The absurdity of Nick's claim was evidently lost on Lee, who said, 'It must be nice. Whatcha want wiv two cars, bof the same sort?'

'I'm keen on Beetles.' He added, 'Anything to do with arthropods, really, not the Liverpool Beatles, you understand.'

For a few seconds, Lee was quiet, itself a blessing, but then he asked, 'What the fuck's that when it's at home? Arfropodge?'

'Arthropods? Insect life, although I'm not terribly keen on wasps, hornets and mosquitos.' Then, remembering the reason for what threatened to be an unpleasant journey, Nick asked, 'How's your ankle, Sharon?'

'Not so bad now, thanks. I've managed to get me boot off, so I don't think it's sprained.'

'That were clever, weren't it?' demanded Lee. 'How are you goin' to get from the car to the house now?'

'You could carry her,' suggested Nick. It seemed the most obvious course to him, and Lee couldn't be all selfishness and incivility, or could he?

Instead of responding to Nick's suggestion, Lee changed the subject completely and said, 'I suppose you'll be on one of them long holidays what you teachers get.'

'No, there's no chance of that.'

'Isn't there?'

'Not in my specialism. I was at the viaduct looking into the possibility of a school trip.'

'Uh?'

'Yes, I think it would be interesting to delve into the history of the viaduct, how it was built and so on, and to study the lives of the illiterate navvies who built it. How they communicated, for example.'

There was no change in Lee's expression, but he asked, 'Watcha wanna do that for?'

'Well, you never know. It might help us solve the question of how to communicate with other ignorant, inarticulate, ill-mannered people in our own time.'

'There isn't any now, is there?'

'What? Ignorant, ill-mannered people?'

'No, navvies.'

'No, I never thought of that.' Glancing sideways, he saw Lee raise his eyes to the ceiling. 'Are you okay in the back, Sharon?' He thought he should ask, and she provided better conversation than Lee.

'I'm okay, thanks. It's good of you to give us a lift. I don't know what we'd have done.'

'Think nothing of it, Sharon. Lee doesn't, do you, Lee?'

'Wha'?'

'Think anything of it.'

'I don't know what you're gettin' at.' He seemed to give the question some consideration before giving up the unequal struggle and abandoning it for easier ground. 'What dya teach, then?'

'Oddly enough, history.' He thought the previous conversation might have established that. It was a silly presumption to make.

'History?'

With a strong feeling of *déjà vu*, Nick said, 'Yes, history.'

'Wha' for? I mean, what's the point?'

'I can't believe you're asking that question.'

Impatiently, Lee asked, 'What's it gonna do for anybody?'

'Are you saying you can't see any future in history?'

'Yeah.'

'Do you mean there's no place for history in the future?' Nick wondered if Groucho Marx might have enjoyed the conversation. He'd possibly have revelled in it and kept it going for at least five minutes.

'Yeah.'

'What about geography? Do you think there's a place for geography somewhere on this planet, supposing we can work out how to get to it?'

'Yeah, well, you've got to be able to find your way about, haven't you?'

'I'm glad you think so, Lee, because we're getting close to Clitheroe and, not being a geography teacher, I'll need help finding your house.'

'I'll tell you how to get there,' said Sharon.

'Excellent. I bet you did geography at school, didn't you, Sharon?'

'Yes, but it was a long time ago.'

'All history now, eh? That's true of everything.'

'What is?' Suddenly, Lee felt obliged to join the conversation.

'Everything becomes part of history eventually, so history must be important.'

'At this roundabout,' said Sharon, 'go left.'

'Thank you, Sharon.' He followed her direction, avoiding the route to the town centre. 'That roundabout, Lee,' he pointed out, 'is now history.'

'How dja make that out?'

'When we were on it, it was part of our present, but now it's part of our past. History is everywhere you look, especially when you look behind you.'

Presumably at a loss to follow Nick's line of reasoning, he said, 'You don' 'alf talk bollocks.'

'You've noticed.'

'Next right, and then right again into Somerset Road.'

'Thank you, Sharon.' He followed her subsequent directions and drew to a halt outside a disreputable house that might have been made for Lee. 'Now, Lee,' he said, 'I want you to open the house door, and I'll bring Sharon in.'

'Wha'ever.' Lee took one rucksack, presumably his, and did as he was asked.

'Now,' said Nick, folding back the front seat, 'pick up your boot and wriggle towards me. Good girl.'

'Are you going to help me inside?'

'Of course. What kind of lout would leave you to struggle on your own?' As she reached the end of the seat, with her feet pointing outwards, one booted, the other bared and swollen, he leant inside and lifted her out of the car, picking up her rucksack at the same time.

'Oh,' she said, pleasantly surprised, 'I didn't realise you were going to carry me.'

'Think nothing of it, Sharon. Any self-respecting history teacher with time to spare would do nothing less.'

'Take no notice of Lee, Nick. He's a gobshite.'

'Yes, I noticed.' With that shared secret, he carried Sharon into the house and deposited her gently on the sofa.

'Thanks ever so much, Nick,' she said. 'It was really kind of you to help us.'

'Yeah,' said Lee without turning away from the TV, 'cheers, mate.'

Nick went on his way satisfied at least that he'd made life easier for an unfortunate but polite young woman.

That evening in the pub was dominated by a number hearty souls assembled in readiness for an assault on the Three Peaks the next day. Whilst he doubted their sanity, Nick felt able to excuse them to some extent, on the basis that none of them was as stupid, selfish and boorish as Lee, but then, where on earth would he find competition?

* * *

The next day promised well. Despite the worst summer he could remember, Nick would make the short journey happily to Hawes, home of the celebrated Wensleydale Cheese. Hoping, then, to avoid loutish walkers, self-opinionated dealers in animal feed, and any other blots on an otherwise wet but pleasing landscape, he left Horton in Ribblesdale and braved the rainswept B6749 and B6255.

It was a short journey, but a pleasant one, partly due to Radio Three. It was a good thing, he reflected, that Lee hadn't insisted on having the radio on, because he would almost certainly have challenged Nick's taste in music. Actually, the defiant quality of Beethoven's *'Eroica' Symphony* provided a very suitable accompaniment to a journey through unceasing rain.

Arriving in Hawes at a little after eleven, he realised he was too early to check in at the Black Horse, and that, in any case, it would be closed until eleven-thirty, so he parked there and went in search of somewhere to sit in warm, dry surroundings and drink coffee.

Having found a table in a nearby café, Nick was enjoying the aroma of ground coffee and the comforting vista of rain falling outside, when a voice that was unmistakably American, interrupted his thoughts.

'One thing I will say for the UK is that you know something about making coffee.' He was middle-aged and tanned, the latter being an unusual sight in Britain, especially in view of the current trough of low pressure.

'That's very generous of you.' Nick looked up as the waitress came to his table. 'Just coffee, please,' he told her.

'A cafetiere, sir?'

'Just a small one, please.'

'Very good, sir.' She made a note on her pad and left him.

'Yes, sir,' said the American, 'the standard of catering in this country leaves something to be desired, but your coffee is on another level. It beats the hell out of the stuff we get at home.'

'I'm gratified to hear it.'

'My wife's gone looking round the town. You know what women are like. You just can't keep 'em away from stores and boutiques, as I'm sure you'll agree. Do you mind if I join you?'

'Be my guest.' If the poor bloke was lonely, who was Nick to refuse him company?

The man extended his hand. 'Randy Webster from Richmond, Virginia.'

'Nick Burnett from Bradford, West Yorkshire. I'm pleased to meet you, Randy.'

'For some reason, English people kinda crease up when I tell them my name,' he confided. 'I have only to say, "I'm Randy", and they just can't stop laughing. It's actually Andrew, but folks have always called me "Randy".'

'I can understand that, Randy. In colloquial English, it translates into American as "horny", but don't worry, because you're in friendly company.'

Shock gave way to relief. 'I'm grateful to you for telling me that, Nick,' he said. 'By the way, do you live hereabouts?'

'I live on the outskirts of Bradford.'

'Not far away, huh?'

'Not really.' All things were relative. 'I'm just taking a short break.'

'Good for you. If you don't mind my asking, what do you do when you're not resting?'

Déjà vu loomed again, but Nick answered honestly, 'I'm a teacher.'

'You teach school, huh?'

'That's right.' Possibly because it was friendlier, Nick found 'huh?' less disturbing than the animal feed salesman's 'hm?' Also, it wasn't all that different from the local 'eh?'

'I'm in plastic extrusion, Nick.'

It sounded painful, but Nick refrained from saying so. Instead, he said, 'It sounds like an industry with a future.'

'I sure hope so. I have two sons and five grandsons lined up to take over from me when they're ready.'

'No granddaughters?' He made room for the waitress to lay out his coffee things.

'I'll have another of those things, as well, honey. Your coffee's most appealing.'

'I'm glad you like it, sir. I'll bring it along in just a minute.'

Returning to their conversation, he said, 'No granddaughters yet, Nick, but time will tell.'

'Good luck, Randy.'

'Thank you, Nick. Tell me, do you enjoy teaching school?'

'Yes, I do. Like any job, it has its downside, but generally speaking, I enjoy it.' He couldn't help saying, 'You know, you're the first person I've spoken to since I left home, who's not complained about teachers having long holidays.'

Randy struggled with the language for a moment, and then made the adjustment. 'Oh, you mean *vacations*. Heck, everyone in this country gets to take long vacations. Having said that, though, we get more public holidays than you do, so I guess that kinda balances things up.'

'I suppose it does. Anyway, it makes a pleasant change, as I said, not to be harangued about it.'

Randy's cafetiere arrived, and he was suitably grateful. 'Thank you, honey. I've been looking forward to this.'

'I hope you enjoy it, sir.'

'Oh, I will.' When she was gone, he said, 'They talk with a funny accent round these parts, a little different from yours, if you don't mind my saying so.'

'Feel free to comment, Randy. I'm bullet proof.'

'Oh, I'm not criticising. You mustn't think that.'

'No offence taken, I assure you.'

'I'm relieved to hear it.' He depressed the plunger in his cafetiere and, possibly in a hurry to change the subject, asked, 'What kind of school is it, where you teach, Nick?'

'It's a comprehensive school. That's all-ability from thirteen to eighteen.'

'So your system's similar to ours, except our kids leave at seventeen.'

'As it stands, but there are murmurs of disagreement at City Hall, and I imagine it's only a matter of time before Bradford changes over to the more common system of two schools: five to eleven and eleven to eighteen.'

'Is that so?' Seemingly unable to imagine such a change, he asked, 'What subject do you teach at your high school?'

Nick braced himself and said, 'History.'

'History, huh? I must say I'm surprised.'

Thrown for a minute at not having to face the usual reaction, Nick asked, 'Why are you surprised, Randy?'

'Well, you see, history is very important in the States. We have a glorious history going right back to the War of Independence, but you guys don't have anything like that, so I'm surprised to hear you say that you teach history.'

It was Nick's turn to be surprised. However, such an unusual challenge begged a rational answer. 'We teach British and European History, and you'll be surprised to learn that in Britain alone we've experienced more than one revolution.'

'You don't say.'

'I do, Randy. There was the Peasants' Revolt in thirteen eighty-one; there were three civil wars between sixteen forty-two and sixteen fifty-one; there was the "Glorious Revolution", as we call it, in sixteen eighty-eight, and the Chartists' Revolt in the nineteenth century.'

'You don't say. I'd no idea you guys had a civil war over here, too.'

'In our own humble way,' confirmed Nick, 'followed by eleven years as a republic, from sixteen forty-nine to sixteen-sixty, such awful years that they led to democratic government and a constitutional monarchy.'

'Democratic government?' It was a cry of horror. 'When was that?'

'Basically by sixteen eighty-eight.'

Randy stared at him in disbelief. 'Do you mean to say,' he said, 'you had a republic and a democracy before we did?'

'I'm afraid so.' He felt almost sorry for the disillusioned man, and he could imagine how parents must have felt when their children learned the unpalatable truth about Santa Claus. 'If it's any consolation, Randy, we weren't the first.'

'No?'

'The Ancient Greeks had democracy two-and-a-half thousand years ago.'

'No.' It was like a plea for mercy.

'That's right. It was the brainchild of Plato.'

'Surely not.'

'It's all there in black and white, Randy. Plato's masterwork *Republic* tells the whole, disappointing story.' He decided not to tell him about Plato's true feelings about democracy. The unfortunate man had already suffered enough.

'Well, waddaya know. I always thought democracy was an American invention, like everything else.'

'I'm sure you're not alone in that, Randy.'

Fortunately for the traumatised wretch, moral support arrived in the shape of a large lady, who shook her umbrella and closed the café door before advancing resolutely on their table.

'So you're still here, Randy,' she said, 'and you've found company, I see.'

'Eleanor,' said Randy, still visibly shaken, 'this is Nick. He teaches history. Heck, how he teaches history!'

* * *

It would have been a great shame to leave Hawes without a quantity of the cheese for which it was famed, Randy's entertaining company notwithstanding, so Nick made the acquisition the next morning before driving to Hardraw.

Access to Hardraw Force, the highest surface waterfall in the country and therefore well worth a visit, was via the Green Dragon Inn, so a leisurely start was both necessary and desirable.

Having allowed the Green Dragon time to open, he went in and ordered a pint of bitter. He found he was alone in the bar, but it wasn't long before a couple came in. They exchanged a quick greeting, and then the woman made for the fire while her companion got the drinks in.

'Hi,' he said, 'do you know if they serve cold beer in this place?'

'Yes.' Nick pointed to two lager signs and asked, 'American?'

'No, we're from Canada.' He added, 'New Brunswick.'

'I'm sorry, my mistake. It was your question about cold beer that threw me.'

The Canadian nodded. 'I just can't get used to drinking beer at room temperature.'

'It's an acquired taste,' said Nick, nursing his pint protectively.

'You know,' said the Canadian conversationally, 'some things in Britain are familiar. Others aren't.'

It seemed unremarkable to Nick, who said, 'I imagine so.'

'One thing that's different is that the roads are so narrow, I can't believe it.'

'You know why, don't you?'

'No, it beats me.'

Nick put his pint down and turned on his stool to explain. 'It's because our roads were built by Roman soldiers, and they marched everywhere two abreast.'

'Is that so?'

'Everywhere,' confirmed Nick, 'so, even allowing for two-way traffic, there was no point in making the roads wider than four generously-sized men.'

'I guess there wasn't.' He broke off to order his drinks. 'Two half-pints of Carlsberg, please.' Turning again to Nick, he said, 'We've just come from Wales. They have road signs in two languages, just as we do in New Brunswick. I guess there's no call for that in England.'

'Not nowadays.' He let the Canadian pay for his drinks and said, 'We've had nothing like that since the Romans left....' He looked at his watch. 'In four-ten AD, it was.'

Incredulously, the visitor asked, 'Does your wristwatch do centuries as well as days of the month?'

'No,' said Nick, 'it's just a habit I have.'

The Canadian handed a glass of lager to his companion and asked, 'You say, "since the Romans left". What did they do before that?'

'They insisted on all public signs being written in Latin. It was an awful nuisance.'

'I guess it would be.' The visitor's features suggested that he was unsure about the matter.

'The worst time came shortly after they'd left, and the Saxons came looting and pillaging. The old signs were still up, and the Saxons couldn't read one of them, the first one they came across, actually, and because of that it was an awful time to be on the move. There was incident after incident on our crowded, narrow roads.'

'What did the sign say?'

'*Magna Britannia vos recipit. Semper iter ad sinistram.*' Recognising incomprehension, he said, 'No, it meant nothing to them, either. It meant, "Welcome to Great Britain. Keep to the left." '

Suddenly, the Canadian grinned and slapped Nick on the shoulder. 'Hey,' he said, 'that was good. You had me going, there. Will you write that down for me? Just the Latin.'

'Okay.' Nick wrote the message on a beer mat with his ballpoint pen, and handed it to him.

'Oh, thanks for that. I'm going to have some fun when I get back to New Brunswick.'

'You're welcome. When I've finished this pint, I'm going through the back to see Hardraw Force. It's the biggest above-ground waterfall we can offer, but I imagine it'll be tiny compared with what you have in Canada.'

'That's not the point, though, is it? We haven't come four thousand miles to see familiar sights, and everything in Britain is in miniature. It's great.'

It was good to meet someone who was truly appreciative.

* * *

Tan Hill was Nick's next stop, and particularly, the Tan Hill Inn. It was reputed to be the highest pub in the country, and that ensured its appeal to Nick, who had long since decided that the happiest pubs were the highest. He'd known some miserable places in the city centre and other locations closer to sea level. He'd also known some dire pubs in Cambridgeshire, but the Raggalds Inn in Queensbury and the Mountain Eagle, while it still existed, were always places of hearty welcome and friendly banter. He put it down to climate. People who frequented high, and therefore cold, places, had to be cheerful, because if they weren't, they'd be rejected by the jovial majority, and then they'd have to go outside and freeze to death.

After a day of sightseeing, albeit through a veil of vertical rain, he arrived at the Tan Hill Inn. There were a few cars in the carpark, so the conditions hadn't deterred everyone.

He found the landlord in a playful mood.

'What can I do for you?' he asked.

'Have you got a single room for tonight?'

'Ah, a single room for tonight.' He consulted his register and said, 'As it happens, I can offer you such a room, and one that commands a panoramic view in suitable weather.'

'Excellent. Of course, it would, wouldn't it?'

'I can guarantee it.' Placing the register on the bar, he said, 'We're actually a bit quiet just now. For some reason, folk don't seem to want to come out. Are you doin' a bit of walking?'

'Only as far as my car tomorrow.'

The landlord laughed, as every landlord should, and Nick knew he'd found the jovial company he was seeking.

* * *

A thoroughly pleasant evening, a dreamless night and an excellent breakfast later, Nick took the short walk to his car and set out for Middleton in Teesdale. His route took him through Bowes and therefore past Dotheboys Hall, originally Bowes Academy and immortalised by Charles Dickens in *Nicholas Nickleby*, hence its new name.

The building was unremarkable. If anything, it suggested an atmosphere of dourness, which certainly matched Dickens's first impression. Apparently, publication of the novel had resulted in several schools, including Bowes Academy, being closed. Dickens had his detractors, but no one could say that his positive influence was less than far-reaching.

He'd booked a room at the Teesdale Arms, so he drove straight into the carpark on reaching Middleton in Teesdale, and went to reception.

I realise I'm a bit early,' he said, 'but it's so unpleasant outside, I wonder if I could have lunch.'

The receptionist checked his reservation and said, 'Your room's available now, Mr Burnett, and we serve lunch from eleven-thirty onwards.'

'That's good news. Thank you.' He completed his registration and took his bag up to his room. There was no need to unpack, as he was only there for one night, so he simply left his bag in front of the dressing table and was about to go down for lunch, when he heard a woman's voice say, 'Bugger.' She could only have been referring to a minor setback or maybe a mildly irritating person, because her tone was quite without emotion; he would even have described it as matter-of-fact. Emerging from his room, he saw the woman in question. She was at the end of the landing, peering through the narrow window.

'If you're referring to the weather,' he said, 'I quite agree. It really is a bugger.'

'Oh, hello,' she said, turning round to face him, 'I didn't know there was anyone there.' She was probably in her twenties, slender, with dark hair and even features. In all, and in the right mood, she might be quite appealing, although her general demeanour seemed to be one of displeasure.

'I wasn't eavesdropping. I was putting my bag in my room and I heard you say, "Bugger". As I pointed out, if you were talking about the weather, I'm in complete agreement.'

'I had it in mind to visit High Force Waterfall, but apparently they've closed it because of the weather. That's the bugger I was referring to.'

'It sometimes happens after heavy rainfall, and let's face it, no one could blame them just now.' He asked, 'Are you alone?'

'Yes.'

'My name's Nick Burnett, and I was just going down for lunch. Will you join me?'

'I don't know. I'm not very entertaining company.'

'Surely, that's for me to find out. For all you know, I may find you quite fascinating. On the other hand, if you turn out to be as dull as you say you are, be assured I shan't so much as hint at it, so there'll be absolutely no need for unpleasantness.'

'All right.' She gave him a half-smile and shook his hand. 'Sally Fordham, and I'll join you.' She locked the door of the room next to his and followed him down the staircase.

He stopped at the entrance to the dining room to ask, 'Have you any preference? Table, I mean.'

'Not really.'

When the waitress approached them, Nick asked, 'Could we have a table in the window, please? I like to see the rain on the other side, where it belongs. It makes me feel cosy.'

'By all means, sir. Would you like to come this way?' She led them to a table for two that matched his request. 'Everything you'll find on the menu is available, sir.'

'Thank you.' He took a menu from her.

'I don't usually eat much at lunch,' said Sally.

'I don't exactly go mad, but we should make an effort. Shall we have a main course and then see how we feel?'

'That's a good idea.' She was beginning to look more relaxed.

'You told me you're not entertaining company, Sally. Did you mean generally, or is it a fleeting mood?'

She hesitated. 'It's a passing thing. Tell me, why have you come to Middleton in Teesdale?'

'I'm driving part of the Pennine Way, basically because it's too wet for walking, and driving's the only other option.'

'You could have stayed at home.'

'No.' He shook his head decisively. 'That's a cop-out.' Then, feeling that he should give her a fuller answer, he said, 'I'm taking a break from some historical research I'm doing. I've reached what looks like a dead end, and I felt that a complete break might help.'

'I see. Is that what you do? History?'

'I'm a history teacher.' He hoped she wasn't about to say the usual thing and, in case a diversion were needed, he said, 'Fair exchange, Sally. What brings you here?' Meeting the awkward look again, he said, 'Forget I asked you that. It's obviously a private matter.'

'No, it's all right, but it's going to sound silly.'

'You wouldn't believe how many silly things I've heard since I left home. I'm so used to it, I shan't turn a hair, honestly.'

Hesitantly, as if she were making a confession, she said, 'I was in a relationship and it broke up. I'm giving myself a spell of my own company in different surroundings as a sort of... comfort, really, I suppose. Actually, I remembered this place from my childhood, and I suppose I thought it might help.'

For an awkward moment, he thought she was going to become tearful, but that passed quickly enough. 'There now,' he said, 'that wasn't in the least silly.'

The waitress came to take their order, so he asked her for a wine list.

'I'll leave that to you,' said Sally.

A surprising number of women seemed happy to do that. They gave their order, and Nick asked for a bottle of Nuits St Georges. When the waitress was gone, he said, 'By all means tell me to mind my own business, but how long has it been since your relationship ended?'

'A few weeks.' Lowering her eyes, she said, 'I didn't intend burdening you with it.'

'There's no question of that. Do you still come across this chap.' As he spoke, he noticed that his question seemed to unsettle her, and he wondered if his use of the word 'chap' were appropriate. Maybe she turned out for the other side. It was always possible, but she set his mind at rest when she spoke again.

'Just to put you in the picture,' she said, 'I'm a nurse, and the man in question is a physiotherapist. I work on an orthopaedic ward, so it's a little difficult, avoiding him, or the… colleague he's now seeing.'

The waitress arrived with the wine for Nick to taste.

'That's good,' he said, 'thank you.'

She poured some into both glasses and left them.

'I really don't know why I'm telling all this to a stranger,' said Sally.

'Strangers are often better than friends in this situation, but if you prefer not to, that's fine. We can talk about nothing in particular and have a relaxing lunch with a drink or two. Let's be honest, there's not much else we can get up to while the weather's like this.' He picked up his glass and said, 'I give you "Peace of Mind".'

She smiled properly for the first time. 'Peace of Mind,' she said, 'and if you can't give me that, at least you've made me feel a little better.'

'That's the spirit.'

'Are you… in a relationship?'

'No, my last girlfriend walked out on me in June.'

'Oh, I'm sorry.'

'I'm not.'

'Oh?'

'Her name was Amanda, but I called her "Acid Drop". It seemed to suit her.'

The thought evidently amused her, because she smiled properly for the second time. 'I'm beginning to get the picture,' she said.

'It doesn't work for everyone, but I find that when things go wrong, it helps to remember the other person's failings. The difference in my case was that I was aware of Amanda's shortcomings from the start, and she left me in no doubt about mine. That way, we were able to part on adverse terms and with no sense of loss on either side.'

'If only life were always so simple.'

'There was nothing simple about it. She accused me of being more interested in Oliver Cromwell than I was in her.'

'Weren't you?' It was almost a tease, an improvement in itself.

'Cromwell?' He shuddered. 'No, it would never have worked. All those warts, not to mention half-an-hour's fervent prayer each bedtime, and insistence thereafter on the Puritan position.'

She closed her eyes for a moment and then opened them, saying, 'I may regret asking you this, but what's the Puritan position?'

'The same as the missionary position, but performed throughout in a thoughtful, sombre and sanctimonious mood.'

Their main course arrived and, when the waitress was gone, Sally asked,

'Was Cromwell central to your research?'

'Not Cromwell himself, but the social, political and religious ethos the Protectorate created, and its effect on the good people of Bradford.'

Her question had evidently arisen from good manners rather than genuine inquiry, because her next one came with a change of subject. 'What will be your next stop?'

'I don't know. I was going to continue to the end of the Pennine Way, but I really can't see the point if I can't see the scenery.'

'And to think I was going to visit a waterfall, as if enough water hasn't fallen already.'

'Try to think of it in a positive light,' he suggested, refilling her glass.

It was clearly a challenge. 'You think I should view this miserable, endless rainfall as a positive feature?'

'Think of it this way. This afternoon, you and I can sit in the warmth and shelter of the hotel lounge, drinking coffee, chatting idly and thumbing our noses at the rain outside, rather as children snuggle cosily in bed and enjoy the sound of rain lashing against the window panes.'

'You should work for Walt Disney.'

'It's a thought,' he agreed. 'Someone needs to stop the screenwriters rewriting history, but why cross the Atlantic when there's so much to waiting to be done here?'

As Nick had suggested earlier, they chatted about nothing in particular and spent a lazy and enjoyable lunch in each other's company. When the waitress brought the bill, Nick signed it and added his room number. At his suggestion, they decided to take their coffee in the hotel lounge.

'Are you sure I can't contribute half?' asked Sally.

'Perfectly sure. You've suffered quite enough.' Offering her his hand, he said, 'Come and listen to the raindrops. Chopin actually wrote a piece of music about them.'

'Who?'

'Frederick Chopin. "Fred" to his friends.'

'If he's a friend of yours, there's no telling what funny ideas he might have.'

'I'll tell him that when I see him,' he said. 'Meanwhile, let's sit in comfort.'

They each took an armchair on either side of a low table, and coffee was brought to them. As she poured it out, Sally asked, 'Do you believe in ghosts, Nick?'

In view of recent experiences, her question took him quite by surprise, but he was careful not to react. 'I have an open mind,' he told her, wondering what had prompted the subject.

'The nurses' home at the hospital where I work is said to be haunted.'

'Is it really?'

'Yes, apparently a student nurse who was there in the early sixties took her own life. She swallowed an overdose of Nembutal and was found dead the next morning.'

'Poor girl. I can't imagine anything worse than to feel hopeless enough to do that.'

'You really mean that, don't you?'

'Of course I do.'

'You see,' she said, handing him his coffee, 'you give the impression that you don't take life all that seriously. It was a surprise, that's all.'

'I don't take my own life seriously, but that doesn't mean I'm not sympathetic to others.' Still intrigued by the ghost story, he asked, 'Have you had an encounter with the ghost?'

'No, and I don't know anyone who has, but I've heard of various incidents.' She paused. 'You won't laugh, will you?'

'You know I won't.'

Reassured, she continued. 'The story that's told is that every now and again a student nurse finds herself at a low ebb – it happens more frequently than you'd think – and that's when the ghost walks, or however ghosts move around. Girls have been reported as saying that they were scared at first, but who wouldn't be? Then, the next morning, it's as if they've been given new heart.'

The story appealed to Nick. 'Comfort and support from beyond the grave,' he said. 'I like that.' Remembering his own experiences, he asked, 'Has anyone described the way the ghost manifests herself?'

'They most likely have, but I haven't heard anything. They do say, however, that they're left feeling far more positive in the morning.'

'Yes,' he agreed, impressed by the whole story, 'I like this girl, whoever she was. She must have felt desperate to do what she did, and now she goes out of her way to bring comfort to other girls. I can see, as well, how such a situation can occur. A girl of maybe eighteen is away from home for the first time, and she's seen something horrible, maybe a fatality, on the ward. It would prey on her mind....' He shuddered at the picture he'd created.

'You really are sympathetic.'

'I hope so.' A question that had been at the back of his mind now occurred to him, and he asked, 'What made you think of that story?'

'It was an association. Apparently this building was once said to be haunted.' She laughed. 'Naturally, the advertising blurb makes light of it.'

'In any case,' he said, 'don't give it a moment's thought. I'll be in the next room. If I hear you scream, I'll give you moral support.'

'What will you do?'

'I'll scream as well, and then it'll be two against one.'

'You're hopeless.'

He was confused, as well, as he often was in exchanges with the opposite sex. She said he was sympathetic, which was a welcome compliment, but he was hopeless as well. By the loose association of chatting with a nurse, he remembered his conversation with the two girls at school, and he said, 'A girl asked me recently if Florence Nightingale was as good as she was made out to be.'

'What did you tell her?'

'I said she was a truly great person. Not only did she save a great many lives, she also fought her corner, and for a woman of her time, that was remarkable. I said that if I'd been around in the mid-nineteenth century, I'd have wanted her to have my children.'

'You didn't tell children that, did you?'

'No, I thought of that later, but my admiration for her is genuine enough.'

Like a parent giving disappointing news, she said, 'In any case, she wouldn't have had your children, Nick. She wouldn't even have married you.'

'Did she turn out for the other side?' If she did, it was something he'd never considered.

'If you're asking if she was a lesbian, no, she wasn't. She received several proposals of marriage, but she turned them all down so that she could continue with her work.'

'What a woman, and what a legacy.'

They talked the afternoon away quite happily, while rain continued to fall outside.

* * *

After dinner, that evening, the subject of Sally's broken relationship re-emerged, although she seemed somehow to have distanced herself from it.

'What you really need,' said Nick, 'is something that works as an emotional enema, to get him right out of your system.'

'What a horrible thought.'

'In the absence of such a process, it seems to me that you have possibly two courses open to you. You could ask to be transferred to another ward, department or whatever, or you could apply for a job in a different hospital.'

'I've already applied for a job in Lancaster,' she said, 'and I did that with a view to getting away, but you know, I have to say, I feel so much better after spending time with you today.'

'I'm glad to hear it. Stick around and you'll soon be as footloose and carefree as I am.' The lounge was quite busy, and they'd found themselves on a sofa, so it seemed quite natural for Nick to take her hand. She made no objection.

'I wish I hadn't remembered that ghost story today,' she said. 'I can't get it out of my mind.'

'I'll be next door, as I told you. Scream once, and I'll be there.'

'That's very reassuring. I'm going up to bed now, so keep your ear to the wall.'

'Better than that,' he said, 'I'll escort you to your room and let the spectre know you're under my protection. That way, she can't say she hasn't been warned.'

'Phew! I'm glad you're here.' She got up and followed him to the stairs.

'I'm not getting any vibes so far,' he said, mounting the stairs with elaborate care.

'Don't, you'll scare me, saying things like that.'

'You've nothing to fear as long as I'm around, Sally. Just hang on to my coat tails.'

'You're not wearing tails.'

'I meant it figuratively.' He stopped on the landing, peering theatrically in all directions. Finally, he stood outside her door, listening intently. 'Okay so far,' he reported.

'You're not taking this seriously, Nick,' she said, unlocking the door.

'But I'm right behind you.'

She flicked on the light and went in. 'Are you going to check my room?' she asked.

'It's probably a good idea.' He took a cursory look beneath her bed and behind her dressing table. 'That seems to be okay,' he said.

'What about inside my wardrobe?'

'I'd never dream of looking inside a lady's wardrobe or her... lingerie drawer... for that matter, but if you insist....' He opened the wardrobe and pronounced it free of spectres.

'You're enjoying this, aren't you?'

'I've told you,' he said, placing his hands on her waist, 'you've nothing to fear.' He kissed her on each cheek, and then, as a studied afterthought, again, full on the lips.

'How did I know this was going to happen?'

'I've no idea,' he said. 'I only thought of it just now.' As if to demonstrate the merit of his idea, he kissed her again. 'You must have been kissed better at some time. Everyone has.'

'Not for a long time.' Even so, she accepted another kiss.

'Doesn't the NHS prescribe it nowadays?'

'I don't know that it ever did. In fact, it draws a firm line at familiarity with patients.'

'I'm under no such constraint.'

'I've… noticed. Have you… got,' she asked between kisses, 'the… necess… ary?'

'Yes.' He saw no need to tell her he'd acquired some from the machine in the gents that afternoon.

'I never expected this when I booked the hotel.' She looked at him in surprise when he unfastened her clasp and ran her zipper down. 'I wasn't expecting that either,' she said, stepping out of her dress.

'I'll turn my back while you take off your tights,' he said.

'This is no time for an attack of modesty.'

'It's not that. I just find that tights tend to put me off.'

They finished undressing, and Sally got into bed. 'I'll leave you to switch the main light off,' she said, lighting the bedside lamp.

'Do you know,' he asked, kissing her again, 'the Mandarin word for what we're about to do?'

'Oddly enough, no. Do you?'

'Yes, it's "*xing jiao*". Unlike you and I, they find it easy to say. It just rolls off the Chinese tongue as easily as "prawn crackers", and I suppose that's why there are so many of them. If they found it harder to say, it might deter some of them from doing it.'

She made no reply, which was always better than struggling with the unpronounceable.

* * *

It seemed a long time since Nick had woken up to the sound of teaspoon and china in productive partnership, and he lay for a while with his eyes closed, enjoying it while he could.

Suddenly, from nowhere, he felt a kiss, and he opened his eyes to see that he was being offered a cup of tea.

'Thank you,' he said. 'I thought for one awful minute the ghost had got among the china.'

'No, it was only me.' She slithered beneath the duvet again and snuggled up to him. 'It's such a shame,' she said, 'that last night was our first and last.'

'Oh no, the cure takes a little longer than that. You're here for the next three nights, aren't you?'

'That's right,' she said, suddenly more cheerful, 'until Saturday.'

'In that case,' he announced, 'so am I, and by the end of the week, you'll have forgotten what you ever saw in him.'

'Who?' she asked. Then, feigning recollection, she said, 'Oh, him. Yes, another three nights should do it.' Watching him, she asked, 'Are you going to drink that tea?'

'That's my intention. Have you something in mind?'

'Yes, I need more therapy.'

'Okay.' He put down his cup and saucer. ' "Tote that barge, lift that pail". There's no rest for the talented and good-looking.'

9

A PICTURE AND A NAME

By the end of the week, Nick was able to chalk up a complete cure and was therefore able to leave Sally happier than before. They both knew their liaison could only ever have been a fleeting one; with Sally based in Manchester and possibly Lancaster, and Nick in Bradford, anything more ambitious would have been fraught with difficulty, so their parting was painless, with just a hint of regret.

Nick returned to find messages on his phone. Most of them were unimportant, but one gained his immediate reaction, because it was from Angela at Newbury Hall. As soon as he was unpacked and his laundry was in the washing machine, he phoned her.

'Newbury Hall. How can I help you?' It sounded like the inarticulate youth who'd answered earlier.

'Good afternoon. It's Nick Burnett returning a call from Angela.'

'Hang about. I'll see if I can find her.'

He was right. It was the inarticulate youth.

After half-a-minute or so, he heard a woman's footsteps and then Angela's voice. 'Hello, Angela speaking.'

'Angela, it's Nick Burnett. Didn't he tell you?'

'Oh, don't, Nick. It's taken until now for him to learn which end of the phone to speak into.'

'I got that impression.'

'Where've you been? The Costa del Sol? I wouldn't blame you.'

'No, I drove part of the Pennine Way, just to have a break from my research.'

'Fair enough. Did you have any joy?'

'Eventually.' There was no need to tell her more than that.

'Good, I rang you for two reasons. One is that the document we found has turned out to be quite interesting. It's not ready to be handed over yet, but it shouldn't be long.'

'Why is it interesting, Angela?'

'Well, it turns out it's a list of what Sir William Newbury called "False and Unjust Arrests". We can only imagine he was saving the list for a time when he could give the information to higher authority, or when he hoped to see the local military under the command of a more enlightened officer.'

'That's excellent, Angela. Obviously, it's not what I'm looking for, because Sir William was still alive, but it must help with the overall picture. Did he name the officer in charge at the time?'

'Yes, he did. It's slipped my mind for now, but as soon as I remember it, I'll let you know.'

'Oh, thanks, Angela. It sounds very promising.'

'Yes, it does. Our other "find" should please you as well.'

'Don't tease. What is it?'

'It's a portrait of Lady Newbury. We put it away a few years ago and basically forgot about it, but it was restored in nineteen seventy-eight, so it's in good condition.'

'That's good news. It doesn't help with the research, but it'll be interesting to see it. Can I come over?'

'I don't see why not. We're not open to visitors, but you can come to the office and I'll show it to you.'

'I'll come over this afternoon. I'm back at school on Monday.'

'Okay, I'll put the kettle on.'

'And I'll bring you some Wensleydale cheese.'

'In that case,' she said with sudden enthusiasm, 'I'll get the biscuits out.'

* * *

Nick parked beside the Transit pick-up that had taken his usual place. As he hadn't been there for some time, he swallowed his resentment and walked round to the office door.

It was a while before his knock was answered, and when it was, he recognised a face from the near past, but the name eluded him. Sounding like a child on an errand, the youth announced, 'There's no visitors allowed in 'til further notice.'

'I know, but I arranged to meet Angela.'

'Right.' He went, presumably in search of Angela, leaving Nick on the doorstep with the less than useful knowledge that the inarticulate youth now had a face. He returned after a short time with Angela.

'It's all right, Scott,' she told him. 'I can find my way to the office, thank you.' Seeing Nick at the door, she said, 'Come inside, Nick. At least it's not raining now, but you'll feel more welcome.'

Nick stepped inside and closed the outer door behind him. 'Open your bag, Angela,' he said.

'Oh, this is my lucky day,' she said, picking up a shopping bag and holding it with her eyes closed.

'There, two baby Wensleydale cheeses.'

'Two?'

'Because you're worth it.'

'Oh, thank you, Nick.' She put her bag back in its place beneath her desk and accepted a kiss on her cheek. 'I asked Scott to put the kettle on,' she said, looking at the brewing facilities, 'and that's just what he's done. He's put the kettle on and walked away from it. I hope he remembered to fill it.' She checked the electric kettle and, with her suspicion confirmed, unplugged it and topped it up at the sink.

'I remember him vaguely, but I don't think I ever taught him.'

'That was a lucky escape,' she said, dropping teabags into two mugs. 'Tell me about your holiday. It's the closest I'll get to experiencing one this year.'

'I'm sorry to hear that, Angela.' He didn't want to crow, but she had asked. 'I met a man in Malham, who told me that teachers were clueless and that history was a waste of time. In Hawes, I met a very pleasant American, who couldn't understand why history was taught over here, when we lack their glorious past. He was surprised to hear that we'd had three civil wars and various upheavals, and he was sickened to learn that, not only had we experienced democracy and a republic before they had, but that Plato had written reams about both in the fourth century BC. He'd previously believed democracy to be an American invention, like every other wonder on this planet.'

'Oh dear,' said Angela, pouring water on the tea. 'If he lives long enough, he's in for a few more unpleasant surprises. Who else did you meet?'

'A friendly Canadian with a sense of humour.'

'No misgivings about the teaching of history?'

'We didn't touch on it.' Thinking again, he said, 'In Middleton in Teesdale, I met a nurse from Manchester, who was recovering from a broken relationship.'

'Milk, but no sugar, isn't it?'

'Yes, please.'

'Were you able to offer her sympathy and comfort?'

'Yes,' he said, taking a mug of tea, 'I left her in a much better frame of mind.' He couldn't help smiling, and that triggered a reaction from Angela.

'You didn't... did you?'

'She was more than compliant, and I did leave her in a happier state than before.'

'Well,' she said, viewing him with exaggerated wonder, 'you must have something special.'

'I do my humble best.'

Chuckling to herself, she took a packet of Hobnobs from a cupboard and examined it. 'Scott's been at these again,' she said, turning out the last two biscuits. At least he left us one each.' Looking through the office doorway, she said, 'Talk of the devil.' When he was within earshot, she said, 'The kettle's boiled, Scott, but you'll have to make it yourself. It serves you right for being a greedy sod.'

Unabashed, Scott made himself a mug of tea with a mountain of sugar, which he stirred in, creating a wave that spilled over the brim of his mug. Nick watched him, fascinated, but Angela ignored him, being used to his ways. Having made his tea, he addressed Nick. 'Did you used to be a teacher at Delius High School?' he asked.

'Unless you've heard something I haven't, I still am.'

Scott nodded. 'I remember seein' you there.'

Going back two conversations, Angela said to Nick, 'I can't believe you sorted out that girl's problem by…. Was she really in a bad way when you met her?'

'Not really. It had happened a few weeks earlier. I think she just needed to get him out of her system.'

'Well, she did that all right.' She reached for her bag and took out a purse. 'Will you be a good lad, Scott,' she asked, 'and nip round to the shop?'

'All right.'

She gave him some money. 'Get a packet of Hobnobs, will you? By rights, you should be paying for these, but I'll let you off.' She waited until he'd gone, and said, 'While Prince Charming's out of the way, I'll show you that portrait. If I let him anywhere near it, it won't last two minutes. Bring your camera and follow me.'

She led him to one of the rooms off the hall, now serving as a lumber room, presumably for the duration of the restoration, and showed him a framed painting. The frame measured something like six feet by three, and it was carved, like so many things, out of dark oak. 'Just take a look at this,' she said, turning it to take advantage of the available light.

For Nick, it was more than a surprise. It was painted extremely well in the Renaissance style and, whether or not the artist had set out to flatter Lady Newbury, Nick had no idea, but it was the portrait of a very striking woman. The main surprise, though, was that, having formed a mental picture of her, with nothing to call on but his imagination, he now found that the artist's depiction was uncannily like his own.

'A very attractive woman, I'd call her,' said Angela.

'She had a sensitive face,' he agreed. 'Her eyes were quite remarkable, weren't they? Very expressive.'

'She doesn't look like a woman who's spent the early years of her marriage having children.'

'The first five years, I suppose,' said Nick. 'The eldest was in his fourth year when he died.' He opened the camera case and removed the lens cap. Berating himself for not bringing a tripod, he steadied the camera on the back of a chair and zoomed in on the painting.

'You can always come again,' said Angela, watching his make-shift preparations.

'It's just as well. I might bring the right equipment another time.' He took several exposures before he was satisfied.

'Fred Flintstone's back,' said Angela. 'I'd better put her away.' She gave Nick an odd smile and said, 'You can come back and see your lady-love another time.' She returned the painting to the lumber room, shaking her head and saying, 'I wonder what she'd have thought if she'd known what you were up to last week.'

Not surprisingly, the thought had also crossed Nick's mind, but for no more than a moment before he dismissed it as fanciful.

They returned to the office, where Angela put the kettle on again, now that biscuits were once more available.

* * *

The photographs might take a day or so, depending on how busy they were at the Kodak shop, but Nick remembered the painting, almost as if it were in the room with him. It had pleased him to think of Lady Newbury as physically appealing and, assuming that the artist had produced a fair representation of her, the portrait had certainly reinforced that fancy. It shouldn't have made any difference, but it did seem to make the barbarous crime committed at Newbury Hall more terrible than ever.

Because there was nothing he could do immediately, he began putting things together for the new term. The new intake, or Year Nine, as they now had to be called would be in on Monday, with Years Ten and Eleven joining them the next day. Lastly, Years Twelve and Thirteen would make up the numbers on Wednesday. Free time on Monday and Tuesday would be given over to staff and departmental meetings. For the next term, Nick would support Kirsty Watford as far as he could, using his own resources, and then, after Christmas, everything would be in the hands of the Omniscient Owl. It was a chilling thought. Maybe he should have applied for the job after all.

He was thinking about that and lubricating the thinking process with cheap Bordeaux, when the phone rang.

'Hello?'

'Nick, it's Angela. Sorry to bother you at this time, but I've just remembered the name of that Roundhead officer. It was Captain Josiah Edmunds.'

10

DAMNING EVIDENCE

So, Captain Josiah Edmunds was the villain of the piece. Nick almost wished he could check that with Lady Newbury, he was so delighted to have made at least some headway. Of course, academic rigour demanded something more worldly than an accusation levelled by a victim who'd been dead for three hundred years, but her confirmation would have been rewarding from his point of view, albeit in the form of a dislodged ornament or a pile of dust on a dressing table.

His first job the next morning was to take the film to the Kodak shop, which he did soon after opening.

'We're not very busy,' the assistant told him. 'It's probably down to the weather. Anyway, your photos will be ready this afternoon.'

'Oh, that's good. Look, there are just four exposures on the film, but they're important. Could you do me a ten by eight enlargement of each, please?'

'Certainly.' She made a note. 'They'll be ready by three o' clock this afternoon.'

'Thank you.' All too often, the good things in his life came and went, but the Kodak shop was one blessing, he felt, that remained reassuringly constant.

His next job was to speak to Norman Lumb, which he did as soon as he arrived home.

'Nick,' said Norman, clearly pleased to hear from him again, 'I trust you had a pleasant break. My wife and I spent a fortnight in Aegina, which was infinitely preferable to what I understand you've had to contend with at home.'

'It was pleasant enough, thanks, Norman.' There was no need to go into detail, not that Professor Lumb would have appreciated it.

'Now, Trevor Raymond tells me that Newbury Hall has found corn in Egypt, and I must say it sounds more than exciting. Would you like to tell me about it?'

'That's the reason for this call, Norman. I haven't seen it yet. It's been undergoing all kinds of scientific treatment at the University of Bradford and apparently it's not yet sufficiently robust to be handed over to the Public Library.'

'These things always call for patience, Nick.'

'I'm being as patient as I know how, but I do know something about it. It seems to be a list of victims of what Sir William Newbury, in his capacity as a JP, called "False and Unjust Arrests". I suppose we could be looking at offences against the Puritan way of life: frivolous behaviour, working on the Sabbath and so on. At all events, the fact that Sir William hid the list securely suggests to me that he was hoping to show it at a later date to someone in authority, someone more sympathetic, I would suggest, than the current enforcer of the law.'

Enthusiastically, Norman asked, 'Do we have a name for this over-zealous Puritan?'

'A name and a rank, Norman. He was Captain Josiah Edmunds, about whom I know absolutely nothing apart from his perverted sense of righteousness.'

'But this is absolutely central to your enquiry. I must say, it's very exciting. From your point of view, as well, it couldn't have happened at a more opportune time.'

'Naturally, it doesn't help with the question of the Newbury Hall murders, but it does fill a hole, as you say, Norman.'

'It does more than that, Nick.' For one who counselled patience, Norman was beginning to sound increasing enthusiastic. 'The subject of your enquiry is how the Protectorate affected the local population, and this latest find sounds eminently promising. On the other hand, the murder of Sir William and his family is a very large bee that seems reluctant to vacate your bonnet. Seen objectively, supposing the evidence could be found, it could be a huge bonus. Otherwise, your enquiry could still be complete without it. In fact, I have high hopes for your M.Phil. dissertation. I think the time has finally come for you to start counting your hatched chickens, Nick.'

That wasn't how Nick felt, but he kept his reservation to himself. In any case, he had another concern. 'Returning to the list, Norman, it's only one source of information, isn't it? Chances of corroboration by an alternative source are too remote to consider.'

'Yes, but if you remember, in a case such as this, when evidence is so scarce, triangulation isn't strictly necessary. You can rely on one original source.'

'I remember now. That's a relief.'

'When are you back at school?'

'Monday.'

'Fine. Take the week to settle in, and then come and see me the following week.... Let me check my diary. How does Tuesday the fifteenth sound?'

Nick leafed quickly through his diary and said, 'I'm free after about five.'

'Good. Let's say five-thirty. That's when we'll go through your notes and look at the thing as a whole.'

* * *

As promised, the photographs and enlargements were ready for three o'clock, and Nick carried them home in a state of almost childish excitement. On arrival, he left the enprints and negatives in their wallet and took the enlargements instead from the large, yellow envelope.

Despite the absence of a tripod, they'd come out remarkably well, and he laid them side-by-side on the dining table to compare them in daylight. At first, he could see little difference in quality, but on more detailed examination, he found that one of them stood out from the rest. He'd given it a longer exposure than the others, and the whole thing seemed brighter. The only problem was that, despite the earlier restoration, the colours lacked contrast, and he decided the fault was most likely the aging process. Ludicrous though it seemed, however, the portrait had a quality that he was sure would lend itself to a monochrome copy, and that was something he could do for himself. It was only for his own amusement, anyway.

He took the negatives up to the small darkroom, smiling to himself as he remembered Amanda's reaction when she opened the door to put her cases away. 'What a bloody silly place to leave a sink!' That should have served as a warning, but he failed to recognise it as such at the time.

Fortunately, Amanda was now a memory, and he had room to work. Making a black-and-white print from a colour negative wasn't at all straightforward, but with the right filters and paper, and with a little patience, it was possible.

* * *

After dinner, he brought the print down from the darkroom. It was fairly dry, but inclined to curl up, so he placed it on the kitchen worktop with a salt mill, a pepper mill, a sugar bowl and a cream jug to hold it down. He was very pleased with the print; in fact, he was so pleased that he felt inclined to have it framed. While he was admiring it, he filled the kettle to make coffee. Then, having measured out ground coffee, he looked again excitedly at the print. He could imagine Lady Newbury alive and very much at the centre of her family, a loving mother scarcely out of girlhood, at least by modern standards. He was more determined than ever to expose the truth.

* * *

With the news that Sir William Newbury's list was now in the hands of the public library, Nick lost no time in requesting a microfilm copy. The story was already out and eagerly seized upon by various newspapers as well as local television news, and he imagined there would soon be a demand for copies.

He was able to pick up his copy on Friday of that week, and he took it immediately to the next floor, where they had microfilm readers and, almost as importantly, some with printers. Paper copies would cost him only ten pence each for A4 prints and twenty pence for A3, and there were only four pages, so he paid his money and took the tokens. He was warned that certain pages were permanently damaged, but he hoped he would still be able to form a clear picture of Sir William's concern.

Excitedly, he threaded the microfilm into the film carrier and wound on to the first page. Decay and disuse had combined to disfigure the surface, but Nick could clearly make out Sir William's ornate handwriting.

Sir William Newbury, Baronet and Justice of the Peace,
Newbury Hall, Thornton, Bradforde in the Countye of Yorke.

I, William Newbury, herebye atteste that the followinge Persons were arraigned and punished, as hereby stated, for the said Offences by Capt. Josiah Andrew Edmunds, withoute Reference to me nor to anye othere Justice.

Name and Abode	Offence	Penaltye	Date
Elsie Armley, 42 Top Cottage, Butterworthe Lane, Thornton.	*Witcherie*	*Death by Fire*	*16th. May, 1653*
Henry Long, 46 Bakerye, Long Lane, Thornton.	*Lewde Speche*	*Pilloryed 8 Hrs*	*2nd. June, 1653*
Bessie Fawthrope, 24, Ivye Cottage, Long Lane,S Thornton.	*Carryinge Water upon the Sabbath*	*Pilloryed 8 Hrs*	*19th. June, 1653*
Luke Stephens, 6, Rose Cottage, Carte Lane, Thornton	*Playinge upon the Sabbath*	*Whipped 6 Strokes*	*3rd. July, 1653*

Isaac Russell, 6, Top Cottage, Carte Lane, Thornton.	Playinge upon the Sabbath	Whipped 3rd. 6 Strokes	July, 1653
Naboth Smythe, 43, Well Ende Cottage, Town Streete, Thornton.	Sorcerie	Death by Hanging	6th. Oct., 1653
May Bosworth, 51, Ende Cottage, Carte Lanethe Thornton.	Workynge at Midwyferie upon Sabbath	Pilloryed 8 Hrs	24th. Dec., 1653
Elsie Smythe, 19, c/o Deane House, Thornton.	Syngynge in the Streete	Pilloryed 8 Hrs	15th Jan., 1654

Nick imagined Miss Smythe to have been in service at Deane House, possibly with little pleasure in her life, but for expressing whatever joy she found, by singing as she went about her work, she was fastened in a pillory for eight hours, to be pelted with rotten fruit and vegetables by those mindless or insensitive enough to take advantage of the situation. His sympathies were also with the two little children who were whipped for playing innocently on a Sunday, and to Mrs Bosworth, who had been punished for an errand of mercy. He couldn't bring himself to dwell on the cases of those put to death by hanging or by fire for alleged sorcery and witchcraft.

He read through the remainder of the document, except where the script was illegible, scarcely able to believe the horrors recorded on it. It was undated, presumably because it was incomplete. Clearly, Captain Edmunds went on to commit further excesses, and Sir William was murdered before he could pass the information to some person in authority. In hindsight, it was possible to believe that Cromwell would have been appalled by such a catalogue of evil, but who would have known that at the time? There was every likelihood that most would have seen the offences just as Edmunds presented them.

He rewound the microfilm and put it with the paper copies in his briefcase. As Norman Lumb had said, it would serve him well as part of his dissertation, and that was of prime importance. Unfortunately, however, it took him no closer to uncovering the murders at Newbury Hall.

11

In All But Name – and Salary

Brian Purley, M.A. (Oxon), Headteacher, also known to the irreverent minority as 'The Purley King', was seldom inclined towards frivolity; in fact, he was known to be an habitually solemn man, give or take an occasional heavy and ill-advised attempt at wit, and his attitude was particularly grave at staff briefing on the first day of term.

'I recently received some very disturbing news,' he said. 'Most of you will recall that we appointed Nathan Thorganby as Head of History last term, the appointment to take effect from this coming January.'

Suddenly Nick, who had been involved in his own thoughts, lent the headteacher his full attention.

'I regret to say that I have been informed that Mr Thorganby was arrested last week for an offence that will preclude him not only from taking up his appointment here, but also from teaching anywhere in the United Kingdom. The post will therefore be readvertised. There is, fortunately, time to make a subsequent appointment.'

Barbara Morris, Co-ordinator for Special Needs, who could always be relied upon to lengthen any meeting, inevitably had something to say. 'Mr Purley, if Mr Thorganby was arrested only last week, surely everything must depend, mustn't it, on his trial and the fact that he is innocent until proven guilty?'

'Unfortunately for him, Mrs Morris, although only him, he was caught, as it were, red-handed. He has pleaded guilty to that and other offences, and all that remains is for him to appear in court for judgement.' With a gesture that discouraged further questions or observations, he said, 'As you can imagine, this is a thoroughly distasteful matter and one I prefer not to discuss further.' In dismissing the staff, he looked towards Nick and said, 'Mr Burnett, will you kindly remain behind for a few minutes?'

'Of course.' Nick thought already knew what he was about to be asked, and his suspicion was soon confirmed.

As the staffroom emptied, the headteacher said to him, 'When the post was originally advertised, Mr Burnett, you didn't apply. I know this latest development had taken us all unawares, but are you still of the same persuasion, or would you prefer some time to reconsider your earlier decision?'

'Oddly enough, Mr Purley, I made a decision a few minutes ago. It seems to me that if I don't apply, and the governors appoint another clown, with or without criminal attributes, I shan't be in a very realistic position to complain.'

'So you will apply for the post?'

'Yes.'

'Good. I'm glad to hear it.' He looked and sounded genuinely relieved. Then, in a confidential tone, he said, 'I was never convinced about that Thorganby character. His appointment was made in my absence, as you probably know.'

'I was convinced from the start, Mr Purley, but only of a lapse in judgement on the part of the interview panel.'

'Really?' The headteacher turned to leave. 'Oh well,' he said, 'the post will be advertised shortly, and you may naturally rely on me for a highly supportive reference.'

'Thank you, Mr Purley.'

With only the new entrants in school that day, Nick was temporarily free from tutoring, but he had to attend a departmental meeting under the elusive direction of Ronald Eccles. He left the staffroom and made his way to Ronald's teaching room, where he found his head of department and Kirsty Watford waiting and ready to begin.

'I'm sorry to keep you waiting,' he said. 'The head wanted to speak to me.'

'We know,' said Ronald. 'Did he ask you about this job?'

'Yes.' He could see that Ronald was curious, and Kirsty was desperate to know, so he let them go on wondering while he pulled a chair out from behind one of the front desks and made himself reasonably comfortable. They were still looking to him for some indication of what had transpired from the meeting, so he said, 'He asked me if I was going to apply for it this time, and I said I would.'

'Good,' said Ronald, 'you'd be an excellent choice.'

'Excellent,' agreed Kirsty.

'I just can't bear the idea of them appointing another dickhead like Thorganby.'

'No,' said Ronald, 'he was always going to be a problem for you.' He glanced at the list on his desk and, somewhat reluctantly, addressed the business of the meeting. 'This is basically to make sure everyone knows what he or she is doing this term. Kirsty, you've got one of the first-year groups.'

'That's right, Ronald. Nick's been kind enough to give me a copy of his Year Nine Scheme of Work.'

'Oh, thank you, Nicholas, and well done. You're evidently getting into practice already.'

'I was just trying to be helpful, Ronald.' He was secretly surprised that the head of department could say such a thing without even a trace of shame.

'And you've got your schemes of work for the other years?'

'Yes, written in my own fair hand.' He wondered if there was any limit to the man's brass neck.

'How's the research going?'

'Very well, thanks. I've got all the information I need. It's just a matter of presentation, now.'

Perhaps feeling she should also show some interest, Kirsty asked, 'How long have you been doing it?'

'Nearly three years.'

'I admire your determination, Nick.'

'So do I,' said Ronald, who might have done better to admire Nick's ability to function with no one's direction but his own. 'By the way, the student I told you about will be arriving at the end of the month. When you get around to drawing up his timetable, Nick, feel free to give him as many of my classes as you like.'

'Words fail me, Ronald.' In truth, the only words that came immediately to mind might have caused deep resentment.

* * *

The term began quite smoothly, with Nick 'getting into practice', as Ronald put it, in his capacity as unofficial, acting head of department. He actually had very little to do, apart from pointing Kirsty towards a set of textbooks and making a list of suggestions.

So the month passed, until Nick walked into the staffroom to check the substitution list as usual, and heard his name being called.

'Yes, Ann?' he said, recognising the voice of Ann Moresby, the Doomsday Deputy.

'Come and meet the student.'

He turned to speak to Ann Moresby and found her standing with a young woman. She had lustrous, medium-brown hair, an unblemished complexion, and friendly, blue eyes. Eyes alone were incapable of expression, but these were associated with a genuine, open smile that could only be described as friendly.

'This is Jill Thomas, Nicholas. Nicholas Burnett will be your mentor, Jill. I have things to do, so I'll leave you together to sort things out.'

Nick shook hands with Jill. 'I usually answer to "Nick", he told her, and I can assure you that you've now reached the final link in the chain of command.'

'Have I?' She seemed amused.

'You'll have met the Head, who would no doubt pass you on to Ann, the deputy responsible for students on practice; I've no doubt she would introduce you to Ronald, the head of department, who's already passed you down to me.'

She laughed. 'I'm sure I'm in safe hands.'

'I can't guarantee that, but I will get you a brew, which is more important for now. What do you prefer?'

'Oh, coffee, please. Do I have to pay someone?'

'No, don't start offering to do that, Jill.' He took a mug and inspected it, electing to give it a thorough wash before spooning coffee into it.

'Just milk, no sugar, thank you. What do we do about lunch?'

'You can either eat with the inmates and get it free, or eat with the staff and pay for it. Don't worry, I'll treat you.' He handed her a mug of coffee. 'Today's fairly easy. I'll register my tutor group, give you the schemes of work and your timetable, and then you can shadow me for the rest of the day.

Before Jill could respond, Ann Moresby raised her voice to say, 'Briefing, everybody.'

'Staff briefing,' Nick explained. 'It's a daily event.' They stood as Mr Purley made his entrance.

There was nothing of any immediate interest in the briefing, but as they made their way to Nick's teaching room, Jill asked, 'Does the Head always wear academic dress?'

'Only for assemblies, high days and holidays. We lesser beings are spared fancy dress except on Speech Day, which coincides with your practice, now I think of it. Have you got your own comic attire, or did you hire it for graduation?'

'I hired it, I'm afraid.'

'Don't worry. We'll fix you up with something spurious, or I'll persuade Ronald to lend you his gown and hood. He was at Leeds, and he'll welcome the transaction. It'll give him an excuse for not attending.'

Laughing again, she said, 'I'm sure the poor chap doesn't deserve that.'

'He's retiring at Christmas, although no one will notice the difference. That's why he's left me to look after you.' He opened the classroom door and stood aside to let her in.

Before long, Nick's tutor group arrived, and he greeted them. 'Good morning, ladies and gentlemen. Did you all have an enjoyable weekend?'

There was a mumbled response, and a girl asked, 'Did you, sir?'

'Yes, thank you, but as usual I couldn't wait to get back to work and be with you lot again.' Opening the register, he said, 'This lady is Miss Thomas. She is a teaching student and a highly-qualified historian. I expect you to treat her with the same respect you accord the permanent staff.' He went on to mark the register, finally handing it to the waiting monitor as the bell rang for assembly. 'Thank you, Ten NAB,' he said. 'Let's reconvene in the hall.'

The group left the classroom, and Jill said, 'You have a good relationship with them.'

'It's a two-way thing,' he told her. 'If they're treated as civilised people, they respond appropriately.' After a moment's reflection, he added, 'Most of them do, anyway.' As he led the way to the assembly hall, he said, 'The Sixth Form – I should say, "Years Twelve and Thirteen" – have the responsibility of choosing a record from the Music Department to play us in and out. As you can see,' he said, pointing to a hand-printed placard, 'they display the title for the benefit of those less knowledgeable than themselves, but they usually spell it correctly.' The placard read: *Today's Music for Assembly is Beethoven's Erotica Symphony.*

When everyone was in place, Mr Purley swept into the hall and mounted the platform, where he snapped his fingers at the nearest sixth former and said, 'I'll trouble you to remove that card. There is no "T" in "Eroica".'

'There's no fun in it, now, either,' whispered Nick. The rest of the staff controlled themselves with difficulty.

* * *

At lunchtime, Nick asked Jill, 'Do you live in Hall or do you have your own place?'

'I share a house with several others.'

'Does that work well?'

'Most of the time. It's actually going to be quite a performance, travelling to and fro. I have to set off at the crack of dawn to get the train and then the bus.'

'It's an unnecessary distraction.' It had been on his mind to mention it. 'Don't take this the wrong way, Jill,' he said, 'but you're welcome to my spare room while you're here.'

'Really?' Thinking quickly, she said, 'The thing is, I'm already paying for accommodation in Leeds.'

'It's only for a short time, and you can work your passage by doing the washing-up and making the morning tea.'

She hesitated. 'Are you sure?'

'I live two miles away. It'll make life a lot easier for you.'

'If you're happy with that, Nick, I'll take you up on it, gladly. Thank you.'

It seemed logical to him. 'If I drive you over to Leeds after school,' he suggested, 'you can pack some clothes and come back tonight.'

'Now I really am being a nuisance.'

'Not in the least. I've been wondering how to spend the evening, and a trip to Leeds followed by dinner at the pub sounds as good as anything I've thought of so far.'

* * *

He naturally avoided the King's Head, and with it the risk of embarrassment. He took Jill instead to the Farrier's Arms, where the food was good. The beer wasn't quite so good, but he couldn't have everything, and he hadn't gone there to drink beer, anyway. In fact, he ordered a bottle of a Bordeaux he'd enjoyed on a previous occasion.

'You're very *savoire-faire*,' observed Jill. 'Some men make a performance of it, but you're patently genuine.'

'I should hope so. I was schooled from an early age.'

'Oh?' She waited to hear more.

'Some parents leave their children in someone else's care when they eat out, but mine seldom did. They saw it as a parental responsibility to prepare me for the good life, at least as far as they could.'

'Good for them. Do you still eat out with them?'

'No, they're no longer around.'

'I'm sorry.'

'On a brighter note,' he said, feeling that one was in order, 'Where do you live when you're not in the Silver City?'

'Robin Hood's Bay.'

'Fascinating.'

'My family have a gift shop there. That's my parents and my brother, who's still at school.'

As the thought occurred to him, he smiled and said, 'You know what the kids will say if you tell them you live in Robin Hood's Bay, don't you?' He broke off when the waitress brought the wine for him to taste. 'That's good,' he said, 'thank you.'

'What will the kids say?'

' "As if." It's their stock response to any claim they regard as dubious, and Robin Hood being the stuff of legend, a town named after him has to be fictitious.'

'It's real enough, even though it's only a matter of time before it falls into the North Sea.'

'Quite a long time, I hope.'

'I believe so.'

'One of the kids once asked me where I went to university, and when I told her I was at Cambridge, she asked, "Couldn't you get into anywhere more local?".'

'Well, couldn't you?'

'No, but I am working on a research degree at Airedale Polytechnic, if that helps.'

She shook her head slowly and tutted at the lowering of his standards. Then, more seriously, she asked, 'What are you working on?'

'The effects of Cromwell's Protectorate on the local community.'

'That's interesting. How's it going?'

'I've finally got what I need. I only have to write the dissertation.'

'You sound weary.'

'I am.' He paused until the waitress had brought their meal. 'I spent far too much time trying to unearth evidence of an atrocity committed at Newbury Hall, not far from here. Unfortunately, the Puritans were too good at covering up after themselves, and not without good reason.'

'Was that a Puritan characteristic?'

'Yes, they did it religiously.'

'I asked for that, didn't I?'

'Still, I've got the information I need for the dissertation, and that's what really matters.'

'For you to have devoted so much time to the other matter suggests that it was important to you.'

'Too important,' he agreed. 'It seems that atrocities abounded at the time, but for some reason the Newbury Hall murder appealed particularly to my sense of outrage.'

'Who was murdered?'

'Sir William Newbury and his four children, including a baby. Somehow, his wife was spared the fate. She died two years later, and that's an additional mystery.'

Jill was thoughtful for a moment, and then she said, 'It was a horrible time, wasn't it? But from what I've read, excesses were committed in the name of the Protectorate that must have been none of Cromwell's doing. I'm sure he wasn't the fiend he's been made out to be.'

'You know, Jill,' said Nick, somewhat relieved, 'you and the

Reverend Michael Ellison are the only two people I haven't had to disabuse about Cromwell.'

'I'm in good company, evidently, but where does the Reverend come into the picture?'

'He's the vicar of Saint Radigund's, where the Newbury family are buried.'

Jill appeared to absorb that information. Presently, she said, 'I realise it's not part of a head of department's remit to lay on sightseeing tours for students on practice, but I'd be more than interested to see the scene of the crime.'

'I'll be happy to take you there. We could do it after school tomorrow, now that it's reopened, and for what it's worth, I'm not really the head of department.'

'You are in all but name,' she insisted.

'And salary.'

12

MENTOR AND PROTECTOR

In turning into the carpark at Newbury Hall, Nick was rewarded by an absence of vans, pickups and other commercial vehicles.

'It's good of you to bring me here,' said Jill, perhaps for the second or third time.

'You're very welcome,' said Nick, who appreciated her gratitude as well as her other rare qualities.

'Have you got a girlfriend?'

'Not now. She felt she was competing with Cromwell and the Protectorate, and she found it frustrating, so she did a bunk.' He wondered for a moment if her question had arisen because he was spending time with her that he might have lavished on someone else. It was the kind of thing that might have crossed her mind, Jill being as considerate as she was. 'Have you got a significant "other", a fella?'

'Not really.'

Customs came and went, and it was just possible that a new practice had emerged since his student days, and that between going out with someone and not going out with them there was an indefinite stage known as 'not really'. It was baffling, but he decided not to pursue it. 'There,' he said, parking in his usual place, 'we've arrived at Newbury Hall, built during the reign of Elizabeth the First, as you can probably see. It's original owner, Oswald Newbury, was grandfather to the poor devil who was murdered here. Let's go inside.' He took her through the large entrance, where he found Angela going through the visitors' book.

'Hello, Nick,' she said. 'You wouldn't believe some of the comments people write in this book.'

'Don't be so sure of it, Angela. I mark the scribblings of the hard-of-thinking every day, remember. I'd like you to meet Jill Thomas, a PGCE student on practice at Frederick Delius High School.'

'I'm glad to meet you,' said Jill, shaking hands with Angela.

'How do you do, Jill?' said Angela. 'Have you come to share Nick's frustration at not being able to crack the crime of the seventeenth century?'

'In a sense, yes. I said I'd like to visit the scene of the crime, but I'd be interested to see the rest of the hall as well.'

'Do you want to act as tour guide, Nick?' asked Angela. 'You're as well-informed about the place as any of us.'

'All right,' said Nick, 'we'll start with the ground floor.'

He led Jill round the various parts of the building, including the magnificent dining hall. When they came to the master's study, he pointed out the likeliest hiding place where Sir William's list had been discovered.

'He was a justice of the peace, and yet many people were arrested and punished without his prior knowledge.'

'Have you seen the list?'

'Yes, I have the microfilm and printed copies. It makes grim reading.'

'But what kind of offence could they arrest them for without the magistrate's knowledge?'

'Anything that offended their Puritan ideals. They whipped children for playing on the Sabbath and they pilloried adults who broke the fourth commandment. One was a woman carrying water, another was a midwife on an errand of mercy, and they even pilloried a man for "lewd speech".'

'It's a good thing we got rid of the Puritans,' said Jill, laughing. 'There'd be rich pickings for them nowadays.'

'Worst of all, they burned at least one woman for witchcraft and hanged a man for sorcery. Newbury was unable to prevent any of it, so he made the list in the hope that he might be able to bring it to the attention of someone in authority who was less bigoted than Captain Edmunds.'

'They really had to have total belief in their superstition to put someone to death for it.'

'Yes, let's have a look upstairs.' He took her to the oaken staircase.

'These steps are very shallow, aren't they?'

'People had shorter legs in those days.' He hadn't thought about the staircase since his erotic dream, and he smiled at the memory.

'What's funny?' she asked.

'I was just remembering a dental appointment,' he said.

She gave him a strange look. 'That must have been a funny dental appointment.' Then something else claimed her attention. 'You don't see many minstrels' galleries, do you?'

'It's a landing, not a minstrels' gallery. I suppose nowadays we might call it a mezzanine, except there's no floor above it.'

'So architects had funny ideas in those days, too.'

'It was inevitable. Here,' he said, 'are the main bedchambers.'

'Oh, that's interesting,' she said, peering inside.

'What is?'

'There's an adjoining door.'

'I should hope so.'

'What do you think it was for?'

'Are you serious?' He'd experienced her deadpan sense of humour, so he couldn't be certain.

'Yes.'

'He could knock on it at odd moments. After that, if she was a sport, she'd invite him into her room.'

'You're an idiot, Nick. Are you saying that one of these is the master's room and the other is the mistress's?'

'I thought you'd worked that out for yourself. The room with the dressing table is hers.'

'Well, why didn't you say so?'

'You're a big girl now, Jill. I thought I'd leave you to make the obvious connection.'

Leaving the master's bedchamber for the mistress's, she said, 'Hers was much nicer than his.'

'Of course it was. I imagine he'd say, "Have the larger chamber, darling. You have so many more clothes to hang and things to accommodate." It's a familiar story.'

'So you say.'

'You should have seen the luggage my ex-girlfriend brought to the house, and she'd even more when she left. It was frightening.'

'Was it an amicable parting?' It sounded like an innocent question.

'No, she didn't do "amicable". Her needle tended to spend most of its time flickering between "truculent" and "irritable".'

'It's none of my business....'

'You're wondering why I took up with her in the first place, aren't you?'

'Well, yes.'

'Come downstairs and I'll tell you.'

They went down to the ground floor, where they took their leave of Angela and walked out to the car.

'I'm on the edge of my seat,' said Jill as he joined her in the Beetle.

'Why?'

'I'm waiting to hear about how you and Miss Truculent got together.'

His mind seemed to be elsewhere. 'Do you like spaghetti Bolognese?' he asked.

'Yes.' Her tone suggested that she was still waiting.

'Good. That's what we'll have tonight. At least, it'll be pasta, probably not spaghetti.'

'Lovely. Are you teasing me?'

'The very idea. I was just organising dinner.' He pulled out into the main road. 'Anyway, you want to hear the horror story.'

'Yes, please, if it's not too painful for you.'

'I can tell it now without becoming hysterical. I met Amanda, or "Acid Drop", as I came to know her, at a party, where she told me she was homeless. I confess I wondered a little about how she came to be at a party when finding accommodation might have taken priority, but we all have our ways of doing things, don't we?'

'I suppose we do.'

'Well, we were lurching around to some awful noise on the record player, when she told me about her problem.'

'Maybe that's why she went to the party.' Meeting his glance, she said, 'It's only a suggestion.'

'Yes, well, I told her she was welcome to my spare room until she could find somewhere more suitable.'

'You really do excel at off-the-cuff generosity.'

'I suppose I do, really. She was on her best behaviour that night, but she soon reverted to type, and I began to regret my impulsive gesture. Then, to cut a long, painful story mercifully short, I was about to suggest a change of address, when she surprised me by leaving and going to live at her father's place. If I'd only known in the beginning that he had a house nearby, I'd have suggested it then.'

'Oh, Nick.' She was beginning to sound very philosophical for her twenty-one years. 'I think you'd have offered her your spare room, anyway. It's in your nature.'

'I suppose you're right.'

After a little thought, she asked, 'How long was she with you?'

'Two months, give or take the odd pitched battle.'

'Two months of unpleasantness and disagreement? What on earth made you put up with her for as long as that?'

'It wasn't always as bad as that.'

Jill shook her head as she opened the car door. 'You're a hopeless case, Nick.'

'What can I say? *Mea culpa.*'

'There's no need to swear at me in Latin.'

'I wouldn't dream of it. Let's get that spag bol on. I'm starving.'

* * *

As they shared the sofa after dinner, she said, 'You told me I could do the washing-up, and then I found you had a dishwasher.' It sounded like an accusation.

'It's a hangover from when my parents lived here. I don't usually bother with it.'

'Did you live here with them?'

'Not since I was at Cambridge. They left the house to me, so I moved in.'

'That's awful.'

'What is?'

'Losing your parents like that. I can't imagine it, not that I want to. I'm going to join my family in Spain at Christmas. It's not one of those awful places where they sell beer and fish and chips. They have a place in Andalucia, which is very handy, as they can't get away in the summer.'

'The summer we've just had can't have been all that good for trade.' He picked up the bottle and topped up her glass. 'I did part of the Pennine Way.'

'In all that rain?'

'I didn't walk, I drove to various places. I met a girl who'd sprained her ankle, so I gave her and her ill-mannered boyfriend a lift home.'

'That was you being compulsively kind again.' Having made the observation, she sipped her wine and closed her eyes in enjoyment.

'I also met a woman who'd gone away to nurse her broken heart. Nursing was actually her profession, and her boyfriend had ditched her in favour of someone else on her shift. I stayed there for the rest of the week, and I'm pleased to say she was in a much-improved frame of mind by the time I left.'

She gave him her corner-of-the-eye look and asked, 'Did you administer the panacea for all ills?'

'I helped her find a way through her misery.'

'By helping yourself, I imagine. Still, if it helped her feel happier, fair enough.'

To change the subject, he said, 'I usually get up quite early. I go to the swimming pool, for a shower and a swim. While I'm gone, you can use the bathroom at your leisure. I'll bring breakfast in.'

'I'm being spoiled to death. To be honest, I'd join you in the pool, but I left my cozzie in Leeds.'

'I suppose you could bring it on your next visit.'

'Yes, I could. I must say you lead a very healthy lifestyle.'

'I do now. Three months ago, I decided to break with bad habits. I stopped smoking, I cut down my alcohol consumption by a pint or three, and I started swimming again.'

Clearly impressed, she asked, 'What made you do all that?'

He decided to tell the truth, at least without mentioning his conversation with Miss Bramhope, the dentist. 'I thought I was getting too closely involved with my research project. It was taking over my life, and I needed to change my habits quite dramatically. Does that make sense?'

'Complete sense. One last question....'

'I should hope so. You'd give Torquemada a run for his money. What's your last question?'

'Who's the lady in the seventeenth century portrait?'

'Lady Newbury.'

'I wondered.'

'She usually confines her activities to Newbury Hall, but she turns up here occasionally to go "bump" in the night.'

'You horror, telling me ghost stories at bedtime!' She looked at her watch. 'Well, almost bedtime.'

'You've nothing to worry about,' he told her, with a pleasing sense of *déjà vu*. 'She's a friendly soul, and I'll be just across the landing.' As that thought led to another, he asked, 'Were you comfortable last night?'

'Very comfortable, yes, thank you, but after what you've just told me, I may feel a little bit vulnerable tonight.'

'I've told you,' he reminded her, 'I'll be just one scream away. That's unless you'd prefer us to join forces.' He took her hand in what he hoped was a reassuring manner.

It might have been a pivotal moment; in fact, it was, but for the wrong reason. There was a sudden, familiar fall in temperature and a crash as some object hit the floor. The reason wasn't difficult to fathom, but it was a hell of a time to choose.

'What was it?' asked Jill.

'Nothing to worry about.' The helmet eventually came to rest, and he said, 'Welcome back, Lady Newbury. This is what happens in the twentieth century. If it offends you, perhaps you should return later.' Almost before he'd finished speaking, the temperature began to rise.

'I don't believe this,' said Jill. 'You're actually talking to a ghost.'

'It's possible,' he admitted, although I'm not a hundred percent convinced.'

'This is awful. It's as if she doesn't approve of... you know.' She looked around her, seemingly afraid to name the heinous act where ghostly ears might be listening.

'She's probably gone home, now,' said Nick soothingly.

'I wouldn't bet on it.'

Suddenly the night lacked promise, an impression that Jill confirmed a moment later.

'It was good of you to offer to put me up, Nick, but I can't stay here.'

It was almost half-past eleven. 'Surely you don't want me to run you home at this time of night.'

'Of course not.'

It wasn't clear what she wanted, except that she wasn't in the mood to be sociable, so he said, 'How about leaving your bedroom door open and the landing light on? I'll leave my door open, and then you won't feel completely alone.'

'Do you mind?'

'Not in the least.' Under the circumstances, he felt he had to say that. 'I'll run you home after school tomorrow.'

'Thanks, Nick.'

'It's no trouble. Goodnight, Jill.'

'Goodnight, Nick.'

'Thank you, Lady Newbury.' He uttered those words of irony beneath his breath.

13

THINGS THAT GO 'BUMP'

On the short journey to school, Nick felt he had to refer to the events of the previous night. He didn't want to, but one question had to be asked. 'About the time the Roundhead helmet hit the floor,' he said, 'were you aware of a difference in the room temperature?'

'No.' She looked at him oddly. 'What made you think of that?'

'It's not important. Maybe it was my imagination.'

'Oh, please. I'd rather not think about it.'

'Okay, we'll declare a ghostly moratorium.'

'Some students come to school very early, don't they?' Jill's observation might have been an attempt to leave a disagreeable subject, or it might have been prompted by the number of children already wandering idly about the place, some of whom greeted Nick with a wave, possibly out of friendliness or maybe because his appearance simply interrupted the monotony of their wait.

Nick smiled involuntarily at the recently-adopted practice of referring to children as 'students'. It still sounded strange. 'They have to leave the house when their parents leave for work,' he explained. 'You have to blame circumstances.' He parked as close as he could to his teaching room and got out, retrieving his Roundhead helmet from the back seat.

'What are we doin' in history today, sir?' asked one locked-out urchin, eyeing the helmet with open curiosity.

'That would be telling, Matthew, and I'm not one to spoil a surprise, as you know.'

'Poor little things,' said Jill as they walked on. 'It makes you want to take them home, doesn't it?'

Nick grimaced at the thought. 'I'm not as generous with my spare room as you seem to think.'

'It wasn't a literal suggestion, Nick.'

'Let's get some coffee,' he said, turning towards the staffroom. 'That is a literal suggestion.'

'Who do I need to pay for coffee and things?'

'I've already seen to that.'

'You're too kind, Nick.'

They entered the staffroom and headed for the hot water urn.

''Morning, Nick,' said Geoff Harrison, nodding towards the helmet. 'Are you anticipating trouble?'

'I'd need more than this,' Nick told him. 'Those kids fight dirty.'

'And how. I've been flicked with loaded paintbrushes more times than I care to relate.'

'You need to put a stop to that,' said Ann Moresby, the congenital stranger to levity.

'It's not as bad as chucking clay at him,' said Nick. 'Soft clay would be bad enough, but they bake it first, in the kiln.'

Suddenly alarmed, Ann said, 'You don't allow students to operate the kiln, do you, Mr Harrison?'

'I have to. They're the only ones who know how it works.' He added hopelessly. 'It's a mystery to me.'

'What are you two laughing at?' Perhaps scenting a wind-up, she returned to her original task of pinning various pieces of information to the staff noticeboard. Frustrating experience had taught her that some members of staff were beyond help. She'd even admitted to wondering, on occasions, if they deserved it.

Nick poured two mugs of coffee and he and Jill were making themselves comfortable in time for the morning briefing just as Mr Purley made his entrance.

'Good morning, ladies and gentlemen,' he said. 'I have just a few minor announcements to make.' He performed that duty, and then his eye fell on Nick and his helmet. 'I see,' he said with heavy humour, 'that Mr Burnett has equipped himself with protective clothing. Let's hope he doesn't need it.'

His jest prompted a dutiful laugh from the more sycophantic members of staff, and Nick smiled benignly at Ann Moresby, who simply looked uncomfortable.

After registration and assembly, Nick and Jill returned to Nick's teaching room, where he placed the Roundhead helmet on a windowsill. 'I'll lock it away in the storeroom after school,' he said.

The class arrived and congregated outside the room. 'Good morning, Year Nine,' said Nick. Observing their reaction, he said, 'You thought I was going to say, "Year Three", didn't you? Well, you've been promoted, and Year Three are now tiny tots, just seven years old.'

'Who says we're Year Nine, sir?' asked the one nearest him.

'The Government, Tracy, and their word, as you know, is law. Okay, quiet, please, everybody. In you go.'

When the class were seated, one of the boys noticed the Roundhead helmet and pointed it out to several others. He asked, 'Is that a helmet, sir?' He was rewarded with loud laughter from the boys and just a few of the girls. Jill looked puzzled.

'Yes, it's a Roundhead helmet from the English Civil Wars and beyond. Every soldier of the New Model Army had a helmet like this one.' There was another explosion of gleeful laughter, and the original joker asked, 'What have you put your helmet up there for, sir?'

'Believe it or not, it's to show anyone who's interested what the Parliamentary soldiers wore to protect their heads in the Civil Wars. I didn't put it there to provide humour for the hard-of-thinking. Stand up, please, Nathan.' He waited for the boy to stand, and said, 'Most people realise that a joke is usually short-lived. By that I mean that it may be funny at its first telling, but that the humour wears thin very quickly. Most of us also know that dirty-minded schoolboys refer to part of the male anatomy as the "helmet".' He silenced the laughter with an outstretched hand. 'Remember what I said about it being funny the first time? It's not all that funny now, is it, Nathan?'

'Well, sir, they say everybody's either a Roundhead or a Cavalier, don't they, sir?' He was rewarded by more smutty laughter.

'Do they?'

'Yes, sir. I'm only saying what folk say.' He looked around him for support, but the other boys could already see where the conversation was leading.

'They do, Nathan. At least, grubby-minded boys do. Now, you're obviously very knowledgeable on the subject. While you're standing there, I want you to tell the class about the history of the surgical procedure that converts "Cavaliers" into "Roundheads" and about the reasons for it. Go ahead.' He sat down behind his desk and waited. Nathan, on the other hand, looked uneasy, having realised that the support of his friends had evaporated.

'Go on, Nathan. We're waiting.'

Nathan's face was now bright red. 'I... don't know what to say, sir.'

'No, it's not easy, is it?'

'No, sir.'

'In that case, don't try to make my job harder than it needs to be. Sit down.' Addressing the rest of the class, he asked, 'Will someone – someone sensible, I hope – remind the class of what we were doing in the last history lesson?' He looked at the raised hands and selected a sensible class member. 'Melanie.'

'The Feudal System, sir.'

'Good girl, that's right. The Norman conquerors brought with them the Feudal System, the system whereby communities were divided into lords, ladies and serfs. 'What is a serf, somebody?' He looked around. 'Thank you, Melanie, but we'll have someone else this time. Yes, Lee?'

'They were like slaves, sir, 'cept they got paid. It weren't a lot, and some of 'em nearly starved.'

'They certainly did. Let's look at a few more features of the Feudal System.'

* * *

At lunchtime, Jill said, 'When that boy was going on about helmets, I really didn't know how I'd have handled it. I must say, your way seemed to do the trick.'

'Yes, he wanted to get a cheap laugh by embarrassing both of us, and the best way to play it was to wrong-foot him. What you must never do is play into their hands by showing embarrassment. The straight face will always disarm the joker. Audiences at the Glasgow Empire demonstrated that for generations.'

Almost shamefully, she said, 'I really didn't know about them calling it a "helmet". It was news to me.'

'Slang words come and go with kids, like crazes and fashions.' As something else occurred to him, he said, 'Another word to avoid is "sack", with or without the "k". They'll try to make out you're talking about the scrotal sac.'

Shaking her head in disbelief, she asked, 'Do boys ever think about anything else?'

'Do you mean there are other things to think about?'

A little later, she asked, 'Why did you bring that helmet to school?'

'I'm tired of it falling off the windowsill.'

She rolled her eyes. 'Well, I did ask.'

* * *

The surprise came later that afternoon, when Nick had a marking period. He'd drawn up a timetable for Jill so that she would know which classes to observe more closely, and he was taking her through it when he became conscious of a fall in temperature.

'Do you find it cold in here?' he asked.

'Not particularly. Do you?'

'Yes.' He was feeling very cold, and he knew why, but he tried to ignore it. 'You can usually expect Year Nine to be lively,' he went on, 'but as this is an upper school, they're still getting used to their new surroundings. Nathan Jennings, who provided the entertainment this morning, is an exception. Having said that, if he's particularly troublesome, feel free to send him to me. I'll be—' At that moment, the helmet fell from the windowsill, hitting the hard, wooden floor. 'Excuse me for a minute,' he said, picking up the helmet and taking it into the storeroom. The coldness persisted even as he closed the door. 'Lady Newbury,' he said quietly but firmly, 'I realise that you're offended by my association with Miss Thomas, and I understand your reason for it. The fact remains, however, that attitudes have changed over three hundred years, and modern society now accepts the kind of relationship that… might have developed between us, had you not made your feelings known. Now, will you please stop registering your disapproval and take what satisfaction you can from the fact that your intervention last evening was successful? Thank you.' He found a place on the storeroom floor and positioned the helmet behind a pile of textbooks that he hadn't used for some time. Having done that, he returned to the classroom to find Jill looking puzzled.

'Who were you talking to in there?' she asked.

'I was just talking to myself. I do that quite often. You'll probably find teaching will do that to you eventually, and you'll certainly have a more sensible conversation than you will with the kids— sorry, I mean the students.'

'Do you think it's a retrograde step, calling them students?'

'Not really. It just feels strange, and there's far worse to come.'

'Such as what?'

'There's talk of a nationally-imposed curriculum. I suppose it makes a kind of sense for kids who have to change schools in mid-phase, but I can't think of another good reason for it. Also, I wonder who's going to design the curriculum. Civil servants who went to school so long ago they can barely remember it, or politicians with an axe to grind? At all events, I intend to bale out as soon as I can. If Lady Newbury is upset about the decline in moral standards, it's anybody's guess what she might make of the education system.'

'You might have had an ally there.'

'It's likely. In fairness, though, universal education has only been around since eighteen-seventy. It would be a tall order for her to make anything of it. She knew a damned sight more about totalitarian rule than she did about education.

'When you talk about baling out,' said Jill, 'what have you in mind?'

'Higher education, basically. That's why I'm doing the M.Phil.'

She considered that and said, 'If you go into higher education, research will be compulsory.'

'Yes, I'm still considering what to do for my Ph.D.'

'Traitor,' she said, jabbing him with her elbow, 'you're supposed to be fuelling my enthusiasm for teaching, not trying to put me off it.'

'You'll find teachers who are much more disaffected than I am, Jill. I can still enjoy most of it.'

'So what's the problem?'

'I can see where things are heading.'

* * *

On the way back to Jill's student accommodation, she said, 'I couldn't help noticing your records, last night. I didn't realise you were a Classical buff.'

'I'm not really a buff. I enjoy it, but I don't pretend to know much about it.'

'I had piano and violin lessons until I was sixteen.'

'What happened then?'

'A levels. Something had to go.' Returning to the subject of records, she said, 'I'm surprised you haven't got a CD player.'

'I have too many LPs I like to play. In any case, I'm an old-fashioned, doddery kind of music lover, not a techno whizz-kid.'

'I'm glad you're old-fashioned, Nick. Someone less in tune with the niceties of the past would be less inclined to drive me home.'

He had to agree with that.

Running her eye over the dashboard, she said, 'A car radio is a "sometimes" thing, isn't it?'

'Is it?'

'I mean, you can switch it on, and it's pot luck whether the music they're playing is your taste.'

'My tastes are quite diverse.'

'Yes, I got that impression, looking at your records.'

A little later, she said, 'I'm sorry last night didn't happen.'

'*Didn't* happen?'

'You know what I mean.'

'Yes.' He wondered how many relationships had failed to take-off because of the primness of a tricentenarian spectre. He had to correct that assessment, because Lady Newbury was a good deal more than prim, although that had always been his mother's word for it.

'You've gone quiet,' said Jill. 'A penny for them.'

'I was just remembering how my mother used to say, "I'm not prim, but...." Then she went on to demonstrate the fact that she was downright prudish.'

'People do that, though, don't they? They say, "I'm not racist, but..." and then they say something that would rival Enoch Powell's worst utterances.'

'Yes, I suppose it's a sort of shielding clause or phrase, like, "Far be it from me..." and "With respect...".'

'What made you think of your mother?'

'I don't know. It was just an idle thought that came to me.' It was better to stop referring to the previous evening's disaster, and to close the curtains on it.

* * *

Jill's week at school came to its end, and she returned to university. She would make her second visit in three weeks' time, but not before other distractions occurred. The post of Head of History was advertised in the *Times Educational Supplement*, and Nick had to make his application by the now-shortened closing date before he could begin writing his dissertation.

In one sense, the task was easy; his record at the school was already known, so he had no need to describe it in full. On the other hand, he had to be guarded in mentioning the various ways in which he had so frequently deputised for Ronald, effectively covering his back. Criticising his current head of department would pay no dividends. In any case, he was a fair-minded man, and he had no wish to cloud Ronald's retirement with negative feeling beyond that which already existed. In the end, he steered a middle course that, he felt, highlighted his own administrative flair without damaging Ronald's official record. Although he was largely unaware of it, the current head of department owed a great deal to his assistant's diplomacy, not to mention loyalty.

So much for the letter of application. His CV was up-to-date, and it duplicated nothing already stated on the application form. He placed the form and his CV in an unsealed envelope. He would print the letter the next day, using the school's equipment. He owned a micro-computer, which he used for making notes for his research, but he had no printer of his own. Perhaps, if he were successful in his bid for promotion, he might buy a printer and become, at least technically, self-sufficient.

Before starting work on the dissertation, he took out the photographs he'd taken on the Pennine Way. It was a blatant case of displacement activity, but he didn't care, as he was already feeling quite virtuous after completing his application.

There was usually a limit to the post-holiday nostalgia that could be afforded by photographs in which the common feature was incessant rain, but memories abounded, nonetheless. There was the couple with the German pointer, who'd come as a relief after the self-opinionated feed merchant. Then there was the unfortunate Sharon, whose example of good manners had failed to inspire her monosyllabic companion even slightly. One memory that always raised a smile was that of the American in the café in Hawes, who had made history-teaching a pleasure and an entertainment. The Canadian from New Brunswick also prompted a smile, but the highlight of the holiday was, without a doubt, Nick's meeting with Sally, and not simply for the most obvious of reasons, but because he'd been able to ease her misery. He wondered if she'd been successful in her job application, and how she was faring generally.

He returned his collection of rainscapes to their folder, assured that the holiday had been memorable.

14

ALL WIND AND WHITEWASH

The invitation to attend an interview came, followed by the day itself, both within the fortnight. Nick accordingly arrived at school at the usual time, but clad a little self-consciously in his dark-blue, shadow-stripe interview suit. His unusual garb attracted a variety of comments from his colleagues, some of them polite and even complimentary. Students, who knew nothing of the reason for it, were unfailingly flattering. 'You don' 'alf look smart in that suit, sir,' and, 'Nice bit o' cloth, that, sir,' were among the compliments he received as he marked the register that morning.

'I'm grateful to you for your kind remarks, Year Ten,' he said, 'but all I'm trying to do is set everyone a good example.'

'You're bein' interviewed for a better job, aren't you, sir?' asked one of the more astute members of the group, who had no doubt seen several smartly-clad visitors arriving.

'That as well,' he admitted.

There was a chorus of enquiries as to the exact nature of the job, which he sidestepped, saying, 'I'll tell you about it at Christmas, if I get it.'

There were exhortations of, 'Good luck, sir,' 'Tell 'em what's what, sir,' and 'Give 'em hell, sir.' One devotee of American TV, even said, 'Jus' go in there an' kick ass, sir!'

'I'll do my best,' he promised. 'Meanwhile, let's go to assembly like the civilised people we are when we remember how to be.'

* * *

After assembly, Nick joined the other three applicants in the staffroom, relieved for the time being of his teaching duties. There was the usual, pessimistic, 'Oh,' when they learned there was an internal candidate, but Nick countered it, saying, 'Don't give up yet. It's mine to lose, and it wouldn't be the first time I'd upset this lot.'

'If this is a re-advertisement and you're the internal candidate,' said one of them, 'why didn't they appoint you in the first place?'

'That's what I wondered,' said Nick. 'We'll just have to wait and see.'

The candidates were taken on a tour of the school, and Nick was obliged to take part, to show that the process was egalitarian in every detail. Finally, they were told they would be called into the interview room in alphabetical order. Nick always preferred reverse order, as it enabled him to leave a more recent impression, but the decision had been made, and he had to abide by it. He was duly called as the first candidate.

As Nick had expected, the interviewers were the Chairman of the Governors, the History Advisor and the Head. He acknowledged them each by name.

'Now,' said the Chairman, 'would you like to run through your CV for us?'

Clearly, he hadn't bothered to read it for himself, but it gave Nick an opportunity to emphasise certain details, which he did.

'I see you're engaged in research for an M.Phil.,' said the Advisor. 'You came down from Cambridge with a two-one, but you've chosen to do this thing at Airedale Polytechnic, of all places. Why is that?'

'My research supervisor is Professor Norman Lumb, the country's leading authority on the Stuarts, and Airedale Polytechnic is where he happens to be.'

'I'm a little concerned about this M.Phil.,' said the Chairman. 'Why do you need it, when you're only teaching up to "A" level?'

'I don't need it for teaching,' said Nick, mentally crossing his fingers. 'It's a personal interest, and I'm more interested in learning about history than I am in gaining a higher degree.'

'In that case, why did you put it on your CV?'

'It's common knowledge that I'm pursuing the M.Phil. If I hadn't included it on my CV, it would have looked as if I were hiding something. Don't you agree?'

'Well, yes, I suppose it would.'

'I'm being completely open with you, Sir Henry.'

'I believe you, Mr Burnett.' Speaking to the History Advisor, he said, 'Mr Truelove, I believe you have a question for Mr Burnett.'

'Yes, I have. You know, of course, Nicholas, that the Government is planning to impose a uniform curriculum next year.'

'Yes, I've heard about it, Dennis.'

'What's your reaction?'

Nick had to think quickly. As well as being Chairman of the Governors, Sir Henry Buttershaw was known to be a friend of Mrs Thatcher, which meant that criticism of Government policy was not only foolhardy, but an act of professional suicide. 'If it becomes law,' he said, 'we must implement it. I don't know who's going to write the curriculum, but I hope those responsible will consider the candidates most carefully when the appointments have to be made.'

'I'm sure they will, Nicholas,' said Dennis dutifully.

'Of course they will,' ruled Sir Henry confidently.

A series of less-contentious questions followed, ending with the usual, 'If you were to be offered the post, would you accept it?'

'Of course.'

He was then allowed to resume his place in the staffroom while the other candidates were interviewed. He watched a nervous young woman follow the Head down the corridor. She'd seemed quite collected when he first met her, so he wondered what skulduggery had been enacted during his absence. A likely answer presented itself when he overheard a conversation between the other two candidates. At least, the young woman was trying to take part in a conversation with her fellow candidate, but he seemed to prefer a solo performance.

'I've been in this situation before,' he said, with a quick glance in Nick's direction. 'You have to dominate the interview and let them know that what's really needed is a fresh way of thinking. They need someone to come in from outside and shake things up.'

The young woman was looking far from dynamic until she caught sight of Nick, who shook his head minutely at the nonsense being talked. After a while, the man looked at his watch and said importantly, 'Better make myself comfortable. They'll be coming for me soon.'

'First right down the corridor,' said Nick.

'I know,' said the man, departing.

'Take no notice of him,' Nick told the woman. 'He's a loudmouth.'

'He certainly likes the sound of his own voice,' she agreed.

'Just be yourself when you go in there.'

'Thanks. You don't seem unduly nervous.'

'I'm not,' he confided. 'The last time they interviewed for this job, they appointed a total wally, who went on to prove his unfitness for the profession by being caught in an indecent act. I decided then that if I didn't apply when it was readvertised, I wouldn't be in a position to criticise them if they made a mess of it again.'

'Oh.'

She was possibly digesting the story, when the last candidate returned from the interview room, and the Head asked, 'Is Mr Lomax here?'

'He's in the gents,' Nick told him, 'having an attack of the interview collywobbles.'

'Oh dear. Miss Perry, would you have any objection to coming in now?'

'No,' said Miss Perry. 'I don't mind at all.' She followed him down the corridor.

Less than a minute later, Mr Lomax returned. 'Oh,' he said, 'where's the...?'

'The candidate you were preparing? She's gone in your place. The Head asked her to, as you were nowhere to be found.'

'I was only in the gents. I do think someone might have told me I was needed.'

'Hardly. I mean, you couldn't help it if you were overtaken with nerves—'

'I wasn't!'

'Anyway, the last candidate for this job who went looking for someone in the gents was arrested, so it's not recommended.'

'But I was only—'

'As a matter of fact, that wasn't a smooth move on your part, being absent when the Head came for you. If there's anything he can't abide, it's being buggered about by someone who's never around when he's needed.'

'Oh, heck.' The candidate who had previously exuded confidence was now experiencing the level of doubt he'd tried so hard to inflict on the woman now being interviewed.

'Something else to bear in mind,' advised Nick somewhat brutally, 'is that the History Advisor is very progressive in his approach. He might easily ask you about the planned national curriculum.'

'Yes, a damned good thing, and long overdue, in my opinion.'

Nick laughed mirthlessly. 'Oh,' he said, 'I'd keep quiet about that if I were you.'

'Would you?'

'This is a progressive school. We don't take kindly to politicians telling us how we must do the job. No, if he asks you for your views about the Government's plans, take my tip and rubbish them.'

'Really?'

'It's the only way,' Nick assured him.

'This is incredible.' Glancing at his watch, he said, 'I'll be back in a minute.'

'Now he really is nervous,' said Nick to the second candidate.

'What did you tell him all that for?' she asked.

'I saw what he was doing to… Miss Perry… I think. Call me old-fashioned, but I wasn't impressed.'

'You're a scoundrel,' she said.

'That's an excellent word that doesn't get much use nowadays,' he said.

'You'll hear it a lot more often if you're not careful.' She smiled as she delivered the warning, adding, 'He pulled the same trick on me.'

In due course, Miss Perry returned, and the Head asked if Mr Lomax were available. Lomax accompanied him back to his office.

'Now that we're alone,' said Nick, 'don't let yourselves be psyched out again at an interview by someone like him.' He gestured in the direction Lomax had taken. 'In fact, anyone at all.'

'He had me completely taken in,' said Miss Faulkner, the second to be called. 'I was a bundle of nerves until I got in there. They were all nicer than I'd expected.'

'They're okay,' said Nick. He decided that he wouldn't mind losing to either Miss Faulkner or Miss Perry. 'I think it's Mr Lomax's turn to be nervous.'

'Our friend, here, set him right about a few things,' said Miss Faulkner. 'He wasn't keen on the way Mr Lomax had unnerved you.'

'Oh,' said Miss Perry, apparently impressed, 'a knight errant, no less. Thank you for that, Mr Burnett. I must say, today's been an education for me.'

'You must have come across characters like him,' he said.

'Yes, but I always feel... belittled... by them.'

'Me too,' admitted Miss Faulkner.

It was unbelievable as well as sad. 'Next time you're called for interview, ladies, just remember that loudmouths like Lomax are all wind and whitewash.' Seeing their blank faces, he said, 'No, I don't know what whitewash is, either, but I do know it's not worth very much. Tell yourselves that, though, because it's true, and you won't let yourselves be psyched out again.'

'Thank you,' said Miss Perry. 'That's good advice.'

'Excellent advice,' said Miss Faulkner. 'Yes, thank you, Mr Burnett.'

'And for what it's worth,' said Nick, feeling downright noble, 'I wouldn't mind losing to either of you today.'

'Oh,' they responded in duet, and seemingly unable to find anything else to say, they moved over to sit opposite him, just as Mr Lomax returned from his interview.

'That was quick,' said Nick. 'You must have satisfied them.'

'I'm not sure. I'm not sure, either, that your advice was particularly helpful.'

'I'm cut to the quick, Mr Lomax. Why do you say that?'

'Because they gave me a hard time about being dismissive, and after you told me the History Advisor was progressive.'

'He's fairly open to ideas,' said Nick. 'Of course, it doesn't help that the Chairman's been known to dine at Number Ten and Chequers.'

'You didn't tell me that!'

'There was a limit to what I could tell you. You spent half the morning in the gents.'

'I resent that!' He was no doubt about to expand on that, when the Chairman and the Head came into the staffroom.

'We've decided to offer the post to Mr Burnett,' said the Chairman. Clearly, the decision had not been difficult to make. 'Mr Burnett, will you come this way, please? Will everyone else go with Mr Purley, please? He'll give you your expenses claim forms.'

'Congratulations,' said Miss Perry.

'Yes, congratulations,' said Miss Faulkner.

'Thank you, ladies. Better luck next time.' He shook hands with both of them before following Sir Henry.

'Congratulations, Mr Burnett,' said Sir Henry, once they were in an empty classroom. 'Those two young ladies were very magnanimous in losing to you.'

'Oh well, Sir Henry, I was able to give them some advice for future occasions.'

Clearly, it wasn't what the Chairman was expecting to hear. 'What advice was that?'

'Simply that they shouldn't pay too much attention to interview candidates who come over as omniscient. The fact is, that Lomax character tried his hardest to unnerve them before their interviews.'

'Well, we certainly weren't in the least impressed with him. Would you believe he actually questioned the Government's right to interfere in education?'

'Surely not, Sir Henry.'

'He did, but I've brought you here to congratulate you and wish you every success as Head of the History Department.'

'Thank you, Sir Henry. I'll certainly do my best to justify your decision.'

Looking ahead, the Chairman said, 'I suppose the next step will be for us to find an assistant for you.'

15

Disapproval and Approval

Jill turned up at school, commendably early, having left her lodgings at a time when most people were fast asleep.

'I don't know if I dare ask this,' she said, 'but have they set a date for interviews, yet, for the head of department job?'

'It's been and gone, and yes, I got the job. They're interviewing for an assistant teacher tomorrow.'

'Oh, congratulations! We must celebrate.'

'The same thought has occurred to me.'

As an afterthought, she asked, 'Did anyone else apply for it?'

'Yes.' He tried to sound offended, because he wasn't, really. 'They interviewed three others as well as me. I had to fight off a determined opponent.' He told her the story of the egregious Lomax and his two victims.

'That was sneaky of you, but he asked for it, and he'd have been a rotten choice, anyway.'

'Yes, that was the only reason I applied for it.'

There was a period of puzzled silence, and then she gave in. 'Go on, I'll buy it.'

'After they appointed a weirdo, last term, who celebrated his appointment by attempting an offence that, let's say, prohibits him from further contact with the young and vulnerable—'

'That's too awful for words. I gather the police caught him.'

'Red-handed, according to the Head. As I was saying, I decided that if they appointed another hopeless case, and I hadn't applied, I wouldn't be in a particularly strong position to complain.'

'It's not the most positive reason for applying, but I think you'll be a good head of department, all the same.'

'Thanks.' He rewarded her by handing her a mug of coffee. 'So does Kirsty Watford.'

'Who's she?'

'A member of the English Department. She takes one of the Year Nine groups for History and, in the absence of any kind of directive from Ronald, I've kept her supplied with schemes of work and given her a few ideas about how to go about teaching the Norman Conquest.'

Clearly impressed, Jill asked, 'How could they have denied you the job after all that?'

'They know nothing about it.'

'Don't they?'

'Stabbing Caesar was never an option for me.'

'You're noble as well as everything else, Nick.'

Nick wondered if Lady Newbury thought so. That was supposing she still cared. 'Thank you.' He touched her hand casually in response to the compliment, and as he did so, he was conscious of a gradual reduction in the room temperature. It was no surprise, although he wondered how Lady Newbury had amused herself before he came along. He was resolved to have serious words with his spirit friend just as soon as a convenient opportunity presented itself.

* * *

There were three shortlisted candidates for the job. Once again, they included a bumptious clown and two women, one of whom appeared diffident. The other seemed quietly self-assured, but Nick tried not to pre-judge the contest. In any case, it wasn't his decision to make. He couldn't help noticing, however, that the more confident of the women was quite attractive, with fair, shingled hair and seemingly expressive, blue eyes.

There was a limit to the time he could spend with them, and he was about to return to his classroom when the Head came in and asked for a quiet word. Nick accommodated him by moving away from the candidates.

'I've had a phone call from Mr Truelove, the History Advisor. He tells me he's been unavoidably detained, and he won't be able to join us in time for the interviews.'

'It's all go, being an advisor, Mr Purley,' said Nick, a little unhelpfully. Privately, he wondered how advisors whiled away the hours when they weren't either interviewing, or advancing some exciting but unworkable initiative.

'The point is, Mr Burnett, that his absence leaves us short of subject-specific input.'

'I suppose it does,' said Nick, trying to sound sympathetic. 'I'm sorry to hear that, Mr Purley.'

'Yes, well, the point is that we'd like you to join the interview panel. I'll ask Miss Moresby to find cover for your classes.'

'How could I possibly refuse, Mr Purley?'

'Thank you, Mr Burnett.' Addressing the male candidate, he asked, 'Would you care to come with us, Mr Pringle?'

On entering the Head's office, Nick saw that the empty seat was on the Chairman's right, and after shaking hands with Sir Henry, he took his place, knowing he would never be invited to be his right-hand man in any other capacity.

'Mr Pringle,' said the Head, 'let me introduce you to Sir Henry Buttershaw, Chairman of the Governors, and you've already met Mr Burnett, Head of History Elect.' Smiling at his home-made wit, he invited Pringle to take a seat.

'Now, Mr Pringle,' said Sir Henry, 'perhaps you would be kind enough to run through your CV for us.'

Nick suppressed a smile, convinced by now that Sir Henry always asked for that because he hadn't taken the trouble to read the man's application. It was just possible as well, in fairness to the man, that it was a way of divining whether the candidate had written his own CV, or whether he'd had it prepared professionally on his behalf. For his part, Pringle recounted his schooling and his graduation from university. 'It was most unfortunate,' he told them. 'I was robbed of a "first",' he said, 'by a particularly unsympathetic lecturer.'

'Was that such a hardship?' asked Nick. 'A first-class degree is very laudable, but how useful would it be in teaching to 'A' and Scholarship Levels?'

He treated Nick to a look of annoyance. 'I just feel that I was treated unfairly,' he said.

'Please continue,' invited the Head.

'I went through PGCE, for what that was worth, largely because I was advised to by my tutor, and I… qualified.' He accompanied the last word with a dismissive gesture.

'Tell us more about how you see the Post Graduate Certificate in Education, Mr Pringle,' said Sir Henry.

'Let's be honest,' said Pringle, 'it's a nonsense. No one can teach anyone how to teach. You either can or you can't. It's simply a matter of knowing your subject and having the ability to communicate it clearly.' He reinforced his point by saying, 'I've known far too many teachers who lacked those qualities.'

'A waste of a year, then,' commented Nick.

'You said it.'

'You completed your PGCE in June, this year,' said the Head, 'and yet you're applying for a first post four months later, in early October. Why is that?'

Pringle shrugged, as if the answer were obvious. 'There's a lot of very shortsighted people out there, but I'm confident that my record speaks for itself.' He was so confident that he left his answer there. For his part, Nick had to agree. Pringle's record did speak for itself. As Sir Henry asked another question, he took the opportunity to write a note, which he passed discreetly to Sir Henry, who passed it to the Head. It read, *Do you think we might arrange for interviewed candidates to occupy a place where they can't communicate with those about to be interviewed?*

Eventually, Sir Henry asked the inevitable question, 'Have you anything you would like to ask us, Mr Pringle?'

'No, I don't think so. I take it we'll be informed of your decision before we leave?'

'If at all possible. Now, if you've nothing you wish to ask us, Mr Purley will show you where to wait.'

Pringle looked surprised, but followed the Head to Reception.

'I take your point, Mr Burnett,' said Sir Henry. 'We don't want the other candidates to be disturbed.'

'I think "nobbled" is the term in popular use, Sir Henry. It's dishonest, unfair, and I don't like it.' So that the chairman didn't think it was a one-off occurrence, he said, 'It happened on the day of my interview. I wonder if it might be a useful precaution to adopt on further occasions.'

'Quite. I shall speak to Mr Purley on the subject.'

The Head returned with the next candidate, a seemingly shy young woman called Claire Hutchinson. Nick remembered her coming with the others on a tour of the school, when she seemed nervous of the Year Ten class he was teaching at the time.

The Head introduced Sir Henry and reminded her of who Nick was, and then the Chairman made his usual request, and Miss Hutchinson obliged him with a *précis* of her CV. On this occasion, Nick welcomed it, as he he'd also been grateful for Mr Pringle's sour recital, because he'd had no opportunity to see the applications when they arrived.

The Head asked her about her teaching practices, and the Chairman then surprised Nick by asking her about how she proposed to handle historical events *vis a vis* her own convictions. She was sensible enough to say that she preferred to leave her own political leanings outside the classroom.

'An excellent answer,' said Sir Henry.

'Have you a question you'd like to ask, Mr Burnett?' asked the Head.

'Yes, Mr Purley, I have. Miss Hutchinson, is there a period or event in history that interests you particularly?'

'Yes, I'm interested in nineteenth century English domestic history. It makes a peaceful change from wars and battles, I think.'

'I'm not sure the Tolpuddle Martyrs or the victims of the Peterloo Massacre would have agreed with you entirely, but I take your point.' Noticing that Miss Hutchinson seemed a little deflated by that, he said, 'In general, you're right, of course, and those events did lead eventually to an improved and more equal society.'

She smiled nervously, evidently placated.

The interview ran on, and Sir Henry asked eventually if she had any questions she'd like to put to the panel. His question seemed to leave her floundering, and Nick could only wonder why she hadn't allowed for it. It was a very standard question, after all.

'In that case,' said Sir Henry, 'I have one final question. If we offered you the post, would you accept it?'

'Yes, of course.'

'In that case,' he said, 'thank you for coming, Miss Hutchinson.

Mr Burnett, would you be kind enough to show Miss Hutchinson to Reception?'

'By all means. Come this way, Miss Hutchinson. He guided her towards the Reception area, and because she seemed particularly deflated, he asked, 'Are you all right, Miss Hutchinson?'

'I suppose so,' she said unconvincingly. 'I'm no good at interviews. I come over all tongue-tied and nervous.'

'Well, it's all over now. I suppose it's difficult for you to get advice on interview technique, although there must be books on the subject.' He couldn't remember seeing any, but it seemed fairly likely.

'Yes.' It was as if the possibly had never occurred to her. 'Thanks for that.'

'You're welcome.'

They reached Reception, and Nick was surprised to find that Mr Pringle was no longer there. His first assumption was that he'd nipped out to the loo, but when he looked into the staffroom, there was the errant Pringle, talking to Miss Nolan. 'Mr Pringle,' he said, 'I believe Mr Purley asked you to wait in Reception. We make it a rule at interviews.'

Pringle gave him one of his dismissive looks and said rather predictably, 'Rules are for the obedience of the unthinking.'

'And the well-mannered, I believe. However, it doesn't matter now, because Miss Nolan is the last candidate to be interviewed. Would you like to come this way, Miss Nolan?'

'I suppose I'd better go back to Reception and wait there like a good boy,' said Pringle.

'That would be a worthwhile model,' agreed Nick, taking Miss Nolan to the interview room. On the way, he said to her, 'I would advise you to disregard anything you might have heard just now, and go into the interview without preconceptions of any kind.'

'Yes,' she said, smiling her thanks, 'that's what I intend to do, but thank you.'

He showed her into the room, where the Head and the Chairman greeted her.

After the usual tour of the CV, Sir Henry asked a few questions about her academic record and then invited her views on the PGCE course.

'I can't imagine where I'd be without it, Sir Henry,' she said. 'It was an eye-opener for me, and I got a hundred percent out of it.'

'The reference your course tutor's given you certainly supports that, Miss Nolan.' He held it in front of him, and Nick could see that she came well recommended.

'Oh good, I'd no idea what she was going to say.'

'But you gained a distinction in Teaching Practice,' said the Head.

'Oh well, if the job's worth doing....'

'Quite. Mr Burnett, have you a question for Miss Nolan?'

'Yes, Sir Henry. Have you a specialist period or event in history, Miss Nolan?'

'I try not to think of myself as a specialist, but I'm very interested in nineteenth and twentieth century European history.' With a look of mock-guilt, she said, 'I hope that wouldn't cause a problem.'

'Not in the least,' he assured her. 'One more question, if I may, Miss Nolan, and this is a question I've been asked quite recently. What do you think is the usefulness of teaching history?'

The other two looked at him sharply, but Miss Nolan was ready for the question. 'The Russians say that to understand them, it is necessary to know their history, but I think that applies to all races and societies.' She favoured Nick with a smile, knowing his question was tongue-in-cheek. 'As well as that, though, I think we both know that it's important to recall history clearly, rather than haphazardly, so as not to fall into the trap of repeating its mistakes meticulously.'

Nick met her smile and said, 'I couldn't agree more.'

Once again, the Head referred to the time that had elapsed between completion of the PGCE course and the current interview, and was no doubt surprised by her answer. Nick certainly was.

'I've been searching for the post I really want,' she told him. 'I was unsuccessful in two applications, but I've had three offers that I've turned down. I mean, there's no point in accepting a job if I know it's not going to give me the satisfaction or the start I'm looking for, is there?'

They had to agree. 'In that case, Miss Nolan,' said Sir Henry, 'have you any questions you'd like to ask us?'

'You know,' she said, 'I had several when I got off the train yesterday, but then I had an unofficial look around the site, I learned a great deal, walking round the school with the other candidates, and

I've been able to spend some time with Mr Burnett, asking him about things, so basically, no, I'm very well informed, thank you, Sir Henry.'

'Excellent. One final question. If we were to offer you the post, would you accept it?' It was a fair question, given her earlier answer.

'Yes, I should.'

'Well, thank you for coming today. Mr Burnett, would you be kind enough to escort Miss Nolan to Reception?'

'Of course, Sir Henry.'

Miss Nolan paused before following Nick, to say, 'Thank you, gentlemen.'

It was a minor touch, but an important one, and Nick reflected that she was the only candidate to have thanked the panel that afternoon. Miss Hutchinson was probably too nervous to think of it, and Mr Pringle was clearly too arrogant to consider it necessary. Nick led her back to Reception, where he found the other candidates. 'Feel free to help yourselves to tea, coffee or whatever in the staffroom,' he said.

'Do you mean we're actually allowed in there?' asked Mr Pringle, who was clearly smarting from the earlier incident.

'I issued the invitation. Let's leave it at that. I have to leave you for a while.' He returned to the interview room with his mind already made up. He couldn't answer for the others, of course, but he had a shrewd idea they would agree with him.

'Thank you for that,' said Sir Henry. 'We thought we'd wait for you and make it a fair decision.'

'That's kind of you, Sir Henry.'

'Only right and proper. I suggest we do it the usual way, by eliminating the candidates who impressed us least. I wasn't in the least carried away with Mr Pringle.'

'No.' Mr Purley was firmly in agreement. 'He was too arrogant for words.'

'He also left Reception,' said Nick. 'I found him in the staffroom talking to Miss Nolan. When I challenged him about it, he told me that rules were for the obedience of the unthinking.'

'That settles it,' said the Head. 'I'd just as soon not have him in my school.'

'No,' agreed Sir Henry. 'Let's look at Miss Hutchinson. I found her somewhat timid. Did either of you?'

'Yes,' said Mr Purley, 'very unsure of herself.'

'She seemed nervous of the pupils when she came round the school,' reported Nick. 'It doesn't augur well for teacher-pupil relationships, let alone discipline.

'Which leaves us,' said Sir Henry, 'with Miss Nolan, and I have to say I was very impressed with the way she interviewed.'

'I agree,' said Mr Purley. 'I think you were impressed as well, Mr Burnett, weren't you?'

'Very.'

'In that case,' said Sir Henry, 'I'll speak to Miss Nolan if you'll deal with the others, Mr Purley. Thank you for your kind and expert assistance, Mr Burnett.'

'You're very welcome, Sir Henry.'

They left the room to attend to things, and Nick headed for his teaching room. The school day was almost over, but he wanted to relieve the colleague who was covering for him. That person turned out to be Kirsty Watford, who asked him immediately if an appointment had been made.

'An excellent appointment, unless I'm mistaken,' he told her. 'Thanks for the cover, Miss Watford.'

He saw out the lesson and dismissed the class at the end, in time to receive the Head and Miss Nolan.

'Congratulations, Miss Nolan,' he said. 'You were the obvious candidate.'

'Thank you. My name's Caroline, by the way.'

'Nick.' He shook her hand in congratulation. 'Let me give you my phone number and address in case you need to know anything between now and January. I'm sure you will.'

'Yes, let's swap numbers. I'll be moving from Sheffield, so I'll give you my address when I find one.'

'Fine. Good luck with that.' With a 300-year-old nanny monitoring his private and professional life, he wasn't about to make the same mistake a second time.

* * *

That evening, he was arranging his notes in order. He'd turned up Sir William's list and was wondering yet again at the vile nature of those who used religion as an excuse for tyranny and sadism. It was then that the ambient temperature began to fall.

'Yes, Lady Newbury,' he said, 'I'm appalled by this man's misdeeds, and they will become known. I can promise you that. I only wish I could find evidence of the terrible wrong you and your family suffered, but as you can see, three hundred years is a long time for documentation to survive, even supposing it exists.' He sensed a relaxation in the ambient temperature, but he couldn't let her go without mentioning the other business. 'Before you leave me, Lady Newbury,' he said, 'I must ask you to be less censorius of my behaviour.' He felt that 'censorius' sounded suitably archaic, and it was more closely descriptive of her apparent attitude than 'critical'. 'Much has changed in three hundred years, and mores are no exception. You must understand that what I do in my private life is considered normal by most people in this age.' The coldness seemed to waver for a few seconds, and then the room returned to its normal temperature. He took that to signal acceptance of a kind, although he couldn't be sure.

He looked again at the page copies taken from the microfilm, and it seemed to him that no one had any need to worry in those days about spelling. They had other things to concern them, such as the poor woman who was burned to death for alleged witchcraft, little boys who were whipped for playing on the Sabbath, and the woman pilloried for midwifery on the Sabbath. People of the civilised world had learned about the horrors perpetrated by the Nazis, but how many people knew the truth about Puritan rule during the Protectorate? There had been religious tyranny since organised religion began, and it still happened, but obsession wasn't generated solely by religious fervour; it stemmed from politics as well. The Nazis, the Soviets, the Maoists and the McCarthyites were each a case in point. History was full of them, but it could only warn. That warning had to be heeded.

* * *

He discussed the matter with Jill at lunchtime the next day.

'It's not often you're serious about something,' she observed.

'Isn't it?'

'You know it's not.'

'Well, there's nothing remotely light-hearted about the burning of alleged witches and the whipping of little children.'

'I agree, naturally, but just wandering off the subject a little, and I have to ask this. Have you had a visitation from Lady Newbury lately?'

'No, but I haven't done anything recently to upset her. In any case, I've put all the things she might hurl or otherwise dislodge on the floor, where they can't do any harm.'

'I did ask,' she said, almost to herself. 'Let's talk about something sensible. What do you have to do next with your dissertation?'

'I have to hand-write it, inserting references, and then, very laboriously, type the damned thing.'

'What referencing style are you using? Oxford?'

'No, Harvard. I suppose with references in the text, it's easier to read than it might be with footnotes, and someone's going to have to read it, sooner or later. Also, it's the style the Polytechnic demands.'

She digested that information and asked, 'Can you type? I mean, can you actually touch-type?'

'No, I'm a two-finger typist.'

'I taught myself to touch-type during my gap year. I must say I've found it very useful.'

It sounded like an excellent idea. 'How did you spend your gap year, when you weren't learning to type?'

'I worked as a packer in a boiled-sweet factory.'

'Yum-yum.'

'Yes, to begin with. You see, this was my introduction to pragmatism in management. It was an old, established, family firm, at least until it was taken over, and the managing director let it be known that employees could eat as many of the proceeds as we liked, as long as we didn't carry away boxes of the things. It was much better than threatening us with the sack if we helped ourselves, because after a week or so, we never wanted to taste another one again.'

'Brilliant.'

'Yes, I doubt if the company that bought the firm would be so far-sighted.' Remembering the point of the story, she said, 'Anyway,

I bought an old portable typewriter and a copy of *Pitman's*, and spent at least some of my evenings teaching myself to type. It came in very useful when I had to type my dissertation.' As if she'd only just thought of it, she said, 'I could type yours, if you like.'

'Oh.' It was a generous offer, but one he couldn't possibly accept. 'It wouldn't be fair. On you, I mean.'

'Why not?'

'You'll have all your lesson preparation and reviewing to do, not to mention all the travelling time each way. I haven't forgotten what it's like to be a student on practice.'

'If I do the preparation well ahead, I should be able to do it at weekends as well as fitting everything else in.'

'I still feel awkward about letting you do it.'

'Come on, Nick. You were kind enough to offer me your spare room. Even though that didn't work out, typing your dissertation is the least I can do.'

He was cornered, and she was determined, so he conceded the argument. 'Thank you, Jill. That's a generous offer, and it'll be more than helpful.' Thinking ahead to the evening, he asked, 'This probably sounds like a funny question, but can you throw darts?'

'Can I throw darts? Just watch me.' She sounded serious, at least.

'In that case, let's go to the King's Head tonight. I owe you a drink, at least, and then I'll run you home.'

'All right. Let's do that.'

* * *

They found the usual trio in the public bar.

'Jill,' said Nick, 'meet the local team: the King's Head Undesirables. This is Shaun, Dave and Mike.'

With the introductions complete, Mike said, 'You're an improvement on the last one, Jill. She wouldn't let him play out.'

'Oh, well, I've come to keep an eye on him.' She evidently saw no need to disabuse him of his assumption.

'We were just having a five-oh-one friendly,' said Dave warily. Then, failing to detect any objection, he said, 'You're welcome to join us, if you fancy a game.'

'Thank you.' That was in response to the half of bitter that Nick handed to her. 'Yes,' she told Dave, 'count me in.'

So that everyone was playing with the same handicap, they used the pub's darts, and chivalry dictated that Jill took the first throw. She threw a treble twenty and two doubles. 'Bum,' she said, handing the darts to the open-mouthed Mike.

Mike threw fifty-nine, Shaun followed it with eighty-one, and Dave could only manage forty-three. Nick threw ninety-nine. Jill scored a hundred-and-twenty with her next throw, confirming that her earlier success had not been down to beginner's luck. She remained the highest scorer until Nick threw a hundred-and-eighty, a double-edged achievement, because it meant he had to buy the next round of drinks.

With her third throw, Jill equalled Nick's previous score, by which time the others could see defeat on the horizon. Not even Nick could beat her score, or even equal it, and her final, confident throw of a twenty, a one and a double twenty gave her the sixty-one she needed.

'Meet the Diana of the darts circuit,' said Nick, tucking the money for her round discreetly into her hand.

'What do you do,' asked Dave, 'when you're not beating everybody at darts?'

'I'm a student.'

'Ah, that explains it,' said Shaun. 'Only a student could find time to practice until she got up to that standard.'

'True,' she admitted, 'and it also gives me time to practise my pool. Does anybody fancy a game?'

'Let's have a drink and think about it,' suggested Mike.

'There must be another reason for it,' said Dave. 'Are you descended from that geezer in Trafalgar Square an' all?'

She frowned in puzzlement. 'Who? Lord Nelson?'

'He means Eros in Piccadilly Circus,' prompted Nick helpfully.

'No,' she admitted, 'but I'm told I was conceived after a showing of *Annie Get Your Gun* on television. Westerns and musicals always got my dad revved up, apparently, although I prefer not to think about it, if I'm honest. Anyway, it might have had some influence on my development.'

'Stranger things have been known,' said Nick, not without authority.

16

WRONGLY ACCUSED

November saw Jill arrive for her teaching practice. She also brought with her Nick's dissertation, which she had typed, as far as he could tell, perfectly. Only one person was dismayed.

'I did say the student could have as many of my classes as you wanted to give her,' said Ronald, who couldn't remember Jill's name.

'Oh well, you see I had to give her a representative selection of year groups,' Nick told him. 'As a matter of fact, your Lower Sixth is an important element, covering a period of history that she's made her specialism.'

'Is it?'

'Nineteenth and early twentieth century European history, yes.'

'I didn't know that.'

'No, it must have slipped past you when you were busy, attending to other departmental matters, Ronald.'

'Yes, I suppose it must.' As usual, he showed not even a trace of shame or embarrassment, but simply left the staffroom before someone found him a job to do.

'I suppose we'll have to organise a whip-round when he retires,' said Geoff Harrison, but I'm blowed if I can think of a suitable leaving gift for an idle sod like him.'

'A tea-making machine *cum* alarm clock would be rather expensive.'

'What made you think of that?' asked Geoff.

'It would relieve him of an onerous task each morning.'

'True.' They stopped talking when the Purley King entered the room, attended by the Doomsday Deputy, and waited respectfully for Staff Briefing.

'Good morning, everyone,' said Mr Purley. 'Speech Day is almost upon us, as you know. Attendance in academic dress is mandatory, as usual. Mrs Knowles, is the Music Department ready to regale us?'

'Yes, Mr Purley,' confirmed Mrs Knowles, 'all systems are "go".'

'Really? Is that a musical term?'

'Not exactly, Mr Purley. The Italian term is "*a pronto*", but we tend to be less formal nowadays.'

Nick and Geoff exchanged a wink. Maureen Knowles's ability to wind up the Head was well-known to all but him and his faithful entourage.

'Has the seating for the Governors been organised, Miss Moresby?'

'Of course, Mr Purley.'

'Oh good,' he said with the familiar look that told everyone an attempted witticism was in preparation, 'it seems that all systems really are "go".' Chuckling at his *bon mot*, he said, 'Thank you for that little nugget, Mrs Knowles. I shall remember it.'

'And use it at every available opportunity,' murmured Nick.

When Purley had left the room, Nick spoke to Maureen Knowles. 'Couldn't you prime him with an Italian term that's obscurely pornographic, Maureen?' he asked.

'I've considered it, Nick, but David Williamson is fluent in Italian, and you know what a toady he is.'

Nick did know that, although he hadn't previously been aware of the extent of Mr Williamson's linguistic capabilities. Just then, however, the bell rang for registration, bringing their dissident mutterings to a close, at least for the time being.

* * *

Jill began the week with Year Ten, and bearing in mind some of the characters in the class, Nick rode, or rather sat, shotgun until he was reasonably sure she was secure.

He was impressed by her approach, and the class responded to it well. GCSE was relatively new, having been introduced only a year earlier, but Jill wasn't hampered by years of teaching to 'O' level and CSE. He listened as she introduced the class to the Agrarian Revolution, and found himself drawn into a topic that had previously bored him to death. Jill was pointing out how it was essential at the time for farms to grow more crops and breed more livestock than ever before, and now that he saw the topic in its proper context, he found it much more interesting, as he told Jill after the lesson was over.

'Full marks, Jill,' he told her. 'You brought the Agrarian Revolution to life for me, and for the first time.'

'Really?'

'Yes, it'll go down in your dossier as a flying start. You educated a class of fourteen-year-olds and a teacher at the same time.'

She laughed. 'Are you really prepared to commit that to print?'

'I couldn't care less what anyone thinks about me.'

'Until a job comes up at the university, perhaps?'

'I don't think it's likely to hinge on my ignorance of Jethro Tull's seed drill and his horse-drawn hoe. Anyway, come and let me refresh you with instant coffee.'

'Okay,' she said, returning her lesson notes to her file, 'and thanks for your feedback.'

'You're welcome.' Casually, he put his arm round her and gave her waist a squeeze. As he did so, he heard a faint clatter that seemed to come from the storeroom, and the temperature in the classroom fell noticeably. 'Damn that woman,' he said.

'Which woman?'

'Lady Newbury.'

'What made you think of her?' Her question seemed quite ingenuous.

'Didn't you hear the racket in the storeroom just now?'

'No.' She looked to him for an explanation, but instead, he opened the storeroom door. Where the helmet had stood upright behind a pile of books, it now lay rocking gently on its side. 'That's creepy,' she said.

'And that was because I put my arm round you.'

'It's not as if we haven't been formally introduced. Let's have that coffee,' she suggested. 'Surely she can't object to that.'

* * *

That evening, Nick delivered his dissertation to Norman Lumb at the Polytechnic.

'Well done, Nick,' said Norman. 'It hasn't been easy, but I think you've learned a lot from the process.'

'I certainly have.'

'What's next for you, or is it too soon to ask?'

'Probably.' Smiling at the thought, he said, 'I'd no doubt be creating a rod for my own back, but I've wondered about looking into the question of political and religious excess.'

'Could you be more specific?'

'Yes. We know that Cromwell wasn't the monster that popular fiction has made him, but we also know that outrageous acts of cruelty were perpetrated in his name. I just wonder if there's any mileage in finding out why his followers went to such extremes. It's the only example I can find in which petty officials have committed greater excesses than their leaders ever intended.'

Norman was thoughtful. 'It's difficult to find another,' he agreed.

'No one ever outdid Herod, Hitler or Stalin. I imagine evil on their scale took some matching, let alone exceeding, but it's got to be worth pursuing.'

'There could be a PhD in there for you,' said Norman, but I shan't be able to supervise it.'

'Why not?'

'Because I'm retiring next summer.'

It came as a surprise. Nick had never imagined that Norman was close to retirement age. 'I wish you well, Norman,' he said. 'You'll be missed.'

'Thank you, Nick. Actually, I've been meaning to speak to you about it, basically so that you can keep your ear to the ground. When I go, the department will be minus a seventeenth century specialist, and that could be an opening for you.'

* * *

Nick was still thinking about that the next morning, when he arrived at the swimming pool. Early morning was a good time, because he was able to find a vacant shower; in fact, he was often the first of the day to use it.

His routine was now to swim a series of fast lengths, each with one slow length between them. In total, it worked out at six fast and five slow, a significant improvement on his efforts five months earlier, and he felt much fitter for it. To vary his routine, he sometimes corkscrewed a fast length, and he was approaching the deep end in this way when he thought he saw someone struggling to reach the side. As he drew closer, her head dipped beneath the surface and it became clear to him that she was fighting to save herself.

Cupping her chin with his hand, he supported her and towed her to the steps. 'I've got you,' he said. It was to reassure her, although it must have been fairly obvious. He grasped the ceramic rail and helped her up the steps until she subsided, coughing and choking, on to the side of the pool. 'Lie on your side,' he suggested. Years of teaching left him reluctant to make physical contact with a stranger, but she sank on to her left side, and he arranged her right leg so that she was in the recovery position.

'What happened here?' asked a voice laden with authority and possibly a little guilt at his late arrival. 'I'm the lifeguard,' he explained.

'I pulled her out,' said Nick. 'She's breathing, as you can see, but her airway's impeded.'

'You sound as if you know what you're doing,' said the lifeguard.

'It's just as well.'

'Yeah, well, I can't be everywhere.' Addressing the unfortunate swimmer, he asked, 'Are you all right, love?'

In the circumstances, Nick answered for her. 'Of course she's not all right, you daft sod. Let her cough it up, and she will be.'

'I'll get the oxygen.'

'You do that.' Speaking to the woman again, he asked, 'What was the problem?'

'Stomach... cramp.'

'How awful.' He decided against offering to rub her tummy, as that could so easily be misconstrued. Instead, he waited sympathetically while she continued to cough and retch.

Meanwhile a small group of swimmers had gathered. There were very few at the pool at that time of day, but the incident had attracted them. Not surprisingly, they were full of advice. One said, 'Get her on her front. That's where she needs to be.'

'No,' said Nick, 'this is how she needs to be. Leave it to me.'

141

Another said, 'Here's the lifeguard. He'll know what to do.'

Nick doubted it, but said nothing.

'I've brought the oxygen,' said the lifeguard.

'Okay,' said Nick, 'give her a whiff. It can't do her any harm.'

The swimmer took a breath of oxygen and coughed.

'Take another breath,' said the lifeguard, offering her the mask.

'No... thank you,' she said. 'I'm... all right now.'

'Are you sure?'

In spite of her discomfort, she laughed at the absurdity of his question. 'I'm really... all right, thank you, but... thanks largely to this... man.' She turned her head gratefully to Nick before sitting up. 'I know... you,' she said, still coughing, 'but I'm... afraid your... name escapes me.'

'Nicholas Burnett.' Suddenly his memory threw him a prompt, and masking her nose and mouth with his hand confirmed his suspicion. 'You're Miss Bramhope, aren't you?'

She laughed weakly. 'It's the... swimming cap. It does it every time,' she said. Her coughing fit finally seemed to have reached its end.

'Each time I see you, you're wearing either a face mask or a swimming cap,' he said. 'They both make you anonymous.'

'Well, now that you know who you rescued, thank you, Mr Burnett. I'm very grateful to you.'

'It was nothing,' he assured her.

The onlookers were drifting away, satisfied that Miss Bramhope was alive and well, although one person said, 'I still say he should have laid her on her front and squeezed the water out of her.'

'I bet you're glad I didn't,' said Nick.

'Heartily glad.' Looking at the large wall clock, she said, 'I'm late. I must go.'

'So must I. Let me help you up.' He placed his arm round her and lifted her to her feet, experiencing for the first time, as he did, a dramatic fall in temperature. It was the last thing he'd expected.

'Are you all right, Mr Burnett?' she asked. 'You're covered in goosebumps.'

'I'm fine, thank you, Miss Bramhope. It's probably the reminder that I'm almost due for a dental check-up.'

She laughed properly for the first time, and asked, 'Do I really have that effect on you?'

'I'm just a baby,' he said, glad that she had no idea of the effect she really had on him.

'I'll be all right now,' she said. 'I must go, or I'll be late for surgery. Thank you again.'

'You're welcome, Miss Bramhope.' She headed for the ladies' changing facilities, and the temperature grew warmer.

* * *

When he reached the house, he changed into his school clothes, and now that he was decent, asked, 'Lady Newbury, are you there?' As he spoke, he felt uncomfortably like a medium at a séance. It was the kind of thing they said in films.

After a few seconds, the temperature began to fall.

'You know what I'm going to say, don't you? You leapt to the most damning conclusion this morning. That lady nearly drowned. I only touched her to help her breathe properly and then to get to her feet. It was all absolutely innocent, but you assumed that I was up to no good, and frankly, I feel insulted. Now, will you please go about your business and allow me to attend to mine?' He meant it, too. It was one thing being criticised for actual carnal aspirations, but to be accused of lechery at the swimming pool, when all he wanted to do was save a person's life, was intolerable. He donned his coat and left the house. He had to be at the first period of the day, again, to watch Jill teach Year Nine, and he hoped Lady Newbury would be able to resist placing an unsavoury construction on that.

17

FIRM WORDS

Speech Day, actually held in the evening, was Mr Purley's favourite annual event, providing as it did a shop window for his school, and it was quite fitting that a school bearing the name of Frederick Delius should excel in music, hence Mr Purley's question to Mrs Knowles at staff briefing.

First, the governors took their places at the front of the hall, then the staff entered in order of seniority. Jill walked in beside Nick, wearing Ronald's academic dress. The gown was far too long for her, Ronald being a tall man, but she was able to hitch it up discreetly and hold it at half-mast without alerting too many to her predicament.

'Are we going to hear music by Delius?' she whispered.

'No, they did that years ago, and anything that's left over is too difficult, but don't worry, the choir's usually pretty good.'

Mr Purley addressed the gathering and announced the Choir's first offering: Mozart's *Ave Verum Corpus.*

After the opening two bars, Nick closed his eyes and basked in the glorious sound of the three-times winners of the Airedale Choir Festival. He'd told Jill they were pretty good, but he liked to err on the side of understatement. Maureen Knowles had drilled, cajoled and inspired them to become the school's most outstanding feature.

At the end of the piece, Jill said, 'It was worth coming to hear that alone.'

'Last Christmas, they sang the choruses from Part One of Handel's *Messiah*,' he told her.

'How marvellous.'

It was time for the Head's speech, so they had to stop talking to listen to his review of the past year, which was so tedious that they were thankful when the time came for an item by the Brass Ensemble, which woke them up immediately. It was actually very good, and a fitting prelude to the Chairman's speech. As everyone had expected, Sir Henry told them what a splendid year it had been for all concerned, and how he'd said just that to Mrs Thatcher when he and Lady Buttershaw dined with her recently at Chequers. At that point, a guarded but controlled convulsion ran around the staff, as the Chairman's references to dining either at Chequers or at Number Ten had become an annual feature. It was soon time to calm down, however, and listen to the wind ensemble.

While they were setting out their music scores, Jill asked, 'Why isn't there a string ensemble?'

'There is, and Maureen would normally have given them an airing, especially on the G string, as it were, but they're not the department's best feature,' Nick told her, 'and she was under orders to display only her very best.'

They settled down to listen to a very competent performance, which took them painlessly to the guest speaker's address, the guest on this occasion being Doctor Harley Stewart, Principal of Airedale College of Music, who proceeded to bore the pupils present for a full twenty minutes, on the subject of the organs he had encountered on a recent tour of the churches of Holland and Belgium.

After such an ordeal, resuscitation was in order, and it arrived in the form of the choir, with 'How Lovely is Thy Dwelling Place' from Brahms's *A German Requiem*.

'Oh,' said Jill at the end, 'I want to work here. Will you hurry up and find another job, Nick?'

'I'm working on it.'

The last item on the programme was the presentation of 'O' and 'A' level certificates and prizes, with James Denney of Year 11 accepting the History Prize, having been chosen by Nick in the absence of any interest on Ronald's part. Then the whole company joined in the ritual singing of 'All People That on Earth Do Dwell.' No one knew why the hymn had become a fixture of the school's speech day, but it served as a full stop to the proceedings, and that, in itself, was a welcome feature.

As the company made for the exit, Mr Purley stopped both of them. 'Nice to see you taking part, Miss....'

'Thomas, Mr Purley.'

'Yes, that's right. Good of you to make the effort. I don't remember seeing Mr Eccles this evening, Mr Burnett.'

'Don't you, Mr Purley? It's not always easy, sometimes, recognising colleagues in fancy dress. Don't you agree?'

'If you mean *academic* dress, Mr Burnett,' said Mr Purley stiffly 'I'm inclined to agree with you.'

Nick made a mental note to inform Ronald that, whilst he'd been unaware of the fact, he had officially been present at Speech Day. Thankfully, he wouldn't need to cover his head of department's back for much longer.

When they reached Nick's car, Jill said, 'It's good of you to put me up again, Nick.'

'Yes, I suppose it is.'

'You don't have to agree with me.'

'No, but it helps. Also, when I offered you my spare room, that was what I meant. It would be daft to start something when you've got just three days to go with your practice.'

'Agreed.'

He considered that and said, 'It's not very often I feel virtuous.'

'I'm sure you can handle it.'

'I didn't say it was difficult. It's just different.'

'They say you should try anything once.'

'Within reason.' He didn't want to be drawn into just anything.

'But where do you draw the line?'

It was a fair question. Where did he draw the line? It had to be drawn somewhere. 'I draw the line,' he said, 'at bungee-jumping.'

'Quite understandable. What else?'

He thought again. 'Snake charming, at least without protective clothing.'

'I agree.' She waited, finally prompting him again. 'The best things come in threes. Where do you draw your third line?'

'Pigeon fancying. The only time I can fancy a pigeon is when it's been plucked, prepared and roasted. Otherwise, I find them an unremarkable species.'

'You're a finnicky sort of chap, aren't you?' She asked the question as he pulled in beside the house and she opened her car door.

146

'No, I'm quite egalitarian. I feel the same way towards all breeds of pigeon.'

'I'm not sure pigeons come in breeds, but all right, I take it back.' She followed him into the house.

'Coffee?'

'After such an exciting evening? No thanks, I'll go straight to bed, if that's all right.'

'Perfectly.' He took the portrait of Lady Newbury off its hook and laid it face-down on the floor.

'Why did you do that?' she asked.

'In case she objects to my having you in the house.'

'But as we're not going to get up to anything, why should she be upset?'

'The way she's been lately tells me she's quite capable of hurling her china dolls out of her cradle if I so much as speak to you.'

'I'm sorry, Nick. Goodnight.' She inclined her cheek for a kiss.

'Goodnight, Jill.' Keeping a wary eye on Lady Newbury's portrait, he kissed Jill lightly on the cheek.

He gave her time to use the bathroom, and then went up to bed. Everything seemed to be calm until he passed Jill's door, and that was when he felt the air grow cold. He contained himself, however, until he was in his room, with the door closed. Then, he said sternly, 'Lady Newbury, you know perfectly well what I'm going to say, don't you? What did I say to you after the swimming pool incident? Cast your mind back. Now, let me spell it out for you, Lady Newbury. Jill is in the spare room, I am in here, and although it grieves me sorely, neither twain shall meet. Have you got that? Goodnight!'

18

DECEMBER

NEW FRIENDS

Jill's teaching practice ended without incident, Nick was able to write a highly complimentary report on her performance, and he learned subsequently that her tutor was similarly impressed. He rather missed having her around, but such was life, he supposed, and there were distractions, one of which was the fact that he was about to become Head of the History Department. It made little difference to him, either financially or practically, but he felt it was progress of a kind. The other, more immediate, distraction was his six-monthly dental appointment, that Saturday morning, and he went along to that confident that having saved Miss Bramhope's life he could expect a painless experience. Anything more exciting than that was strictly off the menu.

He was reading a magazine that featured cars he could never afford, when a dental nurse invited him into the treatment room.

'Hello, Mr Burnett.' Laughing, Miss Bramhope lowered her mask and lifted her cap. 'Yes, it's me.' Turning to the nurse, she said, 'Mr Burnett doesn't recognise me in scrubs, or a swimming cap, for that matter.'

'Yes,' said the nurse, 'I heard about you saving her from drowning. What a good thing it was you were there.'

'It was no trouble. I'm just glad, as you are, that I was there at the time.'

'So am I,' said Miss Bramhope with residual feeling. 'Would you like to take a seat?'

'Thank you.' He placed himself on the chair and said, 'By the way, shortly after I was here last, I stopped smoking. You made quite a point of it at the time.'

'It was for your own good, believe me, but well done. Just let me take you back and I'll examine your teeth. Have you had any dental problems lately?'

'Dental ones? No.'

'Any medical problems?'

'None of them, either.'

'Good. Open wide.' She dictated a string of technical mysteries to her nurse while he gazed into her eyes, feeling, he thought, rather like a spaniel unable to understand his mistress's words, but loving every minute of the attention she lavished on him. Then she said to him, 'No problems there. Lift your tongue. Now move it to the right, and now the left. Excellent. I'll just give your teeth a clean and you'll be all set for another six months. Nick braced himself while she wielded the ultrasonic screwdriver, reminding himself that he could at least look into the eyes of his favourite dentist while it was happening. Happily, Lady Newbury hadn't yet found her way to the dental surgery. He based that presumption on the fact that the temperature in the treatment room had been constant since his arrival, despite Miss Bramhall's hands-on approach.

Finally, she triggered the mechanism that caused the chair to bend in the middle, and said, 'Have a rinse-out.'

'All right, but would you mind looking the other way? I get embarrassed when I have to do something uncouth, like spitting.'

'Of course not. I wouldn't dream of embarrassing you.' Obligingly, she turned her back while he cleansed the interior of his mouth.

'All done?'

'Yes, thank you.'

She turned to face him, and asked, 'Now that you've stopped smoking, Mr Burnett, have you given any thought to having your teeth whitened? It's worth it.' She drew her lips back to show him two rows of gleaming, white teeth.

'I'll never look like you, but I think it's a good idea. Will you perform the operation yourself?'

'There's a technician who comes in to do it, but I'll be on hand all the time.'

'With you holding my hand, I'll be fine.'

'I said I'd be *on* hand,' she told him firmly.

That didn't sound too bad, and it couldn't be any worse than the ultrasonic screwdriver. 'All right,' he said, 'I'll volunteer.'

'I'll give you some literature, prices and so forth, and then you can make an appointment.' Adopting a lighter tone, she asked, 'Have you got a lot planned for Christmas?'

'Nothing at all. I've no family, so unless someone takes pity on me, I'll be alone and forgotten.' Naturally, he made no mention of Lady Newbury.

She laughed, and said, 'I never know whether to take you seriously or not.'

* * *

The 'Sold' sign next door had been there for some time, but Nick had only seen movement there recently. Returning from the dental surgery, however, he found a removal van outside and men busily transferring the contents of the van into the empty house. He decided to pay a visit and welcome the newcomers.

He found a young woman inside. Her light-brown hair was caught back in a mysterious contrivance, but she still had a pleasing look. 'Hello,' he said, 'I'm Nick from number twenty-four.'

'Glad to meet you, Nick. I'm Joanne. My husband's upstairs, but he'll be down soon.' She shook his hand, and he braced himself for the plunge in temperature, but mercifully, it never came.

'I wondered if you were ready for tea or coffee.'

'Oh, what a thought! Yes, please. Coffee would be brilliant.'

There was the sound of footsteps on the stairs, and a young man appeared. He was tall and bespectacled, and he looked almost bewildered.

'Daniel,' said Joanne, 'come and meet our neighbour. This is Nick. Is there just you, Nick?'

'Yes, just me.' He shook Daniel's hand.

'Nick's offered to make us a brew. You'd like coffee, wouldn't you, Daniel?'

'Oh, yes.' It was like a sigh.

Nick wrote the particulars on the back of his hand and went outside to take orders from the removal men. He returned after a few minutes, more popular than he could remember, with tea, coffee and biscuits. He learned that Daniel was a mechanical engineer, and Joanne was a bacteriologist. He also learned that they had no children, although not for want of trying.

He asked, 'Have you moved from far away?'

'No,' Joanne told him, 'Horsforth. The trouble was, finding somewhere bigger than our flat meant we had to move away. The north end of Leeds is ridiculously expensive now.'

'Christmas isn't the easiest time to move, is it?' Nick knew very little about moving, but it seemed to make sense.

'It was dictated by the completion date,' Daniel told him. 'We had to move then.'

'Daniel's always been called "Daniel", not "Dan",' Joanne explained. 'At six-foot-two, he needs a long name, and "Daniel" is as long as it gets.'

'What do you do, Nick?' asked Daniel, only a little embarrassed by that disclosure.

'I'm a teacher.'

'Hard luck.'

'It's not as bad as you'd think.' He considered that and qualified the statement by saying, 'Not yet, anyway.'

Joanne said, 'When we arrived this morning, we saw there was no car outside your house, and we wondered if yours was empty as well. The whole neighbourhood seemed deserted.'

'It is fairly quiet round here,' said Nick. 'I was at the dentist. That's why my car wasn't there.'

'You poor thing.'

'Not at all. I'm secretly in love with my dentist. She can do things to me that usually call for anaesthetic, but I feel no pain in her chair.'

'Oh.' Joanne was evidently taken with the story. 'An old friend of mine from university is a dentist somewhere about... somewhere in this city, anyway.'

'Which university was that?'

'Leeds. Where did you study?'

'Cambridge.'

'Ooh.'

'Don't be like that. I'm quite user-friendly, really.'

'Go on, Nick,' said Daniel, 'tell us what you did at Cambridge, between punting and rowing.'

'Modern History and English. I didn't row, and I only know one end of a punt pole from the other because one of them is usually wet. I played cricket, as a matter of fact.'

'Were you a Blue?'

'No, I wasn't. Does that make me acceptable?'

'We accept you, Nick,' said Joanne, opting for an end to the teasing. 'What are you doing at Christmas?'

'I'm waiting for inspiration.'

'Are you really?'

'Yes, I've no family to speak of, so you won't need to complain about the noise.'

'You can come to us,' said Joanne, 'can't he, Daniel?'

'I don't want to impose on you.'

'No, really, come and join us,' Daniel told him. 'Our families are both in the south, and we'll go down there at some time, but we'll be here on Christmas Day. You're the first Oxbridge friend we've had, so you can raise the tone of the gathering.'

* * *

It was decided, but before that, Nick had to go to the dental surgery to have impressions made of his teeth, so that some clever person could make plastic trays to contain the bleaching chemical that would transform his teeth to a new level of brightness.

He also had the usual end-of-term festivities at school, including the carol service, which was another of Maureen Knowles's annual triumphs.

It was already shaping up to be a better Christmas than he'd expected.

19

JANUARY

A BACK-HANDED WELCOME

The teeth-whitening process was uncomfortable, and regular dunking in the bleach stuff was a nuisance, but the difference was remarkable, and Nick felt that his teeth might have rivalled Rudolph's nose for forward illumination in difficult driving conditions. On reflection, though, Christmas probably wasn't the best time for it, but he was still able to enjoy his neighbours' hospitality, and that was both a surprise and a delight.

Caroline Nolan was naturally keen to ask questions, so Nick invited her over to his house rather than the austere surroundings of the History Department.

'I see you decided to give Christmas a miss,' she said, looking around the undecorated sitting room.

'It all happened next door,' he said. 'I was on my own, so the neighbours invited me round, and we all had a whale of a time.'

'Have you no family?'

'None to speak of. There's just me and the ghost.' He'd finally given up concealing the matter, and as most people didn't believe him, it hardly mattered.

'You have a ghost living here?'

'Well, "living" is hardly the word, but yes, she spends a lot of time here.' He showed her the portrait.

'Who is she?'

'Lady Newbury, widow of Sir William Newbury, Bart, JP, of Newbury Hall.'

'You've whetted my appetite, Nick. Tell me more. I love a ghost story.'

'Come and join me in the kitchen while I make coffee.' He explained, 'She could appear at any time, though not in visible form. The first intimation I have of her presence is a sudden plunge in temperature. She has been known to express her disapproval in other ways, haven't you, Lady Newbury?' He directed the last four words at the portrait, but there was no response. 'She's probably sulking after the last telling-off I gave her,' he said.

Caroline leaned against the kitchen counter, laughing silently. 'You're mad,' she said.

'Be warned. This is what teaching does to you.' He measured ground coffee into the filter and switched on the electric kettle.

'What's the story about Lady Newbury?' she asked.

'In a nutshell, considering I've just written seventy-five thousand words on the excesses of the Protectorate, Sir William and his four children, including a baby, were probably murdered by Roundhead soldiers in sixteen fifty-five. I don't know why Lady Newbury was spared, and I never found documentary evidence of the atrocity. I was fortunate enough to find enough alternative examples of Puritan thuggery to complete my dissertation, but I'd still like to be able to bring the truth to light of what happened at Newbury Hall.'

Now that she knew he was serious, she asked, 'Where is Newbury Hall?'

'It's about four miles from here. If you're interested, I'll take you up there when you're settled. It was built in the Tudor period, and it's beautifully preserved.'

'I'd like that.'

'Good.' He switched off the kettle as it approached boiling, and poured its contents into the filter jug.

'Don't you wait for it to boil?'

'No, I think tea and coffee are best made with water that's not quite boiled. I'm a bit fussy about that kind of thing, but I still drink the rubbish they keep at school. I don't want everyone to think I'm effete.'

'How could they possibly think that, Nick?'

They went back to the sitting room, where Caroline walked over to the portrait and examined it. 'She was rather lovely,' she said. 'Not a classic beauty, but very attractive, and with a softness in her eyes that invites sympathy. I think I'd see that, even if I hadn't heard her tragic story.'

'I don't know when that was painted, but she was only in her twenty-third year when she died, and that was two years after the murder of her family.'

Obviously still amused by his earlier disclosure, she asked, 'Why do you think she haunts you?'

'I'll give you a serious answer, even though you don't deserve it. I think she wants me to find evidence of the atrocity and make it public knowledge, as well as citing the culprit.'

Taking a mug of coffee from him, she said more seriously, 'You're a historian, Nick. You deal in hard evidence, so how can you be sure they were murdered?'

'They all died on the same day, the tenth of August, sixteen fifty-five. It would be too much of a coincidence for typhoid or cholera to have made a clean sweep in one day, so I'd say that points to the general belief that they were murdered.' Keen to make his point, he said, 'Bear with me a minute. I have something to show you.' He went to his study and returned with the hard copy of the microfilm. 'This is how the Puritans hereabouts carried out what they saw as the will of God,' he said, handing her the file. 'Sir William Newbury recorded those atrocities, but he died before he was able to denounce Captain Edmunds.'

Caroline studied the catalogue of brutality, narrowing her eyes occasionally in revulsion at what she read. Finally, she said, 'You believe he was keeping this record to denounce Captain Edmunds, but where would he take his appeal?'

'I don't know. Possibly to Cromwell himself, or one of his staff.'

'Do you think they'd have been sympathetic?' It was a fair question from someone who wasn't necessarily familiar with the topic.

'Very likely. Cromwell reserved the death penalty for murder and treason. Also, there's evidence to suggest that he saw belief in witchcraft as nothing more than ignorant superstition.'

'Not the Cromwell of popular fiction, then?'

'Far from it.' Realising that they'd departed from the purpose of Caroline's visit, he said, 'Let me give you the syllabuses and schemes of work. If I give you the floppy disc you'll be able to print them at school. I've also got copies of the textbooks we use. You can take them as well.'

'I can see I've fallen on my feet with you as head of department.'

'I hope so. I've had to write my own syllabuses, schemes of work and study aids. Ronald was bone idle.'

'I imagine he was selfish, too, leaving you to do everything.'

Recalling the most recent instance of Ronald's *laissez faire* policy, he said, 'When Kirsty Watford joined the English Department, she was given a Year Nine History class as well, so she asked Ronald for details, and he told her, "They do the Norman Conquest. It's all in the textbook." She came to me and I fixed her up.'

'That's criminal, on his part, I mean.'

'It was how Ronald worked, if I can use the word "worked" in his case.'

Still shocked, she asked, 'Did no one ever find him out?'

'No, I always covered his back. I'd little enough respect for him, but there are enough bloodstained togas in our business without my adding to the pile, and he's an unhappy case anyway.'

'You're a noble fellow, Nick.'

Looking up at the portrait, he asked, 'Did you hear that, Lady Newbury?' Not surprisingly, there was no response.

* * *

Nick made several trips to the swimming pool, all of which left him feeling fit and healthy, but there was no sign of Miss Bramhope. He wondered at first if her near-drowning incident might have unnerved her, but he dismissed the idea promptly. She was an experienced swimmer and a health professional. If she had an ongoing problem with cramp, she would surely have something done about it. Meanwhile, he concerned himself with more immediate matters. The new term beckoned and, whilst Caroline's search for accommodation didn't affect him directly, he was no less concerned on her behalf. During one anxious phone call from her, he felt obliged to ease her worries.

'You're always welcome to my spare room until you find something,' he told her.

'Oh really? Thank you, Nick. That's a huge load off my mind. I had visions of expensive hotel accommodation.'

'You don't know yet what I charge.'

'What do you charge?'

'I haven't decided yet. I'll have to discuss it with Lady Newbury.'

'Naturally.'

Thinking quickly, he said, 'Look, with two days to go before the start of term, why don't you bring some stuff tomorrow and move in temporarily. If Lady Newbury doesn't like it, she can haunt somewhere else.'

'You're losing patience with her. I can tell. All right, I've got my car back on the road, so I'll be with you by about twelve, if that's all right.'

'Do you swim?'

She must have thought it was a strange question, or maybe one she wasn't expecting, because she hesitated before answering. 'When I can, yes.'

'The reason I ask is that I swim every morning before breakfast. If you'd like to join me at the pool, bring your cozzie.'

'All right, I will.'

* * *

Caroline arrived shortly after eleven-thirty with two suitcases, a briefcase and a canvas grip.

'Did you leave an empty house behind?' asked Nick.

'What do you mean? I'm travelling light.'

Nick picked up the two heavy suitcases and carried them up to the spare room. 'I'll come back for your grip,' he said, 'when I've got my breath back.' He returned to find that Caroline had taken him at his word. The grip was almost as heavy as each of the suitcases, but he lifted it on to the bed beside the two cases, to make it easier for her to unpack them. 'I need a drink after that.' It was something of an understatement. 'Have you eaten yet?' He looked at his watch. 'Of course not,' he said. 'Shall we go?'

'Are we going to your local?'

'No, that's no place at all for a lady. We'll go somewhere posh today – the Farrier's Arms.' Hopefully, Lady Newbury would stay at home, as she was unfamiliar with the place. In any case, ladies had never frequented taverns in her time.

'Shall we take my car? I feel as if I've contributed nothing so far.'

'It's not very far, but let's do that if it makes you feel better.'

* * *

The Farrier's Arms was quiet for a Saturday, and they had no difficulty in getting a table.

'So this is your posh option,' said Caroline looking around the restaurant appreciatively. 'It's very nice, but where do you usually go?'

'I usually drink at the King's Head. It's populated by beer-swilling persons of low intellect, but they help to keep me sane and socially well-balanced. The locals regard me as a novelty because, despite having gone to university, I can beat them at darts.'

'I don't suppose they know many Cambridge graduates.'

'They don't even know where Cambridge is. For that matter, all they know about Oxford is that there must be a marmalade factory there, somewhere behind the car factory, so that car workers can get marmalade-filled toasted teacakes for their breakfast break.'

She considered that only briefly, and said, 'That's based on their experience of life, but how do you know about breakfast breaks?'

'I worked in a mill when I was an undergraduate.'

'Of course.' She nodded solemnly. 'You Oxbridge people were never mere students, were you?'

'But,' he insisted, 'I worked in a mill. It was J. W. Rawlinson, Worsted Spinners, to be exact.'

The waitress came to them, and they gave her their order.

'Will you choose the wine?' asked Caroline.

'If you insist.' He glanced at the wine list and said, 'I'd like a bottle of the 'seventy-six Chablis, please.'

The waitress made a note of the order and left them.

'I didn't ask you to do that because you're a Cambridge graduate,' said Caroline.

'Why, then?'

She shrugged, as if it were obvious. 'Because I'm an ex-student of just twenty-three, untutored in the ways of sophisticated society.'

'I don't believe you.'

'In that case, it demonstrates that you're not the only one who can tell whopping-great fibs.'

Feigning righteous resentment, he asked, 'What fib am I supposed to have told?'

'The one about sharing your house with a ghost.'

'You'll see.' He hoped she wouldn't, but if Lady Newbury was on her usual form, he was expecting a cautionary experience before the day was done.

They continued to tease each other through lunch, because that seemed to be an emerging feature of their relationship, but eventually, it was time to leave. Nick called for the bill and replaced the cork in the quarter-full bottle.

'Why are you doing that?' asked Caroline.

'I'm paying for it, so I'm taking it home. Lady Newbury enjoys a small glass of white Burgundy occasionally.'

'White Burgundy?'

'That's what Chablis is. She doesn't know that, of course. They didn't grow it in her day, but she does care for a drop now and then, even though it makes her giddy.' He paid the bill and picked up the bottle, giving it a wipe with the cloth that came with it.

On the way home, Caroline said, 'If you keeping talking about your Lady Newbury, it won't be long before you convince me she exists.'

'She'd like that.' He just hoped she wouldn't be too persuasive.

They reached the house, and Caroline went upstairs to unpack, leaving Nick to reflect on how things had gone so far. She was good fun, teasing, but not undermining, like some women. All that apart, though, he didn't envisage anything major happening yet, supposing it ever did, but it was reassuring to know that he and his new assistant could work together without much disagreement.

His thoughts were interrupted by a sharp cry from upstairs, and he hurried up there to find out what had happened. He found Caroline nursing the back of her hand.

'What's the matter, Caroline?'

'The lid of this case came down on my hand. I don't know why, because it was resting against the wall.'

159

Nick had an idea how it had happened. 'I'll get you a pack of frozen peas,' he said. 'That'll keep the bruising down.'

'Thanks, but there's no need. It'll be all right, honestly. I just don't understand it.'

'I'll leave you to get on.' He had a job to do, and it wouldn't wait.

When he was downstairs, he went over to the portrait and asked sternly, 'Lady Newbury, are you there?' He sensed an immediate reduction in the temperature, that answered his question. 'Caroline – Miss Nolan, that is – is staying as a guest in my house. She will be occupying the spare room that Miss Thomas recently vacated. Do you remember Miss Thomas, the young woman whose virtue you guarded so effectively? In fact, because of you, I've been living like a monk since last summer. Well, don't think you have to protect Miss Nolan, because I have no carnal designs on her. How could I lead a normal love life when I have a disapproving, puritanical, controlling spectre in my house? Now, I suggest you take a well-earned break from moral guardianship and let me offer short-term accommodation to the unfortunate young woman whose hand you've just injured out of sheer bigotry.' For a moment, he felt the temperature grow much colder. It remained extremely cold for probably only a minute, if that, but it seemed a long time, and then it began to rise until it reached normal. He could only imagine that Lady Newbury was very angry indeed, and had gone off in a sulk. Well, maybe that was the way they responded to home truths in the 17th century. He didn't much care.

20
FEBRUARY

SUCCESS AND MAYBE MORE TO COME

Caroline stayed for just two weeks before finding suitable accommodation, and during that time, Lady Newbury was unusually absent. Whether it was that she'd taken Nick's reproach to heart, or whether it was for another reason, he was simply thankful.

Caroline also joined him most mornings, at the swimming pool, and continued to do so after she moved out. Nick learned that she was involved in a long-distance relationship with someone she'd met at university, so it was as well he'd kept things on an uncomplicated level when she moved in.

He was as pleased as he could be with her performance at school, and he'd just told her so when a messenger brought him a note from the office, asking him to phone Norman Lumb at Airedale Polytechnic.

His first opportunity came at morning break, and he phoned as soon as he could, hoping that Norman would be available. A few seconds later, he came on the line to say, 'Congratulations, Nick.'

'Has it been awarded?'

'Not only that, it's been second-marked and put through moderation, and the result is that your distinction has been confirmed. Well done!'

'Thank you, Norman. Thanks for everything!'

'It was well-earned, Nick. Enjoy it.'

It was a marvellous feeling. He'd always expected his dissertation would gain approval, but to be awarded a distinction was a surprise to be savoured. He went to the staffroom and found Caroline, who greeted him by raising her eyebrows inquiringly.

'Yes,' he confirmed, 'and they've awarded me a distinction.'

'Wonderful!' Looking around the crowded staffroom, rather unnecessarily, she said, 'If it weren't quite so public in here, I'd give you a celebratory hug.'

'No one would mind.'

'All right, then.' She wrapped her arms round him. No one seemed to notice, let alone mind, and just for once, there was not even a hint of a visit from Lady Newbury. As well as being a welcome exception, it served as a reminder.

'I have it in mind to pay a visit to Newbury Hall after school,' he said. 'Would you like to join me?'

'Yes.'

'It'll be easiest, I think, if we leave your car at your place and I drive us up there.'

* * *

As usual on a weekday, they found only a few cars at Newbury Hall, but that was of no interest to Caroline, whose attention was taken completely by the Hall.

'It's beautiful,' she said. 'Full marks to whoever's responsible for maintaining it in this condition.'

'Let's go in and meet some of those responsible. We can talk to one of them, at least.'

They found Angela inside, and Nick introduced Caroline to her. You'll be bringing your Year Ten here later this term,' he told her. 'They're usually quite taken with the place.'

'The older ones can be rewarding,' said Angela. 'It's the nine and ten-year-olds that are difficult.'

'Not guilty,' said Nick. 'Our problems begin at age thirteen.'

Suddenly remembering, Angela asked, 'How's the research?'

'Done. I got the news today.'

'Success? Congratulations, Nick!'

'Thank you.'

Turning to the newcomer, she asked, 'Would you like to look round the Hall, Caroline?'

'Yes, please.'

'I'll give you the tour while Nick communes with Lady Newbury. I expect he's been missing her.'

'Thank you.' She gave Nick an odd look, presumably at the mention of Lady Newbury, and followed Angela.

Nick climbed the shallow stairs that led to the bedchambers, and particularly that of Lady Newbury. The ambient temperature in the Hall was quite low already, as the weather was turning wintry, so he was unsure, as he entered the room, of any change.

A few minutes later, as he was looking around the familiar room, he did detect a difference, and as the temperature fell, he asked, 'Lady Newbury, are you there?' It was a silly question by then, but in view of the fact that his last words to her had been less than amicable, he thought it polite to ask. 'I'm sorry I was so severe when we last met,' he said, but I felt as if you were accusing me wrongly and applying your contemporary standards of behaviour three centuries after their time. I now realise, as a historian, that I was equally wrong to judge your attitude according to the accepted ways of my time. I hope we've both learned our lesson.' He detected no change in the atmosphere but continued all the same. 'I can only imagine you're still hoping I'll find evidence of the murder of your family. Am I correct?' He felt the temperature fall again, and was uncomfortably cold by the time it returned to normal, or what was normal by Lady Newbury's standards. 'I thought so. You know that I've been searching for that evidence for three years now, and I haven't found a single word. The closest I've come to it was Sir William's list that was discovered here.' At that point, he felt as if the walls were coated in ice, like a butcher's cold store, and he asked, 'Was Captain Edmunds responsible for the murder of your family?' Immediately, the place became even colder, so that he wrapped his arms about him and shivered in spite of his winter clothing. 'I think that answers my question, Lady Newbury. Believe me, if I could find that evidence, it would give me great satisfaction to make it known.' He could hear Angela's voice below, so he said, 'I must go now. Be assured I've not forgotten you. Farewell, Lady Newbury.'

He could hear Angela and Caroline coming upstairs now, so he stepped outside the bedchamber, surprised as he always was to find the atmosphere infinitely warmer.

'How's Lady Newbury today?' asked Angela.

'I wish I knew.'

'It's been reported,' said Angela to Caroline, 'that Lady Newbury haunts Newbury Hall.'

'These historic buildings give rise easily to such stories,' said Caroline, 'but some people have too much imagination.' She looked meaningfully, but good-naturedly, at Nick, who was extremely thoughtful after his exchange with Lady Newbury.

As he drove Caroline home, he said, 'I'm going to phone the British Library tomorrow, to see if I can find out anything about Captain Josiah Edmunds. It's worth a try.'

'I thought that was all over. You've got your M.Phil. now.'

'It wasn't just about the M.Phil.,' he said. 'I'm as keen as ever to find evidence of the massacre at Newbury Hall.'

'This is bordering on obsession, Nick.'

'That's what Amanda, my girlfriend of last summer, said. Mind you, that's not all she said. You'd have to pick your way through an awful lot of clumsily-expressed invective to find out the extent of what she really thought about me and my research.'

Evidently amused, she said, 'She sounds like dynamite. How long did she last?'

'A little over two months, about nine weeks, I suppose.'

'As long as that?'

'I didn't want to make her homeless, but then, when she moved out of her own accord, I learned that she could have moved in with her father much earlier. I think she saw me coming.'

'You must have appealed to her to begin with.' Caroline seemed quite taken with the story.

'I'm just too easy-going, I suppose, and I put up with an awful lot. Amanda always had to be on top— figuratively speaking.'

Caroline was still laughing when they reached her flat. 'Thanks for the introduction to Newbury Hall,' she said finally. 'Have a good weekend and try not to fall prey to any designing women.'

'It's unlikely. See you on Monday, Caroline.'

* * *

The next morning, Nick phoned the British Library and made his enquiry. The librarian examined his records, and said eventually, 'I'm sorry. I'm afraid I can find nothing in Printed Books. That doesn't necessarily mean a dead end, however.'

'Is it possible there's something in Manuscripts?'

'That is always possible, Mr Burnett. Would you like me to transfer you?'

'Yes, please, if you will, and thank you for your help.'

'Not at all, sir.'

The line became silent, and then a voice answered, 'Manuscripts Room. Can I help you?'

'Yes, please. I'm looking for any information I can find about one Captain Josiah Andrew Edmunds, active during the Protectorate, and particularly in Bradford, Yorkshire.'

'Captain Josiah Andrew Edmunds.' The librarian was presumably talking to himself as he consulted his records. After a while, he said, 'There's a reference here to Captain Josiah Edmunds on his being cashiered, along with a number of other disgraced officers, from his regiment. It's a royal warrant, and it's dated sixteen sixty-one. There's quite a lot here, and it's not easy to read, as you can no doubt imagine, but it's the only reference I can find to that name.'

'Could you send me a microfilm copy?'

'By all means. You need to take down this shelf reference exactly as I dictate it.' He read the shelf number, and Nick noted it to the last colon and full stop. The librarian took a note of Nick's name and address and quoted the microfilm fee. 'There, if you send a cheque, you should receive the microfilm within the next few days, Mr Burnett.'

'Thank you very much indeed. You've been as obliging as ever. Goodbye.'

'Goodbye, Mr Burnett.'

So Edmunds was cashiered from his regiment. Maybe retribution for his past misdeeds had eventually caught up with him. If that were the case, it would be good news indeed.

* * *

The following Thursday, a package arrived in the familiar blue and white box bearing the logo of the British Library. Inside was the reel of microfilm Nick had been waiting for. It was almost impossible to discern anything with the naked eye, and Nick was obliged to wait a while longer, until he could view it on one of the readers at the public library, or the polytechnic library, whichever he visited first.

In the event, he viewed the film and obtained hard copy at the public library. It was very detailed and, as the BL librarian had said, difficult to read after three centuries of decay, so he took it home to examine at his leisure.

* * *

It appeared that Edmunds wasn't the only rotten egg in his regiment. No fewer than seventeen officers were cashiered on that date, and all were said to be guilty of 'vyle actes of Tyrannye contrarye to the Lawes it was eache Officer's Dutye to upholde'. Their punishment was to be dismissed without pension. In other words, if they were unable to find alternative employment, they would starve, and Nick couldn't imagine Captain Edmunds being inundated with offers of work in Bradford. Neither could he imagine that the populace would be terribly sympathetic towards him in his plight.

While he was reading the indictment, he became conscious of the tell-tale loss of temperature that marked the presence of his spirit companion.

'Good day to you, Lady Newbury. In case you are unable to see this document, I have the warrant signed in sixteen sixty-one by His Majesty King Charles the Second, dismissing Captain Edmunds and other officers from his service. If you are unable, for any reason, to read it, I can tell you that they were each punished for vile acts of tyranny. Unfortunately, I can find no mention of the murder of Sir William and your children, but I ask you to make allowance for me. I'm doing everything I can.' His entreaty seemed to trigger an outpouring of emotion, as the room became warmer and colder by turn. The activity occupied almost two minutes, 'Thank you, Lady Newbury,' he said. 'I think we understand each other.' As the temperature returned to normal, it occurred to Nick that maybe he should have been more open with her from the start, but it was easy to say that, when he considered that in communicating with a member of the spirit world for the first time he was treading possibly the least-known path of all.

21

MARCH

A PATH REVISITED

Nick received an unexpected phone call from Norman Lumb. They exchanged greetings, and then Norman gave him a piece of news. 'They interviewed yesterday for my successor, and they appointed Trevor Raymond,' he told him. 'You know Trevor, don't you?'

'We've never met, but we spoke on the phone. It was last summer, after they'd discovered Sir William Newbury's list at Newbury Hall. You were away on holiday at the time. Anyway, please convey my congratulations to Trevor Raymond.'

'Of course. Now, Trevor is a senior lecturer, which means they have to find a new one. They can't just shuffle the cards, obviously. It has to be advertised and done fairly, but unless they appoint someone from outside who's a seventeenth-century specialist, that means there'll be an opening. I'll let you know when anything happens.'

'Thank you, Norman.'

'It's no trouble, Nick. Are you still looking for evidence of what happened at Newbury Hall?'

'Not so urgently now, but yes. I have microfilm of a warrant signed in sixteen sixty-one by Charles the Second for the discharge of several army officers, including Captain Edmunds, for their misdeeds, but that's all so far.'

'Oh, where did you find that?'

'In the British Library Manuscripts Room.'

'Good work. Well, it won't be lost when you start work on your Ph.D.'

It was possibly good news, and so was the Easter holiday. Nick spent some time deciding on how to spend the holiday, or some of it anyway, and in the end, he opted for walking some of the route he'd driven nine months earlier. That way, he might feel less like a softie. He was also less likely to encounter Lady Newbury.

* * *

His holiday began with a train to Skipton, followed by a bus to Malham. He'd already decided, as before, to avoid youth hostels and live more self-indulgently along the way, so he checked into a B & B before going to the pub as he had several months earlier.

After checking around the bar for contentious animal feed dealers, he bought a drink and went to the fire. The weather was pleasant enough outside, but the fire was still necessary. It was also hypnotic, as open fires tended to be, and Nick's eyelids were beginning to droop, when he realised he had company. A large dog, leaner than the average Labrador, but of that general conformation had planted itself beside him and was introducing itself by pawing his knee.

'Hello,' he said, 'where did you come from?'

The dog seemed to take that in the friendly spirit intended, because it laid its chin on his knee and gazed into his eyes.

'Okay, I'm Nick. Who are you?' He found the dog's medallion and read *Barker* and a phone number. 'That's a good name you've got, Barker,' he told his new friend. 'It's sensible and descriptive. I hope you're not a compulsive barker, although you've been very well-behaved so far. You haven't barkered about or played silly barkers at all, I have to say.' The dog continued to look into his eyes in what could only be interpreted as the spirit of friendship. 'I appreciate your company, Barker, but I can't help thinking you might belong to somebody, and they might be searching frantically for you or even alerting the police about your disappearance as we speak.' The dog disagreed, feeling more inclined to climb up with his forepaws on Nick's legs, evidently with the intention of giving him a thorough licking.

'No, I'm sorry, Barker, but you know, I don't allow French kissing on a first meeting.'

His reaction must have alerted someone at the bar, who called to

169

someone else, currently rendered invisible by the screen that divided the public bar and the restaurant. She said, 'If you're looking for your dog, I think she's in here.'

A large woman clad in a Barbour Stockman emerged purposefully from the shadows, and her informant pointed to Nick. 'That man's got her, over there.'

'That's not quite true,' he said. 'She got me.'

'Oh, you'll have hair all over you,' said the large woman crossly.

'It's not my fault. I was just sitting here, and Barker jumped into my lap.'

'Her name's Topsy,' said the woman as aggressively as before. 'My name is Barker,' she barked.

'Here's your owner, Topsy. Nice talking to you. Mind how you grow, because that's what happens to people called Topsy, and have a Happy Easter.'

'She's awful,' said Miss Barker, pulling her aside, 'a typical flat-coated retriever. She goes to just anybody.' Nick was about to tell her he wasn't just anybody, but he never got a chance, because she clipped Topsy's lead on to her collar and took her briskly outside.

'She'd been looking for her for a while,' said the informant.

'I found her quickly enough,' said Nick. 'It wasn't difficult, and I'm not a dog-owner.'

'You don't have to be,' said a man who was now standing with his arm around the informant and with his nose in her hair. Nick presumed they'd known each other for some time. 'That dog knew everybody in here in the first half-hour she was here.'

'Too friendly for Miss Barker,' said Nick.

'Probably. You doin' a spot of walkin', then?'

'Just a spot.' He got up and went to the bar, thinking he might as well be friendly.

'What d'yer do when you're not walkin'?'

'I usually travel by car.'

'No,' said the man patiently, 'I mean what do you do, like, when you're not walkin' in the Dales?'

Nick wasn't going to be caught with that again. 'I'm a refuse collector,' he said.

'A what?'

'A dustbin man.'

The man gave him a look of distaste. 'Don't talk to me about bin men,' he said.

Nick promised he wouldn't.

* * *

It was a pleasant change to be able to admire the Ribble Head Viaduct without having to attend to twisted ankles and uncouth boyfriends, and Nick marvelled again at the achievement of those who'd designed and laboured on it. He was admiring their workmanship when he heard a female voice call urgently, 'Grigor! Come back, Grigor! Grigor!'

Looking around, Nick couldn't see the owner of the voice, but a sandy-coloured dog was running towards him. He imagined he was about to become acquainted with the Grigor whose unusual name was now being called.

The insistent shouting continued whilst the dog approached him, although its owner was still invisible. Timing his intervention as exactly as he could, he crouched and scooped up the runaway, who gazed at him in surprise before licking his ear.

'That is a busy road,' he told Grigor. 'You go on there and you won't last a minute.'

Grigor seemed oblivious, and in case he hadn't understood, Nick simplified his warning. 'You run on road, you flat dog, yes?'

'Oh, thank you.' The mystery voice now had a body, and it was that of a young woman, an attractive redhead, in fact. 'Thank you,' she repeated, fixing a lead to his harness. 'He's always doing that.'

'I wonder if calling him "Grigor" might have been a mistake,' said Nick, returning him to terra firma. 'Maybe if you'd given him a softer name, he wouldn't have run away from you.'

The young woman eyed him sadly, and said, 'You don't know much about dogs, do you?'

'It's not my line of expertise,' he admitted, 'but I'm quite good at fielding.'

'Yes, and I am grateful for that. Please don't take it personally, but dogs don't differentiate between names, cosy or otherwise, and he was called "Grigor" when I rescued him. He was a stray,' she explained, 'living on the streets of some godforsaken place in Eastern Europe.'

'Ah, so English isn't his first language. That could explain a lot.'

Shaking her head slowly, she said, 'You strike me as a very nice man, and I'm truly grateful to you for stopping him, but you really don't understand dogs.'

'I don't specialise in them, but I do seem to find myself rescuing one species or another, human or canine, whenever I visit this place.'

'Really?'

'Absolutely. Last summer, because it was so wet, I did part of the Pennine Way by car, and I picked up a young woman who'd sprained her ankle. That wasn't her only impediment, though. Her boyfriend was selfish and unsympathetic, and he would have earned the disdain of a socially-challenged Neanderthal.'

'What did you do?' Clearly, she found the story at least moderately interesting.

'Once she'd assured me that she didn't want to go to hospital, I drove them home to Clitheroe. She was very grateful, especially when I carried her into their house.'

'I imagine she was. Why did you have to do that, I mean, with her boyfriend on hand?'

'I think he was in a hurry to see something on television, and I couldn't face the idea of her making her own way into the house.'

She digested that information and asked, 'Why is it that I always meet the right people at the wrong time, as well as the wrong people at the right time?'

It sounded like a rhetorical question, and a complex one, but Nick felt obliged to ask for clarification. 'What do you mean?' he asked.

'You're obviously a lovely man,' she said, 'and I'm saddled with my boyfriend, who's an unmitigated bastard.'

'I'm sorry to hear that,' he said. She seemed very nice, too, but it would be asking too much for a re-run of the previous August, as she confirmed when she spoke again.

'He's waiting for me in the car, and he'll go mad if I make him late for his blinking football match on TV.'

'Best not keep him waiting,' agreed Nick. 'I hope things sort themselves out for you.'

'Thanks again. 'Bye.'

''Bye. '*Do svydanyah*, Grigor.' It was a shame for both of them. He went on his way, wondering if dogs were going to be a feature of his holiday. At the very least, they were better than rain.

* * *

He enjoyed the walk to Hawes, although he wondered about the wisdom of visiting such places when the rest of the population was on holiday. The town was full, and he could sympathise with the locals, who must often regret that their town was so popular with tourists. He paid a visit to the Hawes Creamery, which was also crowded, after which he opted for a cup of coffee in the café he'd frequented earlier.

It was also crowded, and it wasn't long before someone at the next table, clad similarly for the outdoors, spoke to him.

'You gonna use all that sugar?' he asked, pointing to the sachets the waitress had brought.

'No, you're welcome to it. I don't take sugar.' He was about to hand him the sachets, when his neighbour reached across his table and took them.

'Cheers,' said the space invader.

'You're welcome.'

'Where you headin'?'

'North.' He was reluctant to be more specific, in case his new acquaintance felt encouraged to join forces.

'Right. What d'yer do, then? For a livin', like.'

Nick could never fathom the wayfarers' curiosity in one another's line of work. He usually took to the hills as an escape from work, however fleeting, but he seemed to be alone in that endeavour. 'I work in an abattoir,' he said, on the understandable presumption that most people would be disinclined to pursue such a topic.

'What's that, then?'

'A slaughterhouse.'

'Where they kill animals for food?'

'Mm.' He sensed that an accusation was imminent. Perhaps the abattoir hadn't been such a good idea after all.

'D'you enjoy that?'

'No, I hate it, actually. When I look into the innocent, trusting eyes of a calf about to meet its maker, I feel more inclined to turn the humane killer on myself.'

'Why d'yer do it, then?'

'For the perks, really. I mean, where else could I get rump steak at cost price *and* know where it came from?'

The sugar-junkie stirred his coffee vigorously. 'You must be some kind of sick geezer,' he said. Happily, they were the last words he spoke to Nick.

* * *

Hardraw Force was only a relatively short distance from Hawes, but it was worth it for the beer at the Green Dragon and the unusual conversation at the next table.

A young, bearded and earnest-looking man was saying, 'The waterfall is truly inspiring!'

'You can say that again,' said the young woman seated with him. 'I had to queue for the ladies. Everyone's got the same problem, and they all blame the waterfall.'

'I was referring to the majestic view,' he told her, somewhat archly.

'Viewed at the right time,' she insisted.

Nick wondered if the public conveniences at Niagara Falls were similarly over-subscribed. It was an aspect of geography that had never emerged at school, but he'd dropped the subject at the end of the third year, so what did he know? He could ask Alan Kirby, Head of Geography, when he returned to school, but he couldn't imagine him regarding such a question as worthy of consideration. Like the man at the next table, he lived his life seriously. It went with the subject, like untidy whiskers, rugged shoes and an elderly Lada Niva.

The young man was saying, 'This beer's rather good. If it weren't for the fact that I'm driving, I'd be tempted to have more than a half.' His voice had a sonorous quality, and Nick wondered if he might have considered a career as an actor before quantity surveying appealed more strongly to his obviously prosaic nature.

'I don't mind driving,' said the young woman.

'I can't allow it on these narrow, winding roads,' said her companion firmly. 'They call for split-second judgement and skilful gear-changing.'

Not to mention more than a hint of self-obsession, thought Nick before going to the bar and ordering another pint, thankful that he was spared the challenge of negotiating the treacherous by-ways of North Yorkshire by road transport.

'Where are you heading for next?' asked the landlord, pulling Nick's pint.

'Tan Hill.'

'I thought so. Are you doing the whole of the Pennine Way?'

'Not this time.'

'I don't blame you.' Changing the subject entirely, he inclined his head minutely towards the young couple next to Nick's table, and said, 'That bloke's been sipping the same half of bitter for nearly an hour, and he's such a miserable-looking sod, he's not good for trade.'

'I feel sorry for his wife, girlfriend or whatever she is. I'd be surprised if she hasn't realised her mistake by this time.'

'Women put up with an awful lot,' said the landlord. 'Mind you, so do a lot of men.'

Nick waited for him to enlarge on that observation, but it seemed to be the extent of it, because instead of pursuing the subject, he asked, 'What do you do for a living?'

Nick decided to be honest on this occasion. 'I'm a teacher,' he said.

'Oh? What age group?'

'Thirteen to eighteen.'

'Very sensible,' said the landlord. 'I wouldn't know where to start with little 'uns.'

'Me neither.' He knew that should have been 'Nor I', but he was in a pub, and he didn't want to come over as a clever dick.

'It's a job for women.'

Nick nodded as passively as he could, not wishing to get into an argument about gender roles.

The young couple got up from their table, and the woman brought their empties to the bar. The man was already on his way out.

'Thank you,' she said, demonstrating that one of them had been well brought up.

'Thank you,' said the landlord.

She bit her lip in afterthought, and headed once more for the loo. After a while, the young man returned, and seeing Nick at the bar, asked, 'Have you seen anything of my wife?'

The landlord pointed to the door leading to the loo. 'It'll be Hardraw Force that's to blame,' he said. 'There's no fighting it.'

The man gave him a look of impatience and then appeared to think again. Without a word, he took his wife's example and made for the loo.

'It's always better to go when you've got the chance, rather than leave it 'til later' said the landlord.

* * *

The Tan Hill Inn was a welcome sight after the walk, and the welcome itself was as hearty as Nick remembered it. He ordered a pint and sat down to enjoy it.

The landlord was in discussion with a casually-dressed man of around forty, who kept looking around the bar, as if he were expecting someone. Eventually, the landlord, who was showing signs of growing boredom, drew his attention to Nick and said, 'Maybe he'll remember you, that chap who's just come in.' He made the suggestion in a tone loud enough to disconcert the man, which was possibly his intention, and now it seemed that Nick was to receive a visitor.

'I was just saying to the landlord,' said the man, 'I was in the vicinity a few years ago, filming with *Emmerdale*, but no one seems to remember the episodes we filmed at the time.'

'I'm not the best person to ask about that,' said Nick. 'I used to watch the programme at one time, but I got out of the way of it when I went to Camb— to university.' He was trying to lose the habit of referring to his *alma mater* by name, in case it attracted the kind of reception he'd encountered when he met Daniel and Joanne next door.

'How long ago was that?' The man had taken the seat opposite and evidently intended to stay there, at least for a while.

'Nineteen seventy-eight. I remember Annie Sugden, Grandad, the two lads, Amos, Mr Wilkes and Seth Armstrong, but that's about all, I'm afraid.'

'Oh, you're talking about when it was *Emmerdale Farm*, back in the old days.'

'That's what I said.'

'I'm Drew Cordingley,' he said, offering his hand.

'Nick Burnett.' They shook hands, but Nick said, 'I spend very little time watching television, and I never watch soaps, so I'm afraid I shan't be asking for your autograph.' He wondered for a moment if that might have sounded unfriendly, but he was becoming bored with the man, anyway, so he didn't really care.

'It was just a thought. I wondered if anyone would remember the story.'

'How long were you in it?'

'Three episodes.'

'That reduces the chances a bit, doesn't it?'

'I'm afraid so. Anyway, nice talking to you.' He got up and, presumably, went in search of someone else to irritate.

'Did that chap annoy you?' asked the landlord.

'Not really, but he might have if he'd hung around longer.'

'We get 'em, I'm afraid. It's the unusual location. It attracts all sorts of misfits.' He added hurriedly, 'As well as a lot of decent, ordinary folk.'

Thereafter, the evening improved, and Nick was able to relax in good company. The unknown actor had evidently given up on his quest and left the pub.

* * *

It was good to see High Force again and to marvel at the eternal nature of the River Tees. He wasn't the only fascinated spectator, either. The path was lined with tourists, and several people stood at the bottom, seemingly mesmerised by the power of the water hitting the base of the fall. One was a young, dark-haired woman who looked rather good in fitted jeans and a T shirt. She turned and saw him raise his camera.

'Do you want me to get out of the way?' she asked.

'No, far from it. I wondered if you'd let me photograph you against the waterfall.'

A little impatiently she said, 'I can't stop you, can I?'

'Yes, you can. It's illegal to make someone the subject of a photograph without their consent.' It wasn't, but he thought it sounded reassuring.

'Is it?' Eyeing his camera, she asked, 'Are you a photographer?'

'No, I just play at it.'

'But you don't know me, so why on earth do you want to take my photograph?'

'Look, if you'd rather I didn't, fair enough. I take photographs so that I've got something to show for my holiday, and I just thought that a particularly attractive woman against a wonderful backdrop would make a memorable picture.'

'At least you didn't call me a pretty girl.'

'I'm sure you were before you grew up and became an attractive woman.' She was certainly over eighteen, so it was a fair distinction to make.

She appeared to give that some thought. Eventually, she said, 'Okay, go ahead.'

'Thank you.' He stepped back to frame the picture, and said, 'Could you turn slightly to your right and flick your hair over your shoulder?'

'Are you sure you're not a photographer?'

'Positive.'

She turned as he'd asked, and he took the picture. 'Now left a little, with your hair still over your shoulder. Magnificent.' He took several more, and said, 'Thank you so much. I'm going back to my hotel, but I appreciate your cooperation.'

'It was no trouble. I'll walk with you, if you like.'

'I'd like that.'

'Are you fairly local?'

'I live in Bradford.'

'I live close by,' she told him. 'I'm on holiday, actually, from university.'

'Where's that?'

'Manchester. I'm studying modern history.'

'Snap.' Seeing her reaction, he explained, 'I teach history.'

'Oh? Where did you study?'

'Cambridge.'

'Gosh.'

'Don't,' he pleaded, 'it's like a tin can tied to my tail. If it improves my human credentials, I've just gained an M.Phil. at Airedale Poly.'

'A research degree too. Should I walk behind you?'

'Don't be silly.'

'All right. What area of history do you specialise in?'

'The Civil Wars and the Commonwealth and Protectorate.'

'Fascinating.' She wasn't too fascinated, though, to turn and observe High Force from the distance. 'Isn't it wonderful?' she said. 'Even though I live nearby, I can't get enough of it.'

'It's truly wonderful,' he agreed, joining her, 'but I learned something recently, about waterfalls.'

'What was that?'

'They make you want to pee.'

She bit her lower lip and said, 'I wish you hadn't said that. I was vaguely conscious of it, and now you've put it into words, it's become more pressing.'

'My hotel's not far. Come back with me and use their facilities. Then, if you're interested, they should be serving tea.'

'Please don't talk about tea.'

'I'm sorry.'

They pressed on in silence until they came to the road, when she ran across to the hotel, taking tiny steps. Nick came with her and led her into reception, pointing the way to the loo while he removed his boots.

'Thanks. I'll see you in a minute.'

He hung around in reception, looking at brochures for attractions he'd never seen, and some he didn't want to see, and several minutes later, she emerged, a very picture of relief and fulfilment.

'Would you like tea?' he asked.

She hesitated. 'Yes… if I can make one thing clear.'

'Feel free.'

'You need to know that I'm otherwise involved.'

'Romantically, I assume?'

'It's heading in that direction,' she confirmed.

'My invitation still stands.'

'In that case, please, I'd like that.'

179

'Follow me.' He led her into the hotel lounge, where they found a tea menu.

'My name's Lorraine, by the way. I thought you should know, as you're buying me tea.'

'It's the civilised way to do things,' he agreed. 'Mine's Nick.'

'Were you "Nicholas" at Cambridge?'

'No, never. Things have changed since the last century, you know. They've even given up ordering muffins for tea, but we could have them if they appeal to you.' Picking up the menu, he asked, 'What do you fancy?'

'Nothing much, thanks. Just a toasted teacake, please.'

'That's a good idea, and it may explain how you maintain your slender figure.'

'No, that's hereditary. My mum's the same.' Looking around her, she said, 'This is a bit posh for a walking holiday. Have you stayed here before?'

'Yes, last summer. I'm a glutton for comfort.'

'I thought you seemed at home. What on earth did you find to do last summer? It never stopped raining, as I recall.'

'When I arrived at this hotel, "I met a maid upon the meads; full beautiful, a faery's child".'

'Sure.'

'Actually, I did meet her in this hotel, and she wasn't really beautiful, but she had her charms. She'd come away to recover from a broken relationship. Her bloke had been stolen away by a work colleague, and she was getting her nose rubbed in the problem on a daily basis.'

A waitress came, and Nick ordered two toasted teacakes. Turning to Lorraine, he asked, 'Is the house blend all right?'

'I imagine so.'

'And a pot of the house blend, please,' he told the waitress.

'Very good, sir.'

'Tell me about this maiden all forlorn,' prompted Lorraine. 'What happened when you met her?'

'We had lunch together, and she told me her story.'

'I imagine you were very sympathetic.'

'How do you know that?'

'Men usually are when they're fancying their chances,' she told him dispassionately.

'You wrong me. I was sympathetic towards the poor woman, and I tried to be helpful.'

'Did you sleep with her?'

He was taken by surprise, but he recovered quickly. 'Not immediately,' he said.

'What then?' She seemed greedy for detail.

'We spent the afternoon together, drinking tea and talking.'

'Lovely. Here comes the tea.'

The waitress arrived with two toasted teacakes and a pot of tea. 'If you want anything else, just say the word,' she said.

'Thank you.'

'So you spent the afternoon together. In here?'

'Yes, and then we had dinner together. It was pouring down outside, so there was nothing else to do.'

'And then you slept with her?'

He hesitated. 'Yes… I did, but it wasn't premeditated. Well, not until the last hour or so.'

Lorraine was laughing openly. 'I know,' she said. 'You couldn't help yourself.' Considering her nineteen or twenty years, she took a sceptical view of the male population.

'It did her a power of good.'

'What, a one-night stand?' There was incredulity as well as inquiry in her tone.

'No, I stayed another three nights.'

'Just to see the thing through properly?'

'Yes.'

'You know, Nick,' she said thoughtfully, 'I can't believe you did it for purely altruistic reasons – no man is capable of that – but I can imagine you were good for her.'

'I hope so. Have a piece of teacake.' He offered her the plate.

'Thanks. I think the tea will be ready as well.'

'I imagine so.' He poured it for them both, aware that she was smiling to herself.

'What's the joke?' he asked.

'Was the photo at the bottom of High Force part of an elaborate pick-up routine?'

'No, it wasn't. It was exactly as I— well, it was to begin with, but when you told me you were involved with someone, I decided that you were good company anyway, if a trifle sceptical… well, more than a trifle sceptical, I suppose, and I do have a conscience, you know.'

'I believe you, Nick.'

They chatted amiably through tea, and eventually Nick saw her to the bus stop.

'Thanks for tea,' she said, offering a cheek.

'I enjoyed your company.'

He meant it. He'd enjoyed the break, too, and the fact that in all that time, he'd had no contact, if that was the word, with Lady Newbury.

22

HERBAL MYSTERIES

Nick delivered Wensleydale cheeses to Caroline and Angela as well as his new neighbours. Daniel asked him if he'd managed to score again this time, prompting Joanne to voice her objection to her husband's choice of terminology, not to mention his intrusive line of questioning, so Nick was spared having to admit that he hadn't.

Later that evening, he realised how long he'd been absent from the King's Head when he was quizzed about the missing Jill, who had apparently made her mark with the darts enthusiasts.

'She's back in Leeds,' he told them, 'and it's anybody's guess where she'll go next.'

There was a trio of disappointment, and when he thought about it, he realised how unusual she must have seemed to them. He'd found her unusual, as well as entertaining.

When he'd made his first throw of ninety, Mike asked him about the 'thing' he'd been engaged in that took so much of his time.

'That's all over and done with,' he told him. 'I should be going to the awards ceremony later this year. I haven't decided yet whether or not to bother.'

'What happens then?'

'Everybody parades in academic dress and receives a certificate from the Chancellor.

'Yeah, I can see why you're not keen,' said Shaun. 'What do they call you now?'

'My name hasn't changed,' he told him, 'but in front of "MA (Cantab)" I'm now "M.Phil.". Don't worry, though. I'll still speak to you if I see you in the street.'

'Have you got any middle names?' asked Mike after some discernible thought.

'Only one.'

'What is it, then?'

'Andrew.'

'Is that all?'

'Yes, the vicar was due to retire shortly after my christening. He was quite old, apparently, and my parents didn't want to give him too much to remember.'

'You know,' said Shaun, sounding like an elder statesman, 'you've got too many initials after your name. You could move some of 'em to the front. You could be Phil NM Canwhatsit Burnett MA, GAD.'

'What's the GAD for?' asked Mike.

'Good At Darts.' His tone suggested that it should have been obvious.

'What's Canwhatsit?' asked Mike.

' "Cantab",' Nick told him, 'short for "Cantabrigia", the medieval Latin name for Cambridge.'

'Is that what the Romans called it?'

'No, the Roman name was Duroliponte.'

His revelation prompted their joint stares of puzzlement. Eventually Mike said, 'No wonder the Romans buggered off when they did. It must have been a total sod finding their way around the country with daft names like that on the signposts.'

Nick was reminded that evenings at the King's Head were invaluable in helping him keep his feet on the ground.

* * *

One item, tabled by the Headteacher in response to 'Suggestions' dominated the first full staff meeting at Frederick Delius High School, and that was the question of whether or not Frederick Delius Day should be adopted in addition to Speech Day.

'There is a feeling in some quarters,' he said, 'that, as some schools celebrate Founder's Day, we should demonstrate our allegiance to the composer from whom the school takes its name. One suggestion I've received is that such a celebration could be held in Saint Radigund's Church.'

'Would that be appropriate, Mr Purley?' asked Maureen Knowles, who was seated beside Nick on that occasion. 'Delius was, after all, an avowed atheist.'

'Was he?'

'So he claimed, and no one has yet had cause to doubt it. His mass, for example, is an atheist work.'

'Oh.' Clearly, that information had taken Mr Purley by surprise. 'I had thought of him as an example to our students.' He paused. 'You're shaking your head, Mrs Knowles. I hope you haven't further bad news for this meeting? You haven't, have you?'

It seemed that Mrs Knowles had. 'You do know that he fell prey to syphilis, don't you?'

'Did he?' It seemed remarkable that Mr Purley knew so little about the esteemed composer.

'He was also a faithless husband and a less-than-discriminating lover, hence the syphilis.'

'Oh dear.'

'But all that came to an end, Mr Purley.'

'I'm relieved to hear it, Mrs Knowles.'

Nick could tell there was a sting on the way.

'Yes, by the early nineteen-twenties he was dependent on two walking sticks and suffering increasing loss of sight. I imagine that inhibited his lascivious activities to some extent.'

There was a burst of laughter from the irreverent few, and Mr Purley looked deflated. 'I realise now, of course, that I should have consulted you earlier, Mrs Knowles.'

'It's an ever-open door, Mr Purley,' she reminded him generously.

'This is such a disappointment.'

'Disillusionment can be unpleasant, Mr Purley,' said Nick, 'but it's fact that we should never expect our heroes and heroines to deliver more than that for which they're celebrated.'

'I do agree,' said Maureen, who had enjoyed the meeting so far.

Nick felt obliged to illustrate his point. 'I've always enjoyed watching Ginger Rogers, especially when partnered by Fred Astaire, but I once saw her in an interview, and she was nothing like the fluffy characters she portrayed. Far from it, she came over as harsh and unsympathetic, but knowing that doesn't prevent me from enjoying her performances as much as ever.'

'You're just a softie, really, Nick,' said Maureen.

'I suppose we all are.' He risked a glance at Mr Purley, and qualified that assessment. 'Well, most of us are.'

'Just as Ginger Rogers is to Mr Burnett, Mr Purley,' said Maureen, 'likewise Frederick Delius. Can't we just enjoy his music and accept the fact that he was a truly magnificent composer? If it comes to that, Mozart wasn't exactly the soul of rectitude, at least according to his father, but that doesn't impede our enjoyment of his music.'

'I'm afraid you're right, Mrs Knowles. Sadly, no one, it seems, is perfect.' Setting his disappointment bravely aside, he consulted his agenda and asked, 'Have we any other business?'

No one had, but Nick was glad he had a Wensleydale cheese to spare. He would give it to Maureen for enlivening the staff meeting. It was unusual for syphilis and licentiousness to feature at the bi-termly gathering. She had also headed off the threat of an additional event, when enough was a great deal more than enough.

* * *

A phone call from Angela at Newbury Hall prompted Nick to make a visit after school. More artefacts had been found, this time in the grounds of the Hall when the Council's Parks Department were working on the flowerbeds, and as Nick had been eager to see anything that might turn up, Angela was quick to contact him.

'They were found while you were away,' she said, showing him two phials that had withstood the onslaught of time, 'and we've just got them back from the university. Naturally it's been impossible to identify the previous contents, but they seem to have held medication of some kind. In those days, of course, it would be herbal – synthetic drugs were unheard-of – but we've no idea what it was exactly, except that their small size suggests something very potent.'

'A potential poison if used in quantity?'

'There was no shortage of those things,' she confirmed. 'You've only to read the Cadfael stories to realise that.'

'Have you any idea of their age?'

She laughed. 'Sixteenth, seventeenth, possibly eighteenth centuries. It really is anybody's guess. If I were to go out on a limb, though, just going by the style of the bottles, I'd say they were sixteenth or seventeenth century.'

'What do you think would be the most common household drug in those days?'

She closed her eyes in thought and said, 'My money would be on belladonna.'

'Deadly nightshade? Why?'

'It was used for pain relief, among other things, quite commonly in childbirth.'

'I don't blame them, Angela, I really don't.' It even hurt to think about it. 'Lady Newbury gave birth four times within the first five years of her marriage, you know.' Thinking about it, he said, 'Those five years represented the extent of her marriage. I feel saddened every time I think of it.'

'You've taken it very personally, Nick.' She spoke without a trace of her usual mockery.

'Yes, I suppose I have. I was warned this might happen, when I first applied to the CNAA.'

'I'm sure it's an occupational hazard. What's your next project going to be, do you think?'

'I'm considering a Ph.D. in religious and political extremism; in particular, what made the Puritans so much more diligent in the persecution of their victims than Cromwell ever intended. It'll be interesting to focus, as well, on how Charles the Second's self-restraint in avenging his father's execution was mirrored elsewhere.'

'It sounds fascinating.'

Returning to the matter of the phials, he said, 'If the apothecary who supplied these things was around during the Protectorate, he must have led an interesting life. For my money, he'd be walking the most awful tightrope with the Puritans watching him eargerly for signs of alleged dealings with Satan.'

'I imagine he would. It just leaves me wondering why Cromwell called himself Lord Protector, when he offered so little protection.'

'His full title was Lord Protector of the Commonwealth. Protecting individuals was an awful lot to ask, but we do know that Charles the Second came down hard on some of the offenders.'

'We know that thanks to you, apparently. Come into the office and have a cup of tea on the strength of it.'

They found Scott in the office. An empty biscuit wrapper lay on the desk in front of him, surrounded by crumbs.

'Make yourself useful, Scott,' said Angela. 'First of all, fill the kettle with water, please, then replace the lid, plug it in and switch it on. There's a good boy.' Repeated experience had evidently led her to making her requests in minute detail.

Without a word, but with overt lack of enthusiasm, Scott did as she asked.

'Thank you. Now, will you go round to the shop and buy a packet of biscuits to replace those you've just eaten?'

'I didn't eat 'em all,' he protested.

'I know. There were two missing, but you ate the rest. Go on, off you go.'

He stared at her stupidly. 'Where's the money?' he asked.

'In your pocket, presumably. Go on, Scott, it's your turn to pay. In fact, your turn's well and truly overdue.'

'That isn't fair.'

'Life's not fair. I'm reminded of that every time I buy a packet of biscuits and find that you've guzzled most of them.'

With a loud *tut*, he left the office.

'I'm sick of that biscuit-gorging little sod,' said Angela. 'One of the Tuesday people had a birthday two weeks ago, and she brought a cake in. You can guess what happened to that.'

'It's a pity you can't lace something with a strong laxative, and then explain to him that his unfortuante condition is caused by greed and over-indulgence.'

'Now, that's an excellent idea,' said Angela, eyeing Scott's Liverpool FC coffee mug with barely-concealed design. 'I'm glad you came.' She stood up to make the tea. 'It's just a shame you never found out more about the Newbury Hall murders.'

'I've not given up on it. There must be evidence of them somewhere. It'll turn up, just as the warrant dealing with Edmunds and the others came to light.' As he spoke, he realised it was a remarkably fanciful remark for a much-qualified researcher to make.

The door opened, and Scott came in with a packet of ginger nuts, which he dumped unceremoniously on the desk in front of Angela.

'You cheapskate,' she said. 'You nick everyone else's Hobnobs and then you buy something at half the price.'

'I don't get paid as much as what you do.'

'You don't do half the work, either. Go and do some dusting.'

'Where?'

'You can do the banister rail and the landing.' She let him go, and said, 'There's not much damage he can do up there.'

Watching him make his clumsy way to the stairs, Nick asked, 'How did he get the job?'

'Council employment policy. We have to take characters like him as well as keen, intelligent ones, and to be fair, he has improved a lot since he joined us.'

'How?' It seemed impossible that in his present state he was an improvement on anything.

'You didn't know him when he first arrived.'

'No, I was spared having to teach him.' He realised he was wrong, of course, to write the lad off in that way.

'I should also tell you that he discovered those phials when he was working with the groundsmen.'

That was a surprise, but he had to give credit where it was due. 'In that case, good for him,' he said, 'and long may he go on finding buried treasure.'

* * *

He told Caroline about the phials when he saw her at school the following Monday.

'Everything was herbal in those days, wasn't it?' she said. 'I expect they knew far more about herbal remedies than we do today.'

'They knew more than I do,' said Nick. 'I'm clueless about that sort of thing, but it would have been a two-edged sword in those days, with over-zealous Puritans ever on the lookout for alchemists and alleged sorcerers. According to Sir William Newbury's list, it was a short-cut to an unofficial death sentence.'

'I've been thinking about that awful business,' said Caroline. 'Just out of interest, I'd like to have a look around that churchyard you told me about earlier.'

'Saint Radigund's? I'll take you up there if you like. I'll provide the paper and crayons.'

'What for?'

'Taking rubbings. It's the easiest way to read the inscriptions on faded headstones.'

23

BURIED TREASURE

Nick led Caroline through the graveyard, firstly to the graves of Sir William and his children.

'The inscription's almost impossible to read,' she said.

'That's why I made rubbings.' Reluctant to sound smugly omniscient, he explained, 'I learned about that the hard way when I took a party to Eyam in Derbyshire.'

'Where they had the plague?'

'That's right. That was three hundred years ago as well, and nature has a brutal way with monuments.

'This looks like a family grave.'

'It is. There's Sir William and the four children. As you can see, they all died on the same day in sixteen fifty-five.'

There was a crunch of gravel on the path behind them, and Nick turned to see Michael Ellison.

'Good afternoon.'

'Good afternoon, Michael. This is Caroline Nolan, assistant history teacher at Frederick Delius High.'

The two shook hands, and Michael asked, 'Are you any further forward with your enquiry, Nick?'

'I completed my research some time ago, but I'm no further forward with the Newbury Hall murders.'

'I must congratulate you, then, on your... MA, wasn't it?'

'M.Phil., and thank you.'

'So what brings you here again, not that you're unwelcome. I'm delighted to see you again.'

'I brought Caroline to see the Newbury graves and, if I'm honest, I can't stay away from them, myself.'

'There is a certain morbid compulsion about them, isn't there?' he agreed.

'Are the burial records extant?' asked Caroline.

'I regret to say they're not. For whatever reason – and we can only speculate – they were removed at some time, which means that the only record remaining is the headstones themselves.'

'This baby must have been no more than a year old,' said Caroline, reading the birth date of James Newbury. 'What kind of savage would do that?'

'If the story is true,' said Michael, 'he was the worst kind of savage, because he believed he was carrying out the will of God.'

'Come and look at Lady Newbury's grave, Caroline,' suggested Nick, thinking it might distract her from thoughts of the massacre of children. 'I have a rubbing of it as well, but it's worth a look.'

They moved to the site of the grave, which was separate from that of the family, for whatever reason, and Caroline traced the inscription with her forefinger. 'Sixteen fifty-seven,' she read, 'two years after the rest of her family.'

Nick was conscious of feeling increasingly cold, but he said nothing.

'It doesn't state the cause of death,' she remarked.

'No, they didn't,' said Michael. 'Those who dictated the inscription concerned themselves with the passing of the deceased and their place in the afterlife, rather than with the earthly circumstances of their death.'

'I imagine the Puritans would find that most convenient,' said Nick, 'and it wouldn't surprise me if they were also responsible for removing the burial register.'

'I was horrified when you told me about this, Nick,' said Caroline, standing up to stretch her legs, 'but seeing these graves makes it all so real.'

'I think so whenever I come here.' The wave of coldness was still there. Not surprisingly, Lady Newbury was also affected by the graves.

'Have you any other graves from the same period?' asked Caroline.

'There are some that can't be identified, because the inscriptions are so worn,' said Michael. 'They would even defy the wax crayon treatment. There is, however, one contemporary grave I can show you, if you'd like to follow me.'

He led them to a grave partly sheltered by the south side of the church. The headstone leant backwards, but when they drew closer, they saw that the inscription was just legible.

'Would you like to take a rubbing, Caroline?' asked Nick, handing her a sheet of paper and a crayon. 'Just go over it gently.'

'Are you all right?' she asked. 'You're shivering.'

'I'm a bit cold.' He saw Michael and Caroline exchange looks. The day had been quite warm.

'I think you must be sickening for something,' said Caroline. Nevertheless, she placed the sheet of paper against the headstone and rubbed gently with the crayon. Now shivering uncontrollably in the extreme cold, Nick watched the characters appear.

Here lye the mortal Remaines
of Edwarde Isaac Martyn Godfreye,
Widower and Apothecarye
borne 1630, departed this Lyfe Avgvst, 1662.
Lovingely reunited with Elizabethe, his late Wyfe.
"Their Bodies are buried in Peace,
but their Name liveth for evermore."
(Ecclesiastes Ch. 44, v. 14)

The Village mourneth his Passinge.

Nick now felt so cold, he was rubbing his arms and stamping his feet.

'I think you need to come into the warm and have a cup of tea,' said Michael. 'Come along, both of you.'

He took them into the vicarage, where he introduced them to his wife, and she set about making tea for them all.

Nick was beginning to thaw. 'I wonder,' he said, when he could concentrate once more, 'what was so special about Edward Godfrey that the whole village was said to have mourned his passing.'

After a little thought, Michael said, 'I've seen similar epitaphs on the headstones of revered country doctors. Of course, in those days, the local medics were called apothecaries.' He thought again and said, 'You know, I can imagine such a man being held in high regard by his ex-patients. At a time of frequent suffering, he may have treated a great many of them.'

Michael's wife came into the room with a tray of tea things, and made another journey to return with an inviting fruit cake. By this time, Nick was warm again and no longer shivering, but very curious.

* * *

'I'm fascinated,' said Nick on the way to Caroline's flat. 'When Angela showed me the phials they'd found, it occurred to me that an apothecary living at the time of the Protectorate would lead a hazardous life, and yet Edward Godfrey survived it by two years.'

'Do you mean the risk of being infected by his patients?'

'That as well, but more particularly because he was dealing in herbal cures, the province of those all too often deemed to be in league with the Devil.' He considered the anomaly a little longer and said, 'He may, of course, have treated the local soldiery at some time, and that would give him a degree of immunity.'

Caroline studied him from the passenger seat and asked, 'Are you all right now?'

'Fine, thank you. I don't know what it was, but it seems to have passed.'

'You looked quite awful.'

'Thanks.'

'You know what I mean.' As they approached her flat, she asked, 'What can you do with the information we've just learned?'

'I'll phone the British Library as soon as I can and find out if they have any record of Edward Godfrey. If he were as highly regarded in local society as his epitaph suggests, there may just be some written record that tells us more. If they have anything at all, I'll investigate it, obviously.'

'Will that entail going to the British Library?'

'Possibly.'

She hesitated, and asked, 'If you have to do that, do you think I might come with you? I've never had anything to do with the place, and the thought appeals to me.'

'I'm afraid not, Caroline. As far as I'm concerned, you'd be very welcome, but to enter the British Library, you need a reader's card, and to get one, you have to provide evidence that you're engaged in post-graduate research.'

'Ah.'

'I'm sorry, but who knows? The trail may end in Saint Radigund's churchyard. With my luck, it probably will.'

* * *

At home, that evening, Nick went over the events at the churchyard. By that time, he was well-used to Lady Newbury's manifestations, so that he regarded the lowering in temperature with almost casual acceptance, but his experience at Edward Godfrey's graveside had been unusually dramatic, and there was no doubting the connection. It had occurred as they moved to the grave, when the cold had been too intense to dismiss, and it had only ebbed when they moved to the vicarage. There was clearly a connection between Godfrey and Lady Newbury, something infinitely more significant than casual acquaintanceship. Maybe he'd attended her at her deathbed. Conjecture was as easy as it was pointless. He could only hope that something would turn up at the British Library.

* * *

He had a marking period the next morning, but he couldn't make a long-distance call from school, so he had to wait until the end of the day, when he was fortunately able to leave promptly.

It was a while before he could speak to the appropriate librarian, and that person had to spend considerable time searching the records, but eventually, he returned to the phone to say, 'I can find nothing in Printed Books. Would you like me to transfer you to the Manuscript Room?'

'Yes, please, and thank you for your efforts.'

'Not at all, sir.' The librarian made the transfer, and when someone in Manuscripts came to the phone, he told him what he was looking for.

After a while, the librarian reported back. 'There is a journal,' he said, 'a diary under the name of Edward Isaac Martyn Godfrey,

Apothecary, of the village of Thornton, near Bradford, Yorkshire. It appears to relate to a period between sixteen fifty-three and sixteen sixty-one.'

'That's the man,' said Nick, he hoped not too excitedly.

'I can give you a shelf reference.'

'Thank you.' Nick noted the reference. 'I'll make a request for a microfilm copy if you would be kind enough to quote me for the fee, please.'

When the librarian returned to the phone, he said apologetically, 'It's going to be very expensive for you, sir. The journal is a lengthy one, of more than three hundred pages, but it is in reasonably good condition, so a copy is certainly possible.'

'I don't care about its being expensive,' Nick told him. 'I suspect it's going to be worth every penny.' He made a note of the charge for copying and thanked the librarian most sincerely. He would write the request and cheque immediately to get them in the post before late collection.

After all that, he phoned Norman Lumb, and found him in his office.

'You're never going to believe this, Norman,' he said.

'I wouldn't like to guess at the number of times I've heard that,' said Norman, chuckling.

Still excited, Nick said, 'I've unearthed the manuscript of a diary kept by an apothecary, a contemporary and fellow villager of the Newbury family. It runs from sixteen fifty-three to sixteen sixty-one, and I've ordered a microfilm copy.'

'That sounds more than promising.'

'The timing could have been better. I imagine it could have been very useful when I was preparing my dissertation, but it's still an exciting discovery.'

'It may well prove useful in your Ph.D. research. That's if you're still thinking along the same lines.'

'I am.' Nick was quite definite about that.

'Let me give you another piece of information while you're on the line. I told you Trevor's job, the senior lecturer post, was being advertised, didn't I?'

'Yes.' Nick was naturally interested, but he was still trying to control his excitement about the journal.

'The job did actually go to an existing member of staff, so the post of Lecturer in History is being advertised, and your specialist area has been identified. Keep your eye on the *HES*. You can naturally rely on me for a reference.'

* * *

The vacancy at the Polytechnic was excellent news, but Nick was preoccupied for the present with his latest discovery. It would be several days before he received the microfilm; the painstaking process of photographing the whole book would be time-consuming, and then he had to allow for the post. He felt like a child waiting for Christmas.

24

A Long-Awaited Rest

Fortunately, the next few days afforded a number of distractions, but the microfilm and the *Times Higher Education Supplement* arrived on the same day. The post at Airedale Polytechnic was advertised, but that could wait a little while longer. Perversely, the microfilm also had to wait twenty-four hours before Nick could take it to a reader. The box in which it arrived was a tantalising sight by itself, and Nick was more than ever conscious of a childlike, helpless impatience, but the time eventually came for him to take it to a reader. On this occasion, because of the unusual length of the document, he chose to use the Polytechnic library, because of its more extensive opening hours.

'I'm going to need a lot of tokens,' he told the librarian, whilst trying to suppress his excitement.

'How many?'

'About three hundred and fifty.'

She laughed and said, 'Tokens can be recycled – we only have to empty the box – I just hope we have enough plain paper.'

'Don't worry about that,' he told her. 'If the worst comes to the worst, I can supply my own paper.'

'It must be important.'

'You could say that.'

'All right.' She took his five-pound note and gave him fifty tokens to get started.

'Thanks. I'll be back.'

'I'll stock up on A-four,' she told him with an amused smile.

Excitedly, he hooked the spool on to the two spindles on the reader and ran it through to the first page of manuscript. Handwriting with a quill pen was notoriously difficult to read, and Edward Godfrey's script was as close to illegible as any Nick had seen, but he tried not to read the content, tempting though it was in those circumstances. For the time being, his intention was to make a usable copy of the diary. He would then be able to read it at home in his own time.

His efforts amounted to almost thirty-four pages before the toner ran out. He reported the fact to the librarian, who suggested moving to another reader while she changed cartridges. She was still highly amused, but he didn't mind that in the circumstances.

Thirty-two pounds, and another two microfilm readers later, he had the whole diary printed on A4 paper. With a heavy briefcase and a feeling of deep satisfaction, he thanked the librarian, left the library and drove home with his precious information.

* * *

Dinner scarcely happened; he was too eager to begin reading the diary to worry too much about food, but he hurriedly made a sandwich so that he could make a start as soon as possible.

The early pages were interesting enough, once he'd managed to decipher Godfrey's ornate, angular handwriting, but if he were honest, he was primarily interested in August 1655. With a feeling of overwhelming excitement, he leafed through the pile until he came to the month in question.

The first week yielded very little, but an entry on the ninth of August caught his attention in the most disturbing way.

That unhappye Maide, Jennye Thwaite, is accused of Wytcherie. I doubt it will be long afore Captain Edmund's Men arryve to tayke her. It is true to saye that she doth take Trade from me withe her Remedyes, yet I feel no Ill towarde her, for the Loss is but little. I have spoken of her to Sir William, and he and I share the same Beliefe, that Wytcherie is an olde Wyves' Fancye, and that poor Jennye is guiltye of Noughte but honest Industrye. Captain Edmunds, though, would have her burned. He is a Simpleton in highe Office, who useth his Power for his owne Pleasinge. His Understandinge of the Scriptures is no better than that of an unlettered Childe.

10th. Day of August.

The Day commenced with Edmunds' Men in brutishe Humore and ended in the moste horrifyinge Waye. Confounded in their Effortes to take Jennye Thwaite, for she was not to be founde at her Cottage, they search'd for her in ev'ry Dwellinge in Thornton, allowinge no Exceptione. My House was as if Cattle had beene driven throughe it, yet worse still was the Fayte of the goode Sir William and his Familie, for I called on him and witnessed for myself what Evile had been done to them. I praye that I may never witnesse its Lyke again. Those accurs'd Levelers had founde Sir William givynge Shelter to Jennye Thwaite and had strucke him downe with the Sworde, lykewyse Lady Newburye and the Children – May the goode Lord take them into his Care and Keepynge. I feare I am unable to continue with thys Accounte. Mayhap tomorne.

The ink was smudged over the last few words, and Nick had no doubt as to the cause of it. He was curious, however. In all the time he'd been reading Godfrey's terrible account of the scene at Newbury Hall, he'd not been conscious of Lady Newbury's presence. He was also puzzled by Godfrey's reference to her having also been put to the sword, when he knew she'd survived the event by two years. Eager for clarification, he turned again to the diary.

I tayke up my Quille once more to tell of thys greate Wronge wiche has beene wroughte. Lady Newburye is nowe in my Care, for she was not put to Deathe with the Otheres, but was sorely wounded and lefte close to dead. Workinge by Nighte, Alfred the Sexton and I layed the Bodies of Sir William and his Children in the Earthe. The Taske troubled us greatlye, yet together we gave them a Christian Burial as well as we were able, the Reverend Thomas being in Sympathie with Captain Edmunds and therefore unworthye of our Trust, for we declared that at the same Tyme, we had also interred Lady Newbury. The Reason for our Artifice was so as to ensure her Sayfety. Meanwhyle, withe God's Helpe, she recovers her Healthe at my House. If anye Person is to speake Wronge of her livinge beneathe my Roof, may the Devil tayke him, for she and I are withoute Blame.

At that point, Nick had to stop reading to assimilate fully the content of Godfrey's account. He had spent three years trying to turn up such evidence, and now the realisation was infinitely more powerful than he had ever imagined, and that was only partly because of Edward Godfrey's understandably impassioned narrative.

After a minute or so, he considered the surprise absence of Lady Newbury, and it occurred to him that the printed copy of Godfrey's diary had arrived so quickly as to take her completely by surprise. It was also of such a size and in an unfamiliar form, that she might be forgiven for failing to recognise it for what it was. She had visited him when he was poring over Sir William's list and the account of Edmunds's dismissal, but they had been brief notes compared with Godfrey's diary. He was also dealing with a woman who knew only the quill pen and, no doubt, parchment. Paper would be an exotic luxury in her time, and print in large quantities would be unknown, except for the Bible and the Book of Common Prayer. It was time she was informed about this twentieth-century development.

Looking up at the portrait, he asked, 'Lady Newbury, are you there?' He waited, and surely enough the temperature began to recede. He switched on the gas fire for his own comfort, and said, 'Good day to you, Lady Newbury. I have news for you.' He felt the temperature fall further. 'This,' he said, holding the sheaf of paper, 'is a fair copy of the diary of Master Edward Godfrey. I located the very journal and had a copy made.' As this was likely to be the most important, as well as his last, conversation with her, he felt obliged to speak to her in words she was likely to understand readily, and that hopefully without delay, because the temperature was now plunging rapidly.

'I have now read of the terrible wrong done to you and your family, and I mean to publish my findings in one of the historical journals. When the staff at Newbury Hall hear of it, however, you may be sure the story will be told in the news sheets so that the entire population may know the truth.' He deliberately made no mention of the other news media. There was a limit, after all, to the modern wonders a tricentarian might be expected to understand.

'Suffice it to say, the nation will know that Sir William and your children were brutally assassinated by soldiers under the command of Captain Edmunds.' The cold was now painfully intense. 'That was your desire, was it not, for the truth to be made known?' Now he felt as if he were packed in ice, like the produce in a fishmonger's window. He moved towards the fire, but it made no difference, because the cold was as severe as ever. 'That being the case, Lady Newbury, although I have enjoyed your company on several occasions this past year, the time has come for us to part, I to make this event known, and you to rest with a quiet mind for the first time in more than three hundred years. Your quest is accomplished, and the time has come for you to enjoy the rest that is yours by right, and which you deserve. I bid you farewell, dear lady.' The agonising cold persisted for maybe ten or fifteen seconds, and then it began to ease so that he was gradually conscious of the gas fire. He moved back to his chair and studied Lady Newbury's portrait once more, because something was different. It may have been his fancy, the product of an emotionally-charged encounter, but just for a moment, he thought he saw the suggestion of a smile.

25

IN THE NEWS

Now that his self-imposed task was almost complete, Nick turned his attention to his application, planning it meticulously and then leaving it alone for twenty-four hours before making minor adjustments. It was unfortunate that he wasn't able to include in his CV a paper he'd written for the journal *History*, but as he'd only recently posted it, the matter was academic in both senses.

After much re-reading and fine-tuning, he delivered his application by hand so that it arrived unfolded. It was a minor detail, but he felt that details were important.

At school, he had to face the disapproval of Mr Purley, who couldn't imagine why his new Head of History could possibly want to be anywhere else, but of course, there was nothing he could do about it, and he agreed to give Nick a reference.

Another development was that the City Council had seized on the development and written a press release that had caused a degree of excitement among the media in general. Nick was obliged to give a press interview and one to *Northern Focus*, the local TV news programme. Norman Lumb had assured him a little wryly that the Vice-Chancellor of Airedale Polytechnic was happy for his institution to be mentioned. It was always advisable, Norman told him, to gain clearance in such matters, as vice-chancellors as a species were sensitive to publicity, both the good kind and the bad.

The *Northern Focus* interview was to be held, for maximum effect, at Newbury Hall, and Nick was there in good time, having persuaded some of his colleagues to cover his lessons at school. He saw the *Northern Focus* van enter the carpark, watched by a few inquisitive individuals. Not surprisingly, TV news teams usually attracted public curiosity.

The camera crew unloaded their equipment while the reporter came to the main door, where he heard Angela greet her.

'Is Mr Burnett here?' asked the reporter.

Nick came forward and introduced himself.

'Oh good, I'm Wendy Hurst from *Northern Focus*.'

He shook her hand. 'Please come inside,' he said. 'This is a new experience for me, so I'm in your hands.'

'You're also on your own,' said Angela, retreating to the office, where he heard her threatening Scott with a lingering death if he dared go near the camera, let alone touch it.

'Oh, there's nothing to worry about,' said Wendy. 'I'm just going to ask you some questions about yourself and about the circumstances that led to your discovery.'

A man's voice from the doorway asked, 'Is it okay to come in and set up?'

'I imagine so,' Nick told him.

'Could we possibly arrange for you to be seated in front of a bookcase?' asked Wendy, looking around the main hall. 'It's the way we usually do it,' she explained.

'I'm afraid printed books were thin on the ground when this house was built,' explained Nick, wondering how this woman imagined people spent the long, winter evenings in centuries gone by.

'There's this fireplace,' suggested Wendy. 'It's quite magnificent. What do you think, Brett? Can we use it?'

The man called Brett stopped chewing long enough to say. 'Yeah, we can stand him in front of that. No probs.'

Nick was glad they'd decided to film the interview at Newbury Hall; it saved him having to tidy up his sitting room. His study, originally the smallest of the three bedrooms, which was usually chaotic, would have been too much of a challenge, even with a television interview at stake.

Wendy took out a pad and pencil and asked, 'Now, is it all right for me to call you Nicholas?'

'Be my guest, but most people call me "Nick".'

'All right, Nick. I'd just like to make a few notes before we start filming. I gather this whole thing arose when you were researching the life and times of Oliver Cromwell. Would you like to tell me something about your academic background?'

'Gladly, but the focus of my research was the way in which Cromwell's rule affected the local community.'

She made a note on her pad. 'Fine. I've got that.'

'I read Modern History and English at King's College Cambridge, and I'm Head of History at Frederick Delius High School. I've recently been awarded an M.Phil. by the CNAA for my research, which was supported and supervised by Professor Norman Lumb at Airedale Polytechnic. I'd completed my research by the time I heard about the diary, and it was too late to include anything arising from it, although I intend to do rather more work on the Commonwealth and Protectorate.'

Wendy finished making a longhand note, speaking as she wrote. 'King's College Cambridge. M.Phil.' She asked, 'What, precisely, does M.Phil. stand for?'

'Master of Philosophy.'

'Ah.' She made a note of that.

Nick hoped she'd gained a clear idea, but somehow, he rather doubted it. 'M.A., Cambridge,' he reminded her, not wishing to cause any misunderstanding, 'M.Phil., brackets CNAA close brackets, Airedale Polytechnic.' He winced when he heard the camera crew banging about behind him.

'When did you first hear about the goings-on at Newbury Hall, Nick?'

'The massacre? I heard an unsubstantiated story about it shortly after I began my research. It had been the stuff of folklore for three hundred years. As I told you earlier, I'd already completed my research when I discovered the diary of Edward Godfrey.'

'Diary of Ed-ward God-frey,' said Wendy, laboriously writing the details.

'Don't you people use shorthand these days?'

She looked at him in mystification. 'I never learned shorthand, Nick. In fact I don't know of anyone who uses it. Most of us use a tape recorder, but I need to be able to refer to the notes during the interview. That's why I'm writing everything down.'

'All set up,' reported Brett, who was evidently more important and efficient than he looked.

'Wonderful. Nick, would you like to lean against the fireplace, maybe with your hand on some part of it, the mantlepiece, maybe, and your foot on the fender?'

'I'm afraid not, Wendy. I'll stand here, if this is where you want me, but we have to be very careful in the way we treat the fabric and artefacts in this building. They've been here now for four centuries, and we'd like them to last a little longer.'

'All right, we don't want to upset anybody.' She looked at Brett, who gave her a casual nod, and the interview commenced.

'I'm talking to Cambridge historian Nick Burnett,' she told the camera, 'who uncovered the secret of the mass murder that took place here at Newbury Hall in Bradford, I believe in sixteen forty-nine.'

Nick suppressed a chuckle. 'It occurred in sixteen fifty-five, Wendy. I think you're probably confusing it with a much-publicised, higher-profile assassination.'

'I beg your pardon, Nick. Now, you were researching the tyrannical rule of Oliver Cromwell and his Roundheads when you discovered the evidence, I believe?'

It was tiresome. 'I'm sorry, Wendy. I have to correct you again. I'd completed my research when I was alerted to the diary of Edward Godfrey. Also, Cromwell was no tyrant, you know. Wrongs were committed in his name, but he's suffered unjustly over the years, largely through political mischief, romantic fiction and low-budget, supporting films.'

'I take your point, Nick. Now, how did you first come to hear about the diary?'

'I'd taken a colleague, Miss Nolan from Frederick Delius High School, to Saint Radigund's churchyard to show her the graves of Sir William and Lady Newbury, and also the Newbury children, and Miss Nolan asked the Reverend Michael Ellison if there were any contemporary graves in the same churchyard. Quite fortuitously, the only one with a headstone that was at all legible was that of the apothecary Edward Godfrey.'

'An apothecary being an early physician?'

'Yes.' She'd got that right, at least.

'So you found his grave and headstone, but how did you learn about his diary?'

'I made what was on the face of it a pot-luck enquiry at the British

Library in London, and they told me about the diary, which has apparently lain untouched for goodness-knows how many years in their manuscript room.'

'How amazing! And what did you learn from it?'

'I learned that Sir William Newbury had taken into hiding a woman called Jenny Thwaite, who was accused of witchcraft. Unfortunately Captain Josiah Edmunds of the local garrison and his men searched every house in the village and discovered Jenny here, in Newbury Hall.'

'What happened then?'

It seemed to Nick that Wendy was adept at asking the most ridiculous questions, as well as being incapable of listening properly. Nevertheless, he had to give her a sensible answer. 'They took Jenny away, presumably to be burned at the stake, which was the usual punishment for the alleged offence, and they slaughtered Sir William and his children, the youngest of whom was a mere baby. The eldest was no more than four years old. Lady Newbury was left for dead, but Edward Godfrey, who found her shortly after the massacre, nursed her back to health.' He left Wendy to make what she would of that, but at least viewers would learn of the story of the massacre.

'But why do you think they murdered those innocent children?'

'Those who opposed the Parliamentarians were known as Malignants, and it wasn't unknown for whole families to be massacred in order, it was believed, to stamp out Malignancy. It was exactly the same as the Nazi principle, three hundred years later, of "Bad Blood". If one person was deemed guilty, the rest of the family had to pay the penalty, too. Some things never seem to go away.'

'And yet you say that Cromwell wasn't the tyrant he's reputed to have been.'

'He wasn't responsible for Edmunds's actions, Wendy. The man was acting on his own perverted initiative, or if you prefer it, out of rampant bigotry.'

'Thank you, Nick. It's been fascinating talking to you. This is Wendy Hurst reporting from Newbury Hall.'

When the news team were gone, Nick vented his frustration in the office. 'That bloody woman has cloth ears,' he said. 'She didn't listen to a damned thing I told her.'

'We've been through it before,' Angela told him. '*Northern Focus* isn't just about news, Nick. It's entertainment as well. After all that, are you going to stay for coffee?'

'I'd love to, Angela. Thanks, but I've got people covering my lessons, so I'd better get back. Thanks for all your help and forbearance.'

'You're welcome. I'm going to miss you. Hug?'

'Definitely.' He held her in a hug that seemed a fitting end to his association with Newbury Hall, at least for the time being.

26

ALL CHANGE

Nick took his turn in the short queue at the reception desk of the dental surgery, and when his turn came, he said, 'My name is Nicholas Burnett. I have an appointment for a check-up at five-fifteen with Miss Bramhope.'

'Five-fifteen, yes, I have you down,' said the receptionist, checking her records. Miss Bramhope is no longer with us,' she told him. 'You'll be seen by Miss Carter.'

'Oh.' It came as an unpleasant surprise, but it probably explained why he hadn't seen Miss Bramhope at the swimming pool lately. 'No disrespect to Miss Carter,' he said, 'but what have you done to the poor woman? I mean Miss Bramhope, of course.'

'Miss Bramhope's gone to another practice.' The receptionist seemed uninterested, even dismissive. 'It happens,' she said. 'In the time I've been doing this job, I've seen a few dentists come and go. It's like an airport at this place, sometimes.'

'Ah well, I'll just have to handle the disappointment.' He took a seat and waited to be called. Suddenly, all the fun had gone out of keeping a dental appointment. Even the cars in the magazines seemed very ordinary and unappealing, and when he'd checked the price of a couple of them, he decided it was just as well.

At about twenty-past five, a nurse came out of what had been Miss Bramhope's treatment room to say enquiringly, 'Mr Burnett?'

Nick followed her in and met a serious-looking woman in a scrub suit, a very poor substitute indeed; in fact, she had a distinctly unsympathetic, not to say menacing, appearance that did her absolutely no favours. In that brief, initial meeting, he was even reminded of Rosa Klebb in *From Russia With Love*. He realised that he was maybe being unfair in making that comparison; in fact, it was blatant exaggeration, but he was still coping with the shock of losing his heart's desire, and that seemed to qualify more than adequately as an excuse.

'Good afternoon, Mr Burnett.'

'Miss Carter, I presume. How do you do?'

'How do you do? Take a seat.'

'Thank you.' He sat on the treatment chair and waited while Miss Carter consulted his record.

'Are you on any regular medication?'

'No.'

'Had any dental problems recently?'

'No.'

'Any health problems at all?'

'No.'

'Any allergies?'

'No.'

'Good,' she said, donning a face mask and a pair of surgical gloves. I'll just take you back and have a look at your teeth.' The chair unbent, and Nick found himself horizontal. 'Open wide.' The unintelligible litany ensued while Nick kept his eyes closed, simply because, without Miss Bramhope's lovely eyes to feast on, he no longer had any reason for keeping them open.

'No problems there, as far as I can see. I'll just give them a clean.'

Nick braced himself and endured the ordeal by ultrasonic screwdriver. It seemed to take even longer than it had in the past.

Eventually, the process ended, and Miss Carter said, 'All done, now. Have a rinse.'

Nick took a sip, cleansed his mouth, and spat it out, no longer worried about the loss of dignity involved.

'Do you brush twice a day?' she demanded.

He nodded. 'And I floss,' he said.

'What kind of toothbrush do you use?'

'An electric one, rotary.'

'Are you confident in its use?'

'I seem to be getting the hang of it. At least, it's no longer the challenge it was when I first used it.'

'Good. I'll see you in six months' time. Make an appointment in reception as you leave.'

'Will do. Thank you both.' He left the room and made the appointment for the following December. It was now no more than a routine process, because life simply wasn't the same without Miss Bramhope.

His life had its compensations, though, he told himself as he drove home. He had a new job to go to, and in the short term, Joanne and Daniel were having a party. He'd forgotten the reason for the party, but he would soon be reminded of it, he was sure.

* * *

He hadn't been home long before Joanne's car drew up in their drive, and she walked across to speak to him.

'Hi, Joanne,' he said. 'Would you like a drink?'

'Yes, please. That would go down well. Gin and tonic, please, if you can manage it.'

Nick poured gin into a tall glass and took a bottle of tonic from the fridge. 'Just remind me, Joanne,' he said, 'because I'm sure you've told me this. What's the occasion for the party? I haven't missed a birthday or anything like that, have I?'

'No, there's nothing in particular. We just thought we'd have a party. Are you still coming?'

'Of course.' He cut a slice of lime and dropped it into her glass with a quantity of ice.

'Lime,' she remarked, 'how posh.'

'Well, I've come up in the world.' He poured a vodka and tonic for himself, also with ice and lime.

'So you have.' She held up her glass. 'Cheers.'

'Cheers.'

'I should say, "Here's to the new job". I'm sorry. Just for the moment, I wasn't thinking.'

'Your congratulations are taken as read, Joanne. I'm not easily slighted, as you know.'

She really was thinking about something else. 'I just remembered why I came here,' she said.

'You're welcome at any time,' he assured her. 'You really don't need an excuse.'

'Yes, I do, in case Daniel gets jealous. I came to ask you first of all if you were coming tomorrow night.'

'And I told you I am.'

'Yes, and also to ask you if you're bringing anyone.'

He pretended to think. Finally, he said, 'No.'

'Why not?'

'The cupboard's bare.' Thanks to Lady Newbury's inflexible moral guardianship, it had remained so for almost a year. It was an unusual kind of record, although clearly not one to be celebrated, much less repeated, if he could possibly avoid it.

'No one to bring?'

'Not a soul.' He wondered why she had to know that, and she answered his question when she spoke again.

'So it's just as well you're coming to the Sycamore Avenue Lonely Hearts Club.'

'Am I?' He thought he was a little old for that kind of thing, and he wondered quite what she had I mind. If it turned out to be anything embarrassing, he might change his mind about going.

'There'll be no shortage of "talent", as my irreverent husband insists on calling the female population. How long is it since you were in a relationship? I mean a meaningful one?'

Maybe she was thinking of his chance encounter with Sally in Teesdale. 'A meaningful one? I can't remember.' He imagined match-making must be a feature of the female DNA, going back possibly to primeval times, and he knew also from repeated and sometimes embarrassing experience that it was both unstoppable and incurable.

'So long ago.' She finished her drink and put down her glass. 'Thanks for the drink, Nick. I must go, but I'll see you tomorrow night. I've got to decide what to wear.' She blew a kiss and disappeared, leaving Nick thankful that he was spared that problem. He would wear his going-to-parties trousers, one of his going-to-parties shirts, and that was about all. There was nothing to be gained by complicating the procedure.

* * *

The next morning, he had a change of heart and went shopping. He'd last been to a party more than twelve months earlier. It was the party at which he'd met Amanda, and mainly for that reason, he decided to break with the past and find something new to wear. For all he knew, a change of habit might even lead to a change in his fortunes. After all, if he could believe in ghosts, surely he could subscribe to mild superstition.

It wasn't easy, and it took care of most of Saturday morning. There were numerous shops for teenagers and one or two shops for middle-aged-to-elderly men, but eventually, he found one that catered for the crucial, fairly-young-but-pushing-thirty market. It was like Aladdin's cave, and he spent some time in there, emerging eventually with two pairs of trousers and three shirts. Now, like Joanne, he would have a choice.

* * *

Armed with two bottles of wine, because he was feeling generous, and because it was a vintage he'd tried out of curiosity and awarded the thumbs-down, Nick joined the party.

'Hello,' said a young woman who'd clearly been drinking herself into the mood, 'I'm Dreb... Dev... Deborah.' She pronounced her name with a final flourish and a look of surprise, presumably at having succeeded in her efforts.

'Hello,' he said, raising his voice above the record that was playing. 'I'm Nick from next door.'

'Have you come to come...?' She looked lost for a second, and then remembered what she'd been about to ask. 'Have you come t' complain about th' noise?'

'Yes.' He hadn't, of course, but it was very noisy, and he would be surprised if one of the other neighbours didn't have something to say at some stage in the evening.

'You'll fin' Joanne or Daliel... Danimel or shomebody in the klitchem... kic... kitchen.'

'Thanks for the tip.' He worked his way delicately through the crowd to the kitchen, where he found Joanne loading a number of items of party food into the microwave.

'Hello, Nick! Lovely man!' she exclaimed, relieving him gratefully of the bottles. 'Let me get you a drink.' Without asking him what he wanted, but knowing him quite well by that time, she poured a glass of red wine from an opened bottle and handed it to him. 'Do you know everybody?' she shouted. Before he could answer, she said, 'Come and meet an old friend of mine from university.' She took his hand and towed him deftly past numerous guests, through the dining room, past yet more guests until, very much to Nick's surprise and delight, they encountered a very attractive, fair-haired woman. He thought he recognised her, but to make absolutely sure, he masked her nose, mouth and hair with his hands. He didn't think she'd mind in the least.

'What are you doing?' asked Joanne, understandably puzzled.

'Just checking,' he said.

'He only recognises me in a scrub suit and a face mask,' said the lady under scrutiny, 'although I sometimes wear a swimming cap to confuse him.' She was wearing a simple, light-blue, cotton dress that was infinitely more inviting than a scrub suit, and her fair hair hung in loose curls over her shoulders.

'You know each other, then?'

Nick recovered his composure to say, 'I'm... I was... one of Miss Bramhope's patients.'

' "Was" is right,' confirmed Miss Bramhope. 'I'm with another practice now, and it's "Sam", by the way.'

'And to think.... I actually imagined I'd never see you again. I do believe in miracles, destiny, serendipity and... all the other things I've rubbished in the past when dreams have gone awry and life has seemed not only meaningless, but merciless as well.'

'You poor thing,' said Sam, gently amused.

'Let me top that up,' said Joanne, taking Sam's glass. 'By the way, Sam, Nick's celebrating his new job.'

'Wonderful. What job's that?' She wrinkled her brow in thought. 'You're a teacher, aren't you?'

'You remembered.' He was rather surprised. He must have made a stronger impression than he'd realised. 'Actually,' he said, 'the job's at Airedale Polytechnic.'

'Oh, grown-up teaching. Well done.' As if she'd only just remembered, she said, 'I saw you being interviewed on *Northern Focus*.

It was very exciting. I told everyone at the practice about it the next day, how you'd saved me from drowning and then become famous, but none of the people I spoke to had seen the wretched programme. They'd all been watching BBC or at the pub.'

He tried not to be mesmerised by her eyes, which seemed to be arched permanently in a smile. 'They probably had the right idea, Sam,' he said. 'It was a dreadful interview, too embarrassing for words.'

'Yes, she wasn't the world's greatest listener, was she? You had to keep correcting her, as I recall.'

'You noticed.'

A man seemed about to move in on Sam, when she said, 'You know, Nick, I never did thank you properly for saving my life.'

In the face of what must have seemed unassailable competition, the man thought better of the initiative and disappeared, no doubt to try his luck elsewhere.

'It was nothing, Sam. I'd do it again anytime, but I haven't seen you at the swimming pool for quite some time.'

'I know. It's not as easy, now that I've changed jobs. The man who owns the practice opened a new branch at the other end of the city, and he invited me to move there.' After a little more thought, she said, 'I suppose I could do it if I got up a little earlier.'

'That would be ideal. We could be what my mother used to call "a good influence" on each other.' Recalling at least one moment from childhood, he said, 'She had plenty to say about the other kind.'

'So had mine.'

Feeling that the moment was right, he said, 'And there's something else we could do, now that I'm no longer under your forceps, as it were.' In the crowded room, and with the deafening noise coming from the record player, subtlety stood little chance, but he still felt inclined to say, 'Now, I'm only floating this as an idea, you understand.'

She nodded, he thought, understandingly, and said, 'Float your idea, Nick, whatever it is.'

'I could pick you up at some time that's convenient to you, and we could eat somewhere that's good,' he suggested, grimacing at the unholy racket that the record player was currently churning out, 'and where we can have a conversation without having to shout above a cacophonous din.' In case further persuasion were necessary, he said, 'If it helps, I promise I'll brush my teeth and floss afterwards.'

Moving closer to make herself heard, she said, 'In that case, how can I possibly refuse?'

He felt success knocking on his door for the first time in a year, but good manners made him say, 'I suppose, to be sociable, we should circulate, don't you think?' He made the suggestion without enthusiasm and in the hope that she would disagree.

'No one else is bothering to circulate,' she observed obligingly. 'As far as I can see, they're all fairly static. In fact, economy of movement seems to have become....'

'*Comme il faut?*'

'If you say so.'

Looking around the room, he could see she was right. Couples were locked together, swaying amorously to a now-gentler offering from their hosts' record collection. Nick was pleasantly surprised that Joanne's and Daniel's library included such comparative subtlety, and he was happy to take advantage of it while it continued to occupy the turntable. 'It seems a shame not to join in,' he said. 'Shall we sway gently?'

'Have you had a busy day, too?' she asked, placing her hands on his shoulders.

'Yes.' He hadn't, but he thought it would be a good idea to sound sympathetic. His hands cupped her slender waist, and they swayed together without a break, even when the record was being changed. When Joanne or Daniel reverted to a louder, more violent example of the popular songwriter's ineptitude, Sam said, 'I'm not convinced that this is really a swaying number, but having said that, I'm not a purist. Are you?'

He made a play of searching his memory, and said, 'It's not one of the insults that have been thrown at me recently.'

'Well,' she said with just a hint of caution, 'I can't imagine it's all that important.'

'I think it depends largely on your *modus operandi*,' he suggested.

'Don't be disgusting.'

'I'm sorry.'

'It's very smoky in here,' she said, narrowing her eyes against a puff of cigarette smoke that billowed their way.

He had to agree. 'It's smoky everywhere. As a fairly recent convert, I'm becoming increasingly sensitive to it, as I'm sure you already are. We could go outside,' he suggested.

'Let's.' She allowed him to take her hand, following him out through the passage, then the kitchen and then outside to the back of the house, where they came to rest. 'You know your way around this place,' she said, as if she were complimenting him on a fine piece of navigation.

'I should. I live next door, and my house is exactly like this one, except it's much quieter, not so full of people, and of course, everything is the other way round.'

'Are you pulling my leg?'

'Would I?' He took her glass and placed it beside his on the dining room windowsill.

'I'm not sure, but I suspect not.' Still swaying to the music, she put her hands on his shoulders again, and he drew her towards him.

'The volume's easier to cope with out here,' he said. 'Easier to sway to as well. Do tell me, though, what's your perfume?'

'Coco Chanel. Why? Do you like it?'

'It's exquisite.' He inhaled deeply, revelling unashamedly in the seductive fragrance.

'So that's why you brought me out here. You're a compulsive perfume sniffer.'

'From earliest years,' he admitted.

'You must be one of those men my mother used to warn me about.'

'I'm not sure. I've never had the pleasure of meeting your mother, but if it makes any difference at all, let me assure you, and her as well, that I wouldn't dream of anything untoward.' As he said that, he remembered he once had. It was curious how things sometimes worked out, and with Lady Newbury finally laid to rest, he now had to answer only to his conscience, confident that it would allow him infinitely greater scope than she ever had.

The End

www.ingramcontent.com/pod-product-compliance
Lightning Source LLC
Chambersburg PA
BHW020838260626
169CB00003B/1038